WANTED II

A Western Story Collection

SECOND IN THE WANTED SERIES

—◆— ■ —◆—

BY THE WESTERN WRITERS GROUP

JAMES D. BEST
DUANE BOEHM
TELL COTTEN
WL COX
BRAD DENNISON
KEN FARMER
ROBERT J. THOMAS

—◆— ■ —◆—

Wanted II
A Western Story Collection

By

James D. Best
Duane Boehm
Tell Cotten
WL Cox
Brad Dennison
Ken Farmer
Robert J. Thomas

Dedication

Once again, we dedicate this to all our faithful readers.
Thank you for keeping the spirit of the West alive.

Contents

Relentless by James D. Best
In a remote wilderness, a band of outlaws chases Steve Dancy. They want his horse. They want his gear. They want his money. And they want his life.

Lady Marshal by Ken Farmer
Deputy US Marshal Fiona Miller isn't aware that two other groups are after two teenage boys and the $5,000 in loot from a bank robbery. One is a band of outlaws and the other is a posse of vigilantes led by the father of a young girl shot during the holdup. Who gets to the boys first?

What's Right by Duane Boehm
Gideon Johann and Farting Jack Dolan find that they get more than they bargained for when they cross paths with a runaway girl while chasing a murderer.

Damsel in Distress by Robert J. Thomas
Jess had finally hunted down and killed the notorious Russell Bell and is on his way to the closest town to turn the corpse in for the bounty.

Along the way, his sometimes partner, Shadow, a huge timber wolf, finds him and leads him to a wagon where a beautiful woman was beaten up during a robbery and her husband shot dead.

Jess helps the woman get to the town of Elk Ridge and then hunts down the three men responsible for the robbery and murder. When he does, things aren't what them seem to be.

Thundering Hooves by Brad Dennison
A prequel to the novel *Thunder*. A story of the McCabes and their early years in the valley.

The Mirror II by Tell Cotten

Lee Mattingly and Brian Clark find a man bushwhacked and left for dead. Blamed for the crime, they are thrown into prison. However, they won't go down without a fight. Along the way, they run into corrupt horse traders, a deputy with a grudge, and a woman with bitter memories.

The Legend by WL Cox

Charles Crawford, a man raised in China by Buddhist Monks after his parents were murdered travels to America and is captured by Sioux Indians as he travels west. This is an episode of Charles' life while living with the Sioux.

Relentless

A Steve Dancy Tale

By
James D. Best

Relentless

Gray sky and gray water made it difficult to discern a horizon. The windless morning raised nary a ripple on the surface of the Pacific Ocean. As I rode my horse along a small rise above a sandy beach, even the small waves seemed listless. *Pacífico* means peaceful in Spanish, and the ocean lived up to its name on this bright, clear morning.

I had risen at daybreak, and after a couple of cups of coffee, saddled my horse, Liberty, and started riding north along the trail called El Camino Real. Walking Liberty at a leisurely pace, I nibbled day-old biscuits and even older bacon. I was content.

Content, but not inattentive. This part of California was known for angry banditos who loved to rob the gringos they believed had stolen their country. I had some empathy for them. The United States had used the Mexican-American War to acquire territory, but that didn't mean I wanted to be an object of their revenge. California was safer than the rest of the frontier, but *pandillas* rustled cattle, counterfeited American currency, and robbed travelers. I enjoyed the ocean in the early morning light but kept a watchful eye on the rolling hills.

The trail was well-worn and clearly marked with stone cairns. Nightly accommodations were readily available in the settlements that had developed around Catholic missions built a day's ride apart. I had spent the night at San Luis Rey de Francía, and with my early start, had plenty of time to reach San Juan Capistrano before nightfall.

Growing up privileged in New York City, I had always wanted to explore the coast that stretched along the edge of the western frontier. I had taken my bride to San Diego for a honeymoon, and we had remained in a seaside cottage for three months. Now I wanted to buy property inside the bay formed by Point Loma. After my father had died, I had sold his gun shop and myriad other interests to invest in railroads, which had done spectacularly well. I now had the wherewithal to develop a commercial harbor that could compete with San Francisco.

California began at Point Loma. When Juan Rodríguez Cabrillo docked on the east coast of a long peninsula in 1542, he named it La Punta de la Loma de San Diego and declared the bay an exceptional port, a port I believed could supply the entire Southwest with products from around the world.

San Diego remained primitive in 1881. A permanent European settlement had been established a little over one hundred years previously, but New Town, deeper in the bay, had been around only a dozen years. New Town, and the potential for dredging the bay, opened the entire inlet to development, which made North Island, situated in the middle of the bay, an invaluable property. Transportation was my preferred investment, and a massive harbor at the southwest corner of the United States looked like a clear winner. The southern tip of the peninsula had already been set aside for the military, but private land still existed further inside the bay. I wanted to own a good piece of North Island, which was perfectly situated for docking dozens of ships.

I had corresponded with a San Francisco attorney named Archibald C. Peachy, who, together with the estate of William Henry Aspinwall, owned North Island. In the settlement of a dispute over a California land grant, Peachy had somehow wrangled ownership of Rancho San Diego for himself and Aspinwall, his New York moneyed partner. Evidently, not all California banditos used guns. Aspinwall had since died, but his interest in North Island remained within his estate. My family had done numerous business deals with the Aspinwalls, so my mother in New York could handle the East Coast negotiations.

After forwarding letters of recommendation from New York and considerable correspondence, Peachy agreed to meet me in Los Angeles, where he had other business. I found this arrangement convenient, because railroads had not yet reached San Diego; thus, my solitary ride up the southern California coastline.

I rode easy and enjoyed the tranquil sea. I was fascinated by porpoises and whales, especially the way they leaped out of the water. I had seen whales off New England, but the slick and graceful porpoises were a new phenomenon. They swam in packs and appeared to effortlessly fly out of the water, twist, and dive back in with barely a ripple. I had no idea what they would do if they encountered a human, but there was slim chance that would happen with me, because I rarely ventured into the sea above my waist. Still, I kept my eyes open in the hopes of catching these animals' playful antics.

deep hatred

A motion behind a hillock caught my eye. After riding for several hours, I had been lollygagging without a care in the world.

Now I had a care.

I brought Liberty to a stop. I saw no more movement, but examining the landscape, I realized it was an ideal spot for an ambush. The terrain had gradually risen until a cliff sat between me and the beach below, and a berm extended out from the coastal hills, narrowing the trail to only twenty feet. Racing through the pinch point probably wouldn't work. If bandits lurked behind the berm, I would risk being driven over a steep cliff that fell to a rocky shoreline.

Maybe I was wrong. Maybe I hadn't seen anything.

I knew better. I hadn't survived on the frontier for the last three years by relying on wishful thinking. Trial by fire and good advice from friends had gotten me through some tough situations. In fact, one of the lessons I had learned was to accept a situation as it presents itself. Don't assume the intentions of bad men can be mitigated by gentleness. When threatened, expect that your assailant means you harm and react immediately.

How should I react? I could fight. I could submit. Or I could retreat. Or perhaps even find a way to go around. I inspected the terrain more carefully. The inland hills weren't impassable, but a determined pursuer could easily get in front of me and have no problem hiding in a fold of the undulating knolls. I carried money in multiple places on my person and my horse so I wouldn't look overly flush when I paid for something. Perhaps if I turned over one of my stashes, the bandits would let me ride on. Unlikely. They would probably search me and take every cent. If they took all my money, would they let me go? Doubtful. Rumors claimed that the Mexican banditos harbored deep hatred for gringos. In the middle of nowhere, their first impulse would not be mercy. A fight with an unknown force appeared foolhardy. That left one obvious choice: pull back and wait for other travelers to come along.

This was not a time for guile. They had seen me, and because of my dalliance, they knew I had seen them. I reined around and spurred Liberty to a gallop. I rode at speed for about ten minutes, but no one pursued, so I slackened the pace to a trot. After another ten minutes, I dismounted and walked my horse. Should I keep heading south until I ran into someone or wait for other parties to come upon me? A wide swale ahead made up my mind. I could set up camp in the recess, where I would be hard to spot but could see anyone who traveled along the trail. I led Liberty up the incline, pleased with my cleverness.

ven aquí

11

I didn't wait long. In under an hour, four riders came along. I came out from hiding and approached cautiously with a friendly wave. I didn't want to be shot for being mistaken for a desperado. They seemed unconcerned with my appearance, greeting me with hearty hellos. All four were dressed as ranch hands and rode good mounts.

When I got close enough not to shout, I said, "Hello, friends." I pointed. "I believe there may be robbers around a berm further up the trail. Almost certain I saw movement, and no one called out a greeting."

The men looked unconcerned. "I think you wrong, señor. Many of my *banda* wait around the corner, but we … we're here … right in front of you." He laughed. "This day not yours, amigo."

My first thought was that these were clever men. Besides wearing American rancher garb, they had not brought enough men to make me wary. They also appeared jocular rather than intimidating. Perhaps they would lighten my load by one of my stashes of money, and I could be on my way.

The leader walked his horse a step closer to mine. "Step off your horse and strip naked."

Or perhaps not.

I didn't move.

He yelled, "Hombres, *ven aquí*!" Then to me, "Get down. Take off your clothes, amigo. Leave your weapons. Leave your horse. Leave your boots. Walk away." He confidently rested both hands on his saddle horn. "All you have is mine. Do it now, señor, and you will not be harmed."

Six or seven more men stormed in a gallop out from behind a hill, whooping with glee. They were also dressed as American ranchers. No sombreros, no bandoleros, no serapes. They evidently intended to add my clothing to their wardrobe. Clever disguise for Mexican highwaymen.

What I did next, I never thought about. Pure instinct. When the charging riders arrived, their horses kicked up dust as they twirled or reared up slightly. I drew my pistol and shot the talkative one in the center of his chest as I spurred my horse past the banditos, then raced away as fast as Liberty could carry me. After I cleared a knoll, I jerked my reins to take me behind a hill that would shield me from flying bullets.

I heard gunfire. Lots of it. What the hell? I moved fast. I didn't give them time to respond. I glanced back but saw no one in pursuit. They were shooting at my image that had already disappeared around a corner. Good. Let them waste ammunition. I bent low against Liberty's neck and urged him up the slight incline that would take me into the hills and to safety.

last stand?

The gunfire grew loud. Taking another peek over my shoulder, I saw that they had recovered their wits and rode after me, blasting away with six-shooters. I had about a fifty-yard head start, a challenging pistol shot when on solid ground, but foolish from a galloping horse. Shooting from horseback took practice. A good cavalryman developed a knack for aiming and shooting with the rhythm of his horse's gait, but it was generally not within a highwayman's expertise.

Something hit me in the butt. Reaching behind, I passed my hand across my rear. No blood. What was that? Reaching back again, I felt a ragged tear in my saddle cantle. I immediately spurred Liberty to greater speed. These vaqueros were either lucky or damn good at shooting from horseback. I needed to put more distance between us.

Liberty was a steadfast runner, possessing a good balance between endurance and speed. With luck, the vaqueros' mounts were lesser animals. In my experience, outlawing seldom generated enough income to buy decent horseflesh. Except. They stole their horses, like they had tried to steal mine. Certainly, a few came from good stock. Another glance showed that we had increased our lead, but I knew we couldn't outrun them forever—not all of them. Eventually, a few would get close enough to put a bullet in more than my saddle. I examined the terrain ahead. If I could find a rock outcropping, I could unsheathe my rifle and possibly drive them away. To ward them off, I needed to make the price too high for them to continue their chase.

I saw something that would have to do. The cluster of rocks was high enough to shelter me if I lay on the ground, but not tall enough to stand or kneel behind … or shield Liberty. Since the outcropping was on an upslope, my legs also might be exposed. As I drew closer, I saw that the rocks were even smaller than I had thought. I spotted something better. At the crest of the hillock we were climbing, a large mound protruding against the skyline looked big enough to conceal Liberty. Would this be our last stand? I immediately regretted the thought. I had been to Little Bighorn, and the landscape looked far too similar for comfort. I desperately wanted a different outcome.

I wheeled around the knoll and flew out of the saddle, pulling out my rifle as I dismounted. I scrambled behind the mound on my elbows and knees until I could peer down at my pursuers. The bandits surprised me. Instead of riding hell-bent after me, they had pulled up just out of rifle range. These men were smart, at least in the art of running a prey to ground. I had hoped to pick off one or two so they would retreat, but they refused to accommodate me. Damn.

I noticed that I was breathing hard. I had no right to complain—Liberty had done most of the work and was breathing even harder. But I needed to get control of my breathing before shooting. The banditos stood not quite beyond range, but far enough away to make the shot difficult. I waited until I could breathe easy, then took a

14

bead on the pack of desperadoes. Just before I could get off a shot, they started to scatter side to side. I threw one futile bullet in their direction, but none fell off his horse. A miss, but I had sent a message that I intended to fight, one that might give them pause about climbing the incline.

I held my fire and watched. What were they doing? Then I saw that they were forming a wide single line. Damn. Another smart move. If they bunched up, I could get lucky, but spreading out with six feet between them lowered my odds of taking down more than one.

Why did they think I was worth the trouble? Did my possessions warrant risking their lives? I had a fine-looking horse, worn but expensive tack, durable clothes, costly hat and boots, but an unknown amount of money or gold coin. They knew I was fast and lethal with a handgun, as evidenced by their dead compatriot. My rifle shot signaled that I would continue to fight. I shook my head. They should go away.

They didn't go away. The far extremes of the line started a slow march toward my position. The riders formed an arc, with every target approximately equal distance. I tried to figure out who the remaining leaders were, but they were all dressed alike, and no one gave obvious orders. Their formation told me that these men had military experience, or at least had served in a highly regimented band of outlaws. I was in trouble.

These were experienced robbers who knew better than to have their leaders ride in the center of the line. I looked behind me. The vaqueros were downhill, and by staying directly behind the knoll, I would be hidden from their view for a hundred feet or so. That would extend my head start. But first I had to slow them down. I picked a rider to the left of center. I rested my rifle barrel on the hilltop, aimed carefully, and squeezed. He fell. I immediately fired three more times in a broad pattern, then turned, grabbed

15

Liberty by the reins, and pulled him after me as I walked away from my pursuers.

I walked because I would come into view sooner mounted. If I heard warlike shouts, I'd turn around and return to my knoll and fight from cover; otherwise, I'd put as much distance as I could between them and me. I heard shots and glanced back. The hill exploded with dirt and debris. The accuracy of the shots told me they had slowed or halted their march to send a volley at the knoll. How far could I travel before an over-shot put a nasty hole in my head? Due to the deteriorating arc of a bullet's flight, it would be prior to their seeing me. I told myself to hell with it and quickened my pace.

committed

A moment later, a bullet dug up dirt ahead of me. The first of the bandits had rounded the knoll. Sorry, Liberty, your rest is over. I swung into the saddle and spurred him up the hill. Without hesitation, he leaped forward. Glancing back, I saw his tail swish side to side as we raced to safety. I hoped it could brush away bullets as effectively as flies. We crested a ridgeline, and I immediately turned north in the direction of San Juan Capistrano. I estimated that the mission was a four-hour ride away … if I could ride as the crow flies. That would never happen. The bandits would herd me inland, away from any fellow travelers who might lend a hand.

I had never taken the time to count the band but had originally estimated a dozen or more. Now, two less rode after me. I needed to get away or whittle their numbers down further. Liberty felt strong and ran at a steady pace, with no indication of tiring. That couldn't last. Again, arithmetic said we could not outrun all of our pursuers. He would have to outlast ten or more horses, one or two of which might be his match. Since I had planned on being

16

gone for over a week, he also carried a hefty load behind the saddle. Could I untie the saddlebags on the run? It would not only lighten Liberty's load, but several of the bandits might stop to inspect their bounty. Not here. I wanted an open space where they would see me drop the bags. They might even present a target as they dismounted to pick them up.

I spotted a flat area in front of me, with low brush and a few scrub oaks. Reaching behind my saddle, I untied the bag flaps and fumbled around until I found the boxes of ammunition I always carried. With difficulty, I shoved the outsized boxes into my overly large shirt pockets. Next, I untied the latigos that attached the bags to my saddle. With the bags riding free, I pulled the reins and jumped off before Liberty came to a complete stop. In one smooth motion, I released the saddlebag flank cinch, threw them to the ground, and jumped back into the saddle. I was at full gallop without drawing a single shot.

When I saw two of the bandits dismount to go after the bags, I pulled around a windswept oak and flew out of the saddle, rifle in hand. The remainder of the band kept after me, so I didn't have much time. I leaned against the tree trunk to steady myself and took three quick shots at the relatively stationary men on the ground. One fell, and the other grabbed his arm as he screamed obscenities. At least, I assumed they were obscenities. My rudimentary Spanish didn't include the more colorful aspects of the language. I leaped back into the saddle and spurred Liberty away from the incoming bullets sprayed around me by the men in pursuit.

The mounted bandits had gained too much ground, and I wondered if I had made a fatal mistake by stopping to throw off the saddlebags and again to shoot at the bandits picking them up.

I wasn't sure if the lightened load made a difference, but Liberty gradually pulled away from the band. I kept looking ahead for a place where I could have an advantage. My hope was a swale that narrowed enough so that they could pursue only in single file. Nothing ahead. I looked back, and although they were still chasing me, the bandits fell further behind. Or maybe *fell* was the wrong word. I suddenly felt like they were herding me. They let me get a lead because they knew what lay ahead. What kind of trouble was I riding into?

More bandits! That must be the answer. They were pushing me up this hill because compatriots waited over the crest. Perhaps their camp lay ahead. They allowed Liberty to pull away as long as I rode in the direction they wanted. I searched left and right, looking for an escape. None. I was committed to going forward.

pang of guilt

As I hit the crest, I saw what they were driving me toward. Nothing. A flat plain that extended north and south as far as the eye could see, with a steep incline to the east. The brown, dried-out grass rose only about a foot, and I couldn't see a single scrub oak. No cover. Lots of room to run, but nowhere to hide. Damn it, they had saved their horses for the real contest.

I felt doomed but turned Liberty north toward San Juan Capistrano. It made no sense to lumber up the steepening incline, so I would head in the direction of the closest mission. I looked back. The bandits had started to lash their horses with their saddle strings, yelping like hunting dogs that had finally treed a fox. Sooner or later, one or more of the bandits would run me down. I needed a gully ... or a tree ... or a mound. Anything to hide behind. Anything.

I spotted a dry creek bed. Not much, but it would have to do. My problem was Liberty. I could lay in the shallow gully, but it was not deep enough to provide cover for my horse. Would they shoot him? Cavalry horses were trained

18

to lie down when a dismounted rider pulled the reins down and to the side. I had never practiced this maneuver with Liberty, but I had forced him at times to lie down. I leaped out of the saddle, throwing my rifle to the position I intended to shoot from, and tugged Liberty toward the ground. He didn't resist. I slid over to the upslope of the gully, picked up my rifle, and moved sideways so Liberty wouldn't be directly behind me. I took aim. They were coming fast and riding low, their heads shielded by their horses' necks. I had a split-second pang of guilt … then shot the horses.

The first horse stumbled and fell, throwing its rider over its head. Then another horse tripped on the first and went down as well. The second horse I shot caused all the other riders to whirl around and retreat. Now I took a bead on one of the tossed bandits as he moved shakily to his feet. He went down hard this time. The other two tossed riders kept their heads. They remained prone as they crawled backward, stopping on occasion to throw a few bullets in my direction. I took a single shot to hurry them along.

ambush

After what seemed like an hour, but was probably less than half that time, I wondered if I should climb back onto Liberty and ride away. The bandits had dropped below the crest of the hill they had chased me up, and I had seen no further sign of them. Had they left? I had now killed four and wounded another. That should make them reconsider. They had my saddlebags, which even empty were worth a week's wages. The clothing and books should fetch several dollars more. The bags also held five double-eagle gold coins worth one hundred dollars. They had no idea if I carried more money on my person. As far as they knew, my clothes and horse, plus maybe some pocket change, were my only remaining valuables.

Wishful thinking. Liberty, an obviously fine animal, would fetch a good price below the border. The men I had killed were probably friends or relatives. A grudge can induce men to do foolish things. Besides, these pursuers had shown no inclination to give up.

I thought. Just because they dropped below the crest several hundred yards back didn't mean they needed to return to this flat area from the same location. In fact, they wouldn't. I looked due west. I was about forty yards from the ridge. If they charged at me from that location, I could get off two or three shots before they overran this position. Or … they could ambush me. The gully curved enough so that I had cover from a sharpshooter lying perpendicular to me below the crest, but I doubted they could hit my head, because I was moving locations and didn't stay exposed for long periods. But I couldn't hit them either, and a couple of shooters from that location could easily pin me down while others charged me from another direction.

Damn. I had to get out of there.

I pulled Liberty to his feet, but instead of riding, I led him on foot in a northerly direction. I wouldn't mount until I saw pursuers. In the meantime, I wanted Liberty to get as much rest as possible. I heard a sharp yell in Spanish. As I suspected, they had someone keeping an eye on me. How long would it take for them to get after me? Not long. I saw the band down the plain emerge first, but two riders soon came up from almost the exact place I had guessed they would wait in ambush.

Another chase. This was getting tiresome.

Instead of mounting Liberty, I walked around behind him and used my saddle as a brace to lay my rifle against. These bandits had been savvy until now, but the two groups were separated by over a hundred yards. I couldn't resist shooting the two on ambush detail. I saw them recognize their error just as I fired. Five dead. The second rider turned back toward his compatriots and lashed his horse mercilessly. I took careful aim. Should I shoot a man in the back as he ran away? I could shoot the horse, but the animal meant me no harm. I shot the man. After all, the bandit had killing in his heart, and if I let him go now, he would return. Next time, the odds might not be in my favor. Besides, I told myself that attempting to assassinate me from behind cover didn't warrant mercy.

Six dead.

hounding my tail

I mounted Liberty and rode away at a leisurely pace. The band rode after me at a full gallop. Good. Let them fatigue their horses. I saw nothing but flatness ahead, so I drove over the edge of an embankment and headed back toward the trail running along the ocean. Perhaps this time I could get support from fellow travelers.

The band followed me back toward civilization. They came on stronger than ever, yelling what I assumed were profanities. For a moment, I wanted to dismount and fight it out. Kill every damn one of them. I hadn't asked for this. I didn't want to kill, but they insisted on hounding my tail with intent to murder me for a few hundred dollars' worth of gear and horseflesh. Damn it, anyway.

Reason prevailed. I had whittled their number down, but I still counted eight men in pursuit. Too many. I needed help … or a narrow path that would require them to approach in single file. I searched left and right. Then I abandoned the idea. I had a canteen of water, but my food had been in the saddlebags. If I hid in a narrow ravine, they would pin me down until hunger forced me to do something stupid. A narrow path would work only if I had an exit that wouldn't require me to pass by the bandits. That was too much to hope for. Better to concentrate on getting back to the trail and finding travelers willing to help.

I could see the ocean, but it looked to be over two miles away. Had I really come inland that far? Evidently. I looked back. The bandits were no longer gaining ground on me. Now they fell behind, not by intent, but because they had worn out their horses. I patted Liberty's neck and continued to ride at an unhurried pace. I smiled. I may not have beat them yet, but if my luck held, I would soon be rid of them.

It occurred to me that I would need to hire guards for the return trip. I wouldn't want to run into this band again without extra gun hands.

I checked behind once again. They had not closed the gap. When I faced front again, my mood instantly turned from pleased to frightened. Four riders approached, all with rifles braced against their legs, barrels pointed up. Riding abreast, these men wore Mexican garb and unpleasant smiles. If I had any further doubts, one of them waved a greeting to my pursuers. I was trapped in a pincer maneuver.

I pulled up. No obstacle prevented me from going left or right, but that would result in a simple horse race that I would eventually lose. Well, hell. I spurred Liberty, and we drove right at the four bandits directly ahead. I pulled my Colt and threw a shot low to spook the horses. Their smirks went away as fast as my good mood had vanished. They hadn't expected a charge. Now I was close enough to aim at the men, not their hapless mounts. I waited a beat. Standing in the stirrups, leaning forward, I put a bullet in the man on the far right, then veered hard in his direction. Two of the bandits were trying to shoot their rifles one-handed. The third was shoving his rifle back in its sheath so he could use a handgun. A smarter play, so I shot him next. By then I was parallel to them, so I put my head down and urged Liberty to run for all he was worth. He was worth all my fortune. I heard shots, but none hit me or Liberty.

We had cleared their secondary force.

let them attack

The downhill slope to the sea allowed me to see all the way to shore. It looked to be over a mile, but Liberty was gliding down with ease. Damn, it felt good to be finally rid of those bastards. No more bandits ahead, and the ones behind appeared to have given up the chase. Then I got angry when I remembered they had taken my saddlebags. I had half a mind to go take them back, but that made no sense. I was free and clear and only ten minutes away from a well-traveled trail.

I slowed Liberty to a walk. He had earned a respite. Besides, I kept an eye on my rear and saw nothing of the bandits. After seven dead and one wounded, I guessed they had finally given up. Out of danger, I dreamed of revenge. I could hire a team of hard men and rid the trail of highwaymen. The thought gave me pleasure, but I knew I didn't want to get involved in a long-running feud.

I felt content until I saw something to the side that made me shiver. About a hundred yards north, riders were racing to get in front of me. I still walked Liberty, but these riders were galloping like there was no tomorrow. This was not over. Damn.

I pulled Liberty to a halt and dismounted. I stopped so I would have a steady shot at anyone riding toward me. If the bandits wanted to race up the hill in front of me, let them attack in the wide open. I'd wait right in this spot and allow Liberty to graze. I pulled my rifle from the sheath and shoved cartridges in the loading gate until it was full. I had an extended fifteen-round tube, so having enough cartridges would not be a problem. The problem would be not getting hit by one of their bullets before I killed them all. I also reloaded my pistol. If they got close enough, I could fire it quicker.

I cradled the rifle in my arms and stared down the slope at the bandits as they gathered at the bottom of the hill. There appeared to be nine. Where did the other one go? I suddenly became wary. Was this a distraction while a sharpshooter ambushed me? I discounted the possibility almost immediately. I was sure they would assume I would run, just like I had done all day. They'd not likely assume that I would stay in place and dare them to attack. At least, I hoped that was the case. A quick perusal of my surroundings showed no threats. In fact, the landscape provided no cover. More likely, the wounded man had died, stayed behind, or made his way back to camp to get help.

The bandits sat astride their horses, glaring at me, their animals pawing the ground and snorting. They wanted to come. They wanted to attack. They wanted to kill me.

Damn it, let them come.

slip right by them

They split up. Five went north, four south. They chose not to charge up an incline for a frontal attack. Instead, they intended to ambush me if I tried to return south to San Luis Rey de Francía or continue north to San Juan Capistrano. I hated to admit that this was the smart move. I was good with a rifle and could have brought down at least four before they got close enough to hit me from horseback. I only needed a little luck or a miscalculation on their part to come out on top.

Now, I was the one who had to make a smart decision. North or south? The odds dictated going south, but my meeting with Archibald Peachy lay to the north. I waited until the bandits disappeared before taking Liberty by the reins to walk north. I would continue my trip to Los Angeles. They would not get the satisfaction of driving me away from my destination.

24

I stayed on high ground. I had never traversed this terrain, and they probably knew it like the back of their hand. They'd guess I'd stay above the trail, so they'd probably set up their ambush in a spot above the coastal thoroughfare. Should I try again to find fellow travelers to help me? Yes. I decided to drop back down to the trail in a mile or so. With luck, they would have repositioned to intercept me inland, and I might slip right by them. In the meantime, I'd allow Liberty a good rest in case we needed to make another run for it.

incredible speed

When I returned to El Camino Real, I ran into no other travelers. People intent on completing the ride between missions would be further along in their journey. Because of my delays, it would be dusk or possibly even dark before I reached San Juan Capistrano. I considered riding hard to catch up with travelers further down the road but wanted Liberty fresh in case of another run-in with the bandits.

The first hour was uneventful, and I started to think my luck had changed. Then I came upon a bend with trees clustered along what must have been a streambed in the wet season. If they wanted to ambush me, this spot would be perfect. The bend in the trail forced travelers to ride hundreds of feet parallel to the tree-lined shallow. I brought Liberty to a stop.

They were there. I knew it. They would never give up.

I could ride straight at them or try to bypass them on the inland side. Closer to the ocean wouldn't work, because the arroyo became wide where the winter stream plunged over the shoreline cliff. I examined the cliff. If I could find a way down, perhaps I could ride through the sand close by the water. I discarded the idea when I realized that I would present a perfect target for potshots from above. I stood in my stirrups but couldn't see anyone hiding ahead. That

25

didn't mean they weren't there, only that I couldn't see a target.

It wasn't the rainy season. No rush of water carved the arroyo deeper. No matter where I looked, I could not see green. The grass and every shrub had been burnt brown by a relentless sun. I held a spit-moistened finger in the air. The wind blew from the ocean. I had a plan.

I dismounted and walked on Liberty's seaward side to the cliff, continuing along the ridge until I reached the arroyo. I pulled a tube of matches from my pocket and lit the dry grass. Then I backed away from the arroyo, keeping Liberty between me and the likely ambush site.

The fire grew fast, taking on a life of its own. I worried that it would consume the entire countryside. What would ever stop it? Were there homes in the way of the fire? I just wanted a small blaze to scare away the bandits, but this inferno moved with incredible speed. The intense heat surprised me. Despite being back from the fire, Liberty neighed as he struggled to get free of my grip.

Thankfully, the fire blew to the east and didn't jump the arroyo, but it did burn up the incline that led to some rolling hills in the distance. I couldn't see if the fire forced the bandits to run, because a smoke curtain made it impossible to see anything beyond the arroyo. Then I noticed something else. The fire subsided quickly after it burnt through the dry grass. In minutes, there was nothing left to burn. As the smoke blew inland, I saw riders scurrying away on the far side of the streambed.

I may have caused a bigger fire than I had intended, but I had accomplished my goal.

trapped

I waited for the sparks to wane so I could lead Liberty over to the other side. I waited too long. A shot rang out from behind. Then two. A quick glance confirmed that the brush fire had drawn the bandits who had headed south. Damn. I mounted Liberty and rode hard for a wooden bridge that crossed the arroyo. When I got to the other side, I dismounted and led Liberty down a steep slope to hide him under the bridge. Then I crawled up the embankment with my rifle. Now I was the one in the ambush position.

The bandits halted their progress to evaluate the situation. I took solace that they were not the smart ones. Otherwise, they wouldn't have thrown random shots that forewarned me. Perhaps they would come right at me. After a few minutes, I realized that they may not have been the smartest of the bandits, but they knew enough not to charge at a man shooting from cover. The thought triggered a glance behind me, but I couldn't see the rest of the band. Now the bullet made more sense. They had fired at me to signal to the rest of their band that they had returned.

I surveyed my position and decided to move to the other side of the bridge where the ravine narrowed so I could move quicker between the north and south banks of the streambed. I had no food and very little water, but plenty of ammunition. I wondered who had my saddlebags. I peeked at the band, but they remained too far away for me to see their gear clearly. Because of my fire, there were no shrubs or tall grass to obscure my head when I lifted it above the ridge. I visually examined the bridge, but it had withstood my fire and looked far too substantial to burn easily.

Suddenly, I heard something behind me. Sure enough, the other portion of the band had returned. They had me trapped.

escape plan

The two bands spread out wide, at least ten feet between each man. They approached slowly. Who leads these bandits? I spotted the man closest to the ocean yell and give hand signals. Others acknowledged his commands, confirming his leadership. My furthest shot. Why would men follow such a yellow dog?

The line from the south seemed to move faster, so I lay on that bank and took careful aim. I was just about to squeeze the trigger when they did something unexpected. They dismounted. Glancing behind, I saw that the other line must have already swung down from their horses, because they were all without riders. The fire had not burned the grass on the north side at all, and the bandits were concealed as they crawled toward me. The ones to the south were not so lucky. The scorched earth provided little cover.

If I stayed and fought, I would soon be dead. Not a desirable outcome. My only choice was to go east. If I followed the streambed west, I'd end up where the land dropped off to the ocean. No escape that way. Going uphill to the east, I would find many of the bandits bunched up below me. That escape route meant I had to leave Liberty under the bridge, because he was too tall to be hidden by the shallow depression, and my escape plan would be exposed.

I took my canteen from Liberty and hunched low to scramble up the incline, away from the coast.

kill them all

Once I had moved about a hundred yards, the streambed became too low to conceal me. I had expected this. I knew the water-eroded channel didn't provide escape, only a better fighting position.

I was now on foot, hunched down in a ditch, with relentless pursuers. I wanted to live, so I had no choice. I had to kill them all.

Tributary water flows had eroded the walls of the swale in places that might provide a position where I could hide from someone sneaking up the streambed. But for now, I wanted as smooth a surface as possible to lie against. I soon found a spot with clean slopes on either side, the walls close enough that I could swing from north to south with ease. I used a bush blackened by the fire to disguise my head peeking over the ledge. The bandits still crawled toward my old location, but now I lay nearly opposite the one furthest inland. This closest bandit thought I was still huddled far below, so he grew careless and failed to keep his head down.

With my first shot, I had the luxury of taking my time. I took aim at his head as he crawled high on his elbows. I squeezed. My bullet caused a plume of blood to spray the air. I quickly readjusted my aim, but everyone else had bent low to the ground. I flipped around to check on my assailants from the north. One idiot was running hunched over. I pulled two shots. Both struck him, but neither might have been fatal. Didn't matter. His injuries were severe enough that he no longer presented a threat. Again, the other bandits ducked so low, they had to be eating dirt for their noonday meal.

Now they realized I was far more inland than they had supposed. Those closest to the ocean on the north side stood and ran to the streambed. I snapped a shot and missed. Damn, I didn't have much time. Soon they would attack from three directions. The streambed meandered, so the bandits who scrambled into it could approach partway without being seen. They presented the greatest risk, but not at the moment. Yelling in Spanish, the leader, now safely concealed, gave orders at the top of his lungs. If I survived this attack, I would need to learn the local language. Checking the south from behind my blackened bush, I saw the remaining bandits moving away from the ocean and toward my position. This must have been what the leader had yelled out. Unfortunately for me, the bandits crawled with their heads in the dirt. I aimed at the movement anyway. Sooner or later, one of them would lift his head to make sure he was crawling in the right direction. Sooner. And uncomfortably close. I shot him before he finished raising his head. Now there were only two to the south.

I returned my attention to the north.

I finally made out one moving bandit. That meant three had made the run for the streambed. He kept low. I kept a bead on him, but he never accommodated me by lifting his head. I could wait until he got so close that hugging the ground wouldn't save him, but that would waste far too much time. Checking south, I saw that the two bandits had veered away from me. Killing two of their compatriots had made them cautious. Good. If they kept to their current track, they would enter the streambed on the ocean side of me. That meant the attack would come from one direction … except for the lone bandit to the north. I needed to kill him so I could concentrate on the streambed.

I took another look. He crawled right at me … close enough to be on me in seconds. I swung my rifle around, hesitated an instant for the barrel to steady, and shot him in the forehead. No time to waste. I scurried up the streambed until I found a crevice deep enough to hide me. Laying my rifle aside, I checked my pistol load. Six bullets. Five killers. Hopefully, the two groups wouldn't join up and coordinate their attack.

quickness

I was a good marksman with a rifle, but quicker with a pistol. Growing up in my father's gun shop, I had practiced with pistols so much that I could fire faster than even a wary person could react. But I needed surprise, so I leaned back against the slope and used only my ears to tell me when they approached.

I didn't wait long. The men trudged heavily, so they must have assumed that I had raced further up the

30

streambed. I wanted them right on top of me before I revealed myself. My sole strategy was quickness. I waited. I tried to breathe shallowly. I relaxed my muscles, especially in my gun hand. This was not a time to think. I needed to rely on instincts bred from hundreds of hours of target shooting.

I leaped up, keeping half my body shielded by the crevice. I fired three times. The first shot hit the lead attacker center chest, but he partially blocked the man behind. My next bullet put a hole into the second attacker's exposed leg. As he collapsed sideways, I shot my third bullet into his chest. Damn. These were the two who had been crawling toward me from the south. Where were the other three?

The leader had sent these two forward to draw fire while he held back. Coward. I hadn't wanted this fight, and killing repelled me, but this man deserved to die. Why would he lead men, men he had probably befriended, to attack me so relentlessly? I had proved capable of defending myself. He had my saddlebags and horse. How much money could he suppose I had on my person? In truth, I had a lot, but he had no way of knowing that. Unless. Unless that banker had forewarned him that I would be traveling El Camino Real with ten thousand dollars. How stupid of me. I had wanted to be ready to close a deal for North Island, but I should have made withdrawals from several banks over an extended period. Without conscious thought, I swept my hand across the thick money belt around my waist. They weren't out for revenge, nor would they be satisfied with five twenty-dollar gold coins. They knew what I carried. And … they needed me dead to protect the banker's fraud. This had happened before. He probably pointed out any traveler who had made a large withdrawal.

That damn banker. He would rue the day I got out of this mess.

31

hard to spot

Now what? If I escaped up the streambed, I'd probably take a bullet in the back. If I stayed put, my last memory would likely be a muzzle flash. Only one thing to do. I crawled out of the streambed to the north side, where long grass still waved in the breeze. Cradling my rifle in front of me, I scrambled directly north as fast as I could. After a few minutes, I squirmed around and faced the streambed. I stopped moving. After reloading my pistol and rifle, I lay as still as possible. While in the ditch, I had spotted the bandits crawling toward me. If I didn't move, I would be hard to spot.

I had a decent line of sight through the grass but saw nothing. Then a head popped up and down. They didn't know where I had gone. Good. They would eventually need to come out of that swale. I could be patient. Then I thought about what I would do in their situation. I would move to the other side of the bridge. Far to the other side. As far away as possible from a potential assassin lurking in the grass. I had vowed not to move, but was that the wrong strategy? The bandits were smart. They would move away from the threat, return to their horses, and hunt from horseback, with the advantage of speed and elevation.

I had to move toward the coast. I started crawling but kept my eye on the streambed. Whenever I saw a head pop up, I stopped moving. The head never changed location. He was a decoy. He was supposed to distract me while the other two bandits made their way to the far side of the bridge. The bandit did not perform his job well. Fearing a bullet in the forehead, he popped up and down so fast, he never got a good perspective on what was in front of him. Emboldened, I crawled faster.

surrender

I saw the bridge. If I could get in a few more yards, I would be in a perfect position to shoot the robbers as they came out of the streambed. Before I could move an additional foot, one of the bandits jumped up and ran for all he was worth. I almost shot him but wondered why he bounced out of the swale all by himself.

I soon had my answer. The presumed leader came charging out on the back of Liberty. The poor sod on foot was yet another decoy. Instead of shooting, I yelled "Hey, horse!" which was the way I greeted Liberty.

Liberty stopped and threw down his neck, and his rider tumbled to the ground. He was obscured by grass, so I swung around and shot the running man, who collapsed like a scarecrow thrown to the ground by a wicked wind. Only two of the band remained.

I scrunched over and kept a bead on where the bandit had been thrown. Liberty felt content to locate me and then graze while I killed the man who had tried to steal him. It occurred to me that the bandit might shoot Liberty for spite.

I yelled, "Do you want to live?"

"Hombre, you couldn't kill me on your best day."

"You're out of luck. This is my best day. Ask your amigos."

"*Antiguo soldados* I picked up in del pueblo. Nobodies. I'm a different breed. An officer. Now stand up with your hands raised, and I won't kill you."

"How about we stand up together with our hands in the air?"

"No, gringo. No fair fight. I kill you my way unless you surrender."

I worried about the bandit behind me in the streambed, but I saw no movement from that direction. I returned my attention to the front. We each knew only the general position of the other. Yelling would alert him to my exact whereabouts, so I kept quiet.

"You like your horse, hombre? Stand with hands in air, and I won't shoot it."

I rolled to the left. I knew his head would be down when he yelled. I waited.

"Hey, hombre, give me your dinero … and you can go."

I rolled left twice.

A shot rang out. Liberty raised his head but returned to grazing.

"Next bullet goes into your *caballo*. Last chance."

Two more rolls, and I cascaded into the streambed. Immediately, I checked for the other bandit. With no one in sight, I scrambled forward until I was sure I was behind the leader. I rose and spotted him not ten feet away, aiming at Liberty.

He never got off the shot.

si, señor

Now I shouted at the last bandit.

"Give up! I won't harm you!"

"Why would I trust you?"

The response came from the last of the band, still somewhere in the streambed.

I yelled again. "Do you know the banker?"

A long pause.

"I know him."

"I want him more than you. Tell the marshal … and you go free."

Another long pause.

"If no?"

"Then you are of no use to me. You will join your amigos."

"Then I say, si, señor."

two weeks later

I stepped into the San Diego bank two weeks later. I hadn't closed a deal on North Island, but negotiations remained open. I had made Miguel, the surviving bandit, bury the dead, collect the horses and guns, and return my saddlebags. He not only accompanied me on my travels, but we had become friends of sorts. His disreputable nature persisted, but he was a gregarious rogue who remained loyal to whoever paid him. I paid him well.

With the U.S. marshal at my side, I asked to speak to the bank president. Unlike Miguel, Mr. Blankenship was not gregarious, and he was disloyal to boot.

He sauntered over, hand extended, "Mr. Dancy, a pleasure to see you again. I hope your business up north went to your liking."

"Not yet, but hopefully soon. I'm pleased with the progress." I detected no surprise at my return, but he probably knew the robbery had not gone well. "However, I did encounter a mishap on the way to Los Angeles."

He looked me up and down. "A shame, but you look well. I hope it was a minor mishap."

"Not really. I killed many men to protect my purse. Men who tried to rob me … at your bidding."

He looked aghast. "Never! I don't associate with riffraff. You're mistaken."

"Am I? Perhaps you wish to tell Miguel Lopez that he's riffraff."

Miguel came forward, wearing a friendly smile. "Señor Blankenship, I have bad news. We failed in our last robbery." He bowed. "*Lo siento*, this Mr. Dancy is *un duro* hombre."

Now Blankenship looked surprised. He said, "I never saw this man before."

The marshal spoke for the first time. "Perhaps you remember Mrs. Harding. Her husband withdrew a large sum to buy horse stock. He never returned from his buying trip." He stepped forward. "Señor Lopez returned a saddle engraved with her husband's name." The marshal pulled his pistol. "There are six men besides Mr. Lopez who say you tipped them about lone riders with large amounts of money. They've all agreed to testify."

Blankenship looked furtively around for an escape path.

"Run," I said. "Please."

"Listen, I may have had too much to drink one evening and blabbed about Mr. Dancy's withdrawal. I meant no harm."

I held out a satchel. "Your money. It's counterfeit. You had me ambushed to hide that you were behind the rash of counterfeit money in San Diego."

"What? No!"

"We have additional witnesses," the marshal said as he handed Blankenship a piece of paper. "This is a warrant to examine your vault."

Blankenship started to wail. "I can give you names, men below the border who print this money. But only if we make a deal."

"Do you admit you had me robbed?" I asked.

Blankenship spoke only to the marshal. "I admit it, but I'm not the only one who passes bad bills. I can provide names. Here, in San Diego, and in Mexico. Can we deal?"

"Mr. Blankenship, you're under arrest."

The End

About the author

James Best is the author of the bestselling Steve Dancy Tales: *The Shopkeeper*, *Leadville*, *Murder at Thumb Butte*, *The Return*, *Jenny's Revenge*, and *Crossing the Animas*. His other novels include *Tempest at Dawn* and *The Shut Mouth Society*. *Principled Action* and *The Digital Organization* are his nonfiction books. James has ghost written three books, authored two regular magazine columns, and published numerous journal articles.

He is a member of Western Writers of America, Western Literature Association, and the Pacific Beach Surf Club. James enjoys writing, film, surfing, skiing, and watching his grandchildren play sports and cavort.

James and his wife Diane live in Omaha, San Diego, and New York City.

His blog, social media sites, and contact information can be found at:

http://jamesdbest.blogspot.com/

His books can be found here.

Lady Marshal

By
Ken Farmer

CHAPTER ONE
JACK COUNTY, TEXAS

"Where'd you git that gun an' stuff, Charlie?" asked thirteen year old Donny Weber as he looked at the big rusty old Patterson Colt, a bullet mold, small can of black powder, bar of lead and a melting pitcher on the rickety kitchen table.

"Traded fer it down to Mister Bagwell's General Store in Antelope," said the fifteen year old as he scraped the green mold from a small slab of fatback, and sliced it into four pieces, placing them in a battered old tin skillet on the top of a potbellied stove.

"What in the world did you have to trade fer it?"

"Mama's gold weddin' ring."

"Charlie! You cain't do that. Her ring was all we had to 'member her by…Tell me you didn't go and do that."

"Well, I did."

Donny paced a quick circle in the tiny kitchen of the ramshackle rural shack. "An' what about that spavined mule you led in behind ol' Ted…Where'd you git him?"

"Same place. Mister Bagwell throwed him in with the deal."

"You'll go to hell fer this Charlie…It's wrong, plumb wrong."

"It was things we needed…" He flipped the slices of sizzling fat back over in the skillet. "…fer what we gotta do."

Donny paused a moment in thought. "No, no, no, Charlie! You still ain't plannin on doin' that, air ye?"

"Dammit to hell, Donny, we got to. They's takin' the farm an' everthang…Now shut up an' eat." He handed his little brother two pieces of the half-burned fatback on a cracked plate.

Donny spun on his heel and tore through the battered old screen door to the outside. "Ain't hungry…Yer a gonna git us kilt."

FLAT CREEK

"Reckon 'nybody might recognize Bo in Antelope?" asked Carson, the youngest of the Standish brothers.

"Don't see as how. We never been in this part of Texas afore," said the oldest, Cougar—a barrel-chested man with a full beard and a face that had been on the receiving end of more than one fight—as he picked up the beat-up old coffee pot from a flat rock next to the fire.

"'Sides, he's good at scoutin' out of the way little towns fer banks, stores an' such…The nearest law's in Jacksboro, I hear tell, an' that's right at twenty miles south of there."

"How'd you know 'bout Antelope?"

"'Member that ol' cowboy cell mate of mine up in McAlister? You know…Slim?"

"Shore. He could take a bath in a gun barrel…Talk the hind leg off'n a mule."

"Well, I done a lotta listenin' to his blather…He wuz kindly entertain' most of the time."

"So?"

"So, he wuz atellin' bout the trail drive days after Lincoln's War an' how they taken several herds up the Texas Trail. Well, Antelope was the last supply point 'fore they got to the Red an' joined up with the Chisholm Trail a headin' north…said it was a wild an' woolly place back then. Had several general stores, a small bank, an' best of all…no lawdogs."

"Well, if'n Bo don't git distracted at the waterin' hole, I mind we'll know if'n they is er if'n they ain't when he gits back."

ANTELOPE, TEXAS

Charlie and Donny tied the old plow horse and the mule to a canopy post at the side of the Merchant's Bank. They each tied a bandana around their necks and pulled them up over their noses, just below their eyes.

"There, that oughta do…Now, you jest do what I tell you an' thangs will go fine, you hear?"

Donny shook his head. "It ain't right, Charlie. It jest ain't right. Mama an' Papa taught us better'n this."

"Well, this here bank killed Mama and Papa jest as sure as we're standin' here…Mama worried so much over payin' the note after the drought that the flu taken her an' Papa died from a broken heart from losin' Mama…All on account of that black-hearted banker…They's gonna pay. Now you jest point that old shotgun like you mean business when we git in there."

"It's broke, Charlie…won't shoot…Even if'n we had cartridges."

"They don't know that. Now, git." He pointed down the boardwalk to the corner of the bank building.

Charlie pushed open the nine foot tall door to the small bank, and stepped inside with the old Colt in his hand. Donny followed tentatively behind him.

"Now, this here's a hold up. Don't nobody move," Charlie said, making his voice as low and gravely as he could. "Shoot anybody that moves, Otho…an' give them yahoos that flour sack to fill with cash from their drawers."

Donny glanced over at his brother. "Otho?…Oh, right…uh, Billy Bob."

Charlie shook his head, and then turned to the nearest cashier. "You there, open the safe an' be quick about it now."

"I, uh, don't have the combination."

"Then git it." He waved the gun about.

"All right, all right. Just be careful with that hogleg."

The president of the bank, T.J. Mortensen strode into the bank lobby from his office at the side of the teller cages. "What the duce is going on here?"

"It's a robbery, Mister Mortensen," said the first teller.

"The devil you say? You boys get out of here and put down that gun."

Charlie poked him in his ample stomach with the Patterson. "No! You open that there safe 'fore somebody gits hurt." He used both thumbs to cock the hammer on the old pistol.

The president threw up his hands and backed up. "All right. Just a minute."

He bent over the safe, spun the dial several times to the right, once to the left and once more back to the right. There was a muted click as he turned the handle and pulled the thick door open.

"Now put them stacks of foldin' money in his sack." Charlie pointed to Donny. "Bring it over here, Otho."

Mortensen grabbed the six stacks of greenbacks and dropped them in the sack. He stared first at Donny and then at Charlie. "Wait a minute, I know you. You're Jason Weber's boys, Charlie and Donny…You hand that money back right now!"

"Oh, Lord, Charlie. The jig's up. He knows," whined Donny.

"Shut'ur face an' let's git outta here."

They turned, ran to the door just as it opened and the attractive eighteen year old daughter of the owner of Youngblood's Mercantile, Regina Youngblood, stepped in.

The three collided, Charlie's pistol discharged, striking the young lady. She moaned and collapsed to the floor.

"Oh, God, no," shouted the president.

"I never meant to, it just went off."

"Charlie, Charlie, what do we do?" yelled Donny.

42

He looked down at the puddle of blood growing around Regina's body, and then back up at Donny. "Run…Go, go."

The two boys sprinted around the corner to their mounts. Charlie quickly tied the sack to his saddlehorn, mounted, and they galloped off as fast as their decrepit mounts could take them.

Across the street in front of the Cool Water Saloon, Bo Standish had stepped out onto the boardwalk at the sound of the pistol shot. He casually took out his makings, rolled a quirley, licked the edge of the thin paper and stuck it in the corner of his mouth as he watched the Weber boys ride out of town, heading east.

Reaching into his vest pocket, he pulled out a strike anywhere match, scratched it on a canopy post, lit the homemade cigarette and sauntered across the street toward the crowd gathering at the bank…

CHAPTER TWO
SHERIFF'S OFFICE
JACKSBORO, TEXAS

Sheriff Mason Flynn was loading a '76 Winchester at the gun rack when Deputy Gomer Platt burst through the front door waving a telegram.

"Sheriff! Got a telegram for you." The young man bent over with his hands on his knees to catch his breath.

"Well, what's it say, Platt? Can't you see I have my hands full?" The mustachioed, broad-shouldered peace officer said without looking up from inserting the last round into the magazine.

"Uh, yes, sir." He ripped open the yellow envelope and unfolded the flimsy. "Sheriff Flynn - Stop - Merchants Bank of Antelope robbed this morning - Stop - Young lady shot - Stop - Not fatal - Robbers were Charlie and Donny Weber - Stop - Both teenagers - Stop - Made off with over five thousand dollars - Stop - Witnesses say boys riding a plow horse and a mule headed east - Please come - Stop - T.J. Mortensen, President - Stop." Platt looked up at Flynn.

"Well, slap Aunt Gussie in the face. Just ain't enough of me to go around today." He laid the rifle on his battered and scarred oak desk and stepped over to the brand new telephone mounted on the wall.

He lifted the black receiver, turned the crank on the opposite side of the wooden box several times, and then spoke into the funnel-like mouthpiece mounted in the center of the box. "Mary, this is Sheriff Flynn. Need you to ring the sheriff's office over in Gainesville. I'll wait."

He snapped his fingers a couple of times at Platt for the telegram. The nineteen year old, sandy-haired deputy rushed over and handed it to him.

"I have your party, Sheriff Flynn," said Mary through the receiver.

44

"Thank you…Sheriff Durbin?"

"I'm here, Sheriff Flynn, how kin I help you?" said Walt.

"Need to get a message to Marshal Miller. You got somethin' to write with?"

SHERIFF'S OFFICE
GAINESVILLE, TEXAS

"You're in luck, Sheriff, she's right here in the office. Just a second."

Sheriff Durbin held the receiver out to a tall raven-haired beauty with a crescent and star Deputy US Marshal's badge pinned to the red paisley bustier she wore underneath a black morning coat.

"Sheriff Flynn! How are you this morning?" she asked.

"Up to my backside in bobcats, Fiona…Could use a little help."

"Be a pleasure, Mason. What do you need?"

"I was fixin' to head out of town south toward Graford. Rustlers made off with 'bout fifty head an' killed the rancher and one of his hands…Then, just a bit ago, the bank up to Antelope…the complete opposite direction…was robbed of over five thousand dollars by two teenagers, plus they shot a young woman, the daughter of the owner of Youngblood's Mercantile. Both trails are hot an' there ain't 'nough of me to go 'round. Don't have but the two deputies an' I need them to stay here in town to watch things."

Fiona glanced over at Sheriff Durbin. "I see…Which one do you want me to take?"

"The bank robbery, if you could…"

"It will be tomorrow before I can get there, Mason. I'll leave right away."

"Actually, you could catch the Santa Fe to Henrietta. Antelope's only 'bout twenty miles south of there…Be a whole lot closer an' quicker for you."

"That sounds good. I'll check at the depot for the next west bound. Anything else I need to know?"

"The boys are ridin' an old plow horse an' a wore out mule an' headed east from Antelope, I'm told…Now, you know what I know."

"Fine, since it's just two teenagers, I'll see about wrapping it up quick as I can and come down and give you a hand with the rustlers…It's still a hanging offense in Texas."

SHERIFF'S OFFICE
JACKSBORO, TEXAS

"It is that." Flynn gave the crank a couple of turns to charge the line for disconnect and hung the receiver back on the side hook.

"Alright, Platt. You and Parker take care of things. I'll try to get back soon as I can. He should be back from making his rounds in a bit…Oh, an' while you're restin' you can scrub down that cell where the drunks were last night. Think the three of 'em musta puked a couple gallons. It's startin' to git rank back there."

"Oh, boy," Platt frowned.

"Part of the job, boy, part of the job."

"Yessir." He took a small brown paper sack from his coat pocket, extracted a lemon drop and popped it in his mouth. "I'll wait till Slim gits back, meby I kin git him to help."

"So long as it's done by the time I git back…Understand?"

SHERIFF'S OFFICE
GAINESVILLE, TEXAS

Fiona waited for the line to go dead, hung up her receiver and then turned to Sheriff Durbin.

"Well, Walt, guess I better go down to the depot and check on schedules." She grabbed her hat from the tree and headed toward the door.

The sheriff cleared his throat. "Ahem…uh, Fiona." He pointed to a chart behind his desk.

She stepped over closer and got an embarrassed look on her classic features. "Oh…Should have looked around," she said while perusing the Santa Fe hourly schedule.

"The depot sends over a new one every time they add or subtract a train. KATY does the same."

"Well, saves a trip…West bound from Paris is due in forty-five minutes. Just enough time to get my gear together and saddle Spot."

FLAT CREEK

Bo pulled rein at the edge of the camp, tied his blood bay to a sapling and loosened the girth.

"'Bout time you got back…They still got a bank there?" asked Cougar.

His younger brother squatted down by the campfire, grabbed the coffee pot with his bandana and filled a tin cup with the stout trail brew.

"Well?" Cougar inquired again.

Bo took a sip and looked back up. "Yep, but robbin' it won't do no good."

"What do you mean? It's a bank or it ain't," said the middle brother, Carson.

"No money in it," said Bo after he took another sip.

"You ain't makin' no sense atall," commented Cougar.

"Somebody beat us to it. Watched it happen. Two teenagers robbed it this mornin', shot the daughter of a local business man an' made off with 'bout five thousand dollars…'cordin' to the bank."

Cougar spat a long stream of tobacco juice at the fire. "Son of a bitch!"

"Hold on, now, brother, you didn't listen to what I said."

The bigger man glared at Bo. "So, you wanna lick that calf again, smart aleck?"

"I said it was robbed by a couple of teenagers…I watched 'em ride out of town on a broke down old plow horse an' a spavined mule…Tracked 'em a little ways…Got no idee how to cover their trail." Bo grinned.

Cougar jumped to his feet. "Hot damn almighty…Mind where you're a goin."

"Uh, huh. We track down the little snot-noses, take the money an' nobody'll ever know we wuz even 'round," said Bo.

"What 'bout them kids?" asked Carson.

Bo glanced over at his brother. "What kids?" He chuckled. "Ain't nobody ever gonna find hide, hair er tallow of 'em when we're done."

"Damnation, Bo, you done thought this all through, ain'tcha?" said Cougar.

"They sendin' a posse out after 'em?" asked Carson.

"Hell, the nearest law is in Jacksboro an' we're a hellova lot closer to Antelope than any posse from there." Bo grinned, took another sip of his coffee, and then pitched it in the fire.

"You say they headed east?" asked Cougar.

"Yep, straight towards that thicket area 'tween Antelope an' Bowie."

"Then we'll jest see as we kin cut 'em off…Mount up."

YOUNGBLOOD'S MERCANTILE

"Regina gonna be alright?" asked the foreman of Carter Youngblood's large cattle operation, Ness McBride.

48

The owner of the mercantile, sitting behind his big ornate desk back in the office, snipped the end from an expensive Cuban cigar, lit a match and held it to the end until he had a good smooth burn. "Doc says she will...lost a lot of blood, though." Carter took a draw and blew a smoke ring over his head. "No thanks to those damn Weber kids...I'm going to see that they pay for hurting my baby...White trash."

He took another draw, turned his swivel chair and looked out the window. "Tell you what, Ness, go out to the ranch and get a couple of the boys that are handy and can keep their mouths shut."

"Sure, boss. What'd you got in mind?"

Youngblood spun his chair back around, blew another cloud of smoke out and leaned forward on his elbows. "We're going to go after the nefarious little bastards and get the money back...Most of it's mine anyway."

"What about them boys?"

Carter squinted at his hired gun. "I imagine they'll resist us taking them back...don't you?"

CHAPTER THREE
SANTA FE DEPOT
HENRIETTA, TEXAS

Fiona led her red and white Tobiano John mule, Spot, down the cleated ramp from the livestock car, tightened his cinch up when she got to the bottom and swung easily into the saddle. She flipped the hostler a silver dollar, touched the brim of her black Stetson Gambler's hat, squeezed Spot into his mile eating single foot road trot and headed south toward Antelope.

Unlike most women of the day, Fiona preferred to ride astraddle when on the trail as opposed to the more genteel sidesaddle. She had a special pair of dark gray gabardine pants made with a doeskin insert down the inside of each leg and covering her bottom. Her long raven hair was tied together at the base of her neck with a beaded leather thong made by her late husband's Cherokee grandmother. The balance of her lustrous tresses was draped over her left shoulder.

LODGE CREEK

Charlie and Donny were letting their jaded mounts rest and drink from the creek. Both of the frightened boys were sitting on the bank, holding their reins.

"What are we gonna do, Charlie? You knowed it was wrong!"

"Hush up, Donny. Jest hush up."

"We ain't got a chance...They'll ketch us...We're a gonna hang."

"Will you hush your mouth and let me think?"

"Why'd you have to go an' shoot Regina fer anyways. She was always nice to us in school."

Charlie jumped to his feet startling his horse. "Shut up, dammit to hell...I tol' you it was an accident."

"Don't make no difference...We'll hang, Charlie, we'll hang...then what good's all that money gonna do?"

"Meby it didn't kill her." Charlie's eyes filled with tears.

"Huh?"

"Meby I only wounded her."

"You think so?"

"They wouldn't hang us for just wounding Regina...would they?"

"What in the world you askin' me fer?" Donny turned away from his brother. "...Never listen to nothin' I say anyways."

"Well, we ain't agonna stay around here to find out...Cinch up."

"Please, Charlie, we're jest makin' it harder on ourselves by runnin'."

"Damnation, Donny, don't argue with me...I'm the oldest. Now, cinch up that saddle...We'll ride down the middle of the creek in case they's 'nybody a follerin' us."

JACK COUNTY
RANCH ROAD

"Well, them kids ain't none too hard to track...A barefoot horse in bad need of a trim an' a mule," commented Ness, glancing at the tracks in the narrow dirt road as they left the outskirts of Antelope.

The other two ranch hands, Skinny Conway and Alder Axline were riding behind McBride and Carter Youngblood. There were short spade shovels tied to each of their saddles.

They pulled rein at Lodge Creek. Alder dismounted while the others watered the horses and scouted for sign.

"Looks like they finally got smart, Mister Youngblood."

"How so?"

"Started ridin' down the middle of the creek. Its got a good rock bottom an' ain't over three foot deep, 'ceptin' at some holes."

"And that means?"

He spat a stream of tobacco juice into the slow moving water. "Well, I figure since they's headed fer that brushy thicket area east of here, an' this here creek cuts back to the south little over a mile downstream…" Alder scratched the stubble on his chin. "…that's where they'll git out an' keep a goin' east…Wuz me, anyways."

"Lead on, then. Going to be dark before long."

EAST JACK COUNTY

"I tol' you we wuz pushin' 'em too hard, Charlie," said Donny as he looked down at Ted, their old plow horse.

"He was old anyways. Git up here behind me on this mule."

"We cain't…He's already limpin' now. He'll keel over an' die too."

"Awright, we'll lead 'im 'nother mile er so an' see as we kin make camp fer the night. Be dark thirty by then…We waded that creek fer better'n a mile. Shoulda lost 'nybody that might a been a tailin' us."

***

"This oughta do." Forty-five minutes later Charlie looked around at the small opening in the mixed cedar and scrub oak trees alongside a nearly dry wet-weather small creek. "I'll unsaddle this mule an' hobble 'im on that grass. You gather up some firewood."

"What er we buildin' a fire for? We ain't got coffee ner 'nythin' to eat."

"Well, mister smart pants, it's gonna git a mite chilly tonight…lessen you jest want to lay there an' shiver."

***

Charlie had built a hat-sized fire close to the bank of the creek. He and Donny sat close to it on a ragged old quilt as he opened the flour sack and took out the cash from the bank and counted it.

"Great jumpin' pollywogs, Donny, you know how much money we got here?"

"Don't know an' don't care, Charlie. It's gonna git us both kilt...You wait and see."

"We got over five thousand dollars!"

"Tol' you I didn't wanna know." Donny rolled over and pulled his knees up to his chest.

A gibbous moon was just rising above the trees as Charlie leaned back and held up a stack of the greenbacks. "Five thousand dollars! Good gosh a mighty."

***

Ness McBride, got to his feet after feeling of the dead horse. "Still a mite warm, Mister Youngblood. Cain't be very far ahead...Not more'n a mile er two, I'd say. Probably up yonder next to Pecan Branch." He looked off to the east where the moon was coming up.

"Then we'll make camp back there next to those trees away from that horse. He'll be stinking before long."

"Why don't we go ahead and ketch up to 'em now, Boss?" asked McBride.

"Because I don't spend all day in the saddle like you boys. My butt's worn out. They'll be there in the morning, especially after losing a horse and didn't you say it looked like the mule was getting lame?"

"Yessir, looked to me like he was favorin' his right front some," said Ness.

"Fine…Now, go make camp, I could use some coffee and something to eat." Carter turned his Saddlebred gelding around and headed back for a grove of persimmon trees.

WISE COUNTY, TEXAS
PECAN BRANCH

There were crimson arrows trimmed in gold streaking across the sky from the breaking dawn in the eastern sky.

Skinny Conway and Alder Axline each kicked one of the boys in the ribs while holding their guns in their faces.

"Wake up, ladies," said Ness.

"Get on your feet you little thieving bastards," added Carter Youngblood.

Charlie and Donny both scrambled to their feet, trying to rub the sleep from their eyes.

"Oh, God, Charlie, it's Mister Youngblood! What are we a gonna do?"

"Shut up, kid," Youngblood slapped Donny across the mouth, knocking him to the ground.

"Leave my brother alone, you big son of a bitch." Charlie flailed at the paunchy owner of the mercantile.

Carter grabbed the fifteen year old by the front of his shirt and slapped him back and forth across the face four times, slung him to the ground, and then kicked him in the stomach. "You shot my baby girl, you worthless piece of shit."

"Here's the money, Mister Youngblood," said Ness, holding up the flour sack.

McBride pitched the sack to Skinny. "Put this in Mister Youngblood's saddlebags."

Carter drew back his foot to kick Charlie again.

"Please don't kick him no more," Donny cried as he crawled over to protect his older brother, who was in a fetal position and bleeding from his nose and mouth.

54

Ness jerked Donny to his feet and cuffed him hard against his left ear. The thirteen year old started to cry.

Charlie struggled to his feet. "Leave my little brother alone. Please don't hurt him…it was all my doin's."

"He was there too. The little shit gets what you get," said Youngblood.

"You got the money…I'll go back with you. Jest please let Donny go."

Carter laughed. "It ain't about the money, kid. You hurt my daughter…put a hole in her she'll carry the rest of her life. Can you change that?"

"Please, Mister Youngblood. I didn't mean to shoot her."

"The road to hell is paved with good intentions," said the forman, McBride.

Charlie looked at Youngblood through his tears. "What 're you a gonna do to us?"

The older man leaned over and got in Charlie's face. "First, I'm going to beat the living hell out of the both of you…You're going to wish you were dead."

"Please, Mister Youn…"

Carter backhanded the youngster across the face again, picked him back up from the ground and then slung him over to Ness. "Then I'm going to stretch your scrawny little necks from the biggest tree I can find…like right over there." He pointed at a large red oak near the creek.

McBride held both of Charlie's arms, but his legs were free. He swiftly kicked Youngblood in the crotch, sending the man to his knees wheezing.

Ness spun him around and hit Charlie up side his head with his fist, knocking him to the ground once again.

Youngblood staggered to his feet with blood in his eyes. "Damn you, damn you to hell." He stepped toward the young man, pulling his Schofield from its holster.

"Boss, hoof beats comin'," said Skinny Conway.

Fiona rode Spot into the clearing and reined the big mule to a sliding halt. She dropped his leathers, stepped to the ground and quickly took in the battered and bleeding boys. "What's going on here?" Fiona asked.

"It's a woman, Charlie," said Donny.

"I kin see," he answered softly.

"We apprehended a couple of bank robbers…and just who the hell are you, lady, to be asking?" replied Youngblood, still holding his pistol aimed at Charlie.

CHAPTER FOUR
WISE COUNTY, TEXAS
PECAN BRANCH

Fiona pulled the lapel of her black morning coat aside to show the crescent and star badge pinned to her bustier.

"Special Deputy United States Marshal F.M. Miller. I was sent at the behest of Jack County Sheriff Mason Flynn…Now, something I rarely do is repeat myself…What's going on here?"

"Like I said, we caught some bank robbers, Marshal," said Youngblood.

"Well, I'm the law around here, so you can turn those boys loose. I'll take care of it from here."

"One of them shot my daughter in the hold up."

Fiona glanced over at the portly man. "You're Youngblood, I take it?"

"I am."

"Well, Mister Youngblood, as I said, I'm not in the habit of repeating myself, so, unless you want to join your daughter in the town hospital, you let go of those boys…Right now."

Carter and McBride released their grips on the lads and the two ran over next to Fiona.

"Are you boys all right?"

"Yes, Ma'am…But jest barely," said Charlie.

She nodded. "Just call me Marshal, if you would, son…Ya'll look abused." Fiona looked back at Youngblood. "What did you do to them?"

"We don't have to answer your damn questions, lady."

"This badge and my Colts say you do."

"They were a fixin' to kill us, Marshal," said Donny.

"That's a lie…We just slapped them around a little, that's all," said Ness.

"He's the liar…They wuz gonna hang us from that big red oak over yonder." Charlie pointed.

Youngblood grimaced. "We were just trying to scare the boys some…Dammit to hell, they shot my daughter!"

"All right, everybody shut up…You boys go over and set down next to my mule. I'll deal with you later." She looked back at Youngblood. "I understand your feelings, but the law doesn't work that way…"

One of Youngblood's gunhands, Alder Axline, standing several feet to his right, moved surreptitiously toward the Colt on his hip.

Fiona drew and cocked her left hand pistol in a blur without even looking at the tall slim cowboy. "If you're wanting me to kill you that bad, Sunshine, I can certainly oblige you…Sun Tzu said, 'He who knows when he can fight and when he cannot, will be victorious'. And trust me, you wouldn't last very long."

Alder looked over at his boss. "What'd she say, Mister Youngblood?"

"She said, go for that gun and you'll die right here…Correct, Marshal?"

"Close enough…Now, all of you, unbuckle those gunbelts and drop them to the ground." Fiona turned to the boys. "Donny, you go over and collect those guns…Charlie, you get the rifles from their saddles."

As the older Webber boy passed McBride, he kicked him sharply in the shin.

Ness jumped around on one leg, holding the other. "You little bastard!"

She looked back at Youngblood. "Where's the bank money?"

"It's over here in Mister Youngblood's saddlebags," said a smiling Charlie from over by the horses as he was collecting the saddle guns.

"Bring it over here," said Fiona.

As Charlie was pulling the flour sack from Youngblood's saddlebags, he noticed a Colt birdshead Lightening with a cut-down barrel in the bottom. He glanced back at the others, and then slipped the small .38 caliber revolver into the rear pocket of his baggy bib overalls, turned and headed back.

"Mister Youngblood, just head on back to Antelope…Oh, leave one of your horses for the boys to ride."

Carter didn't move. He just stood there and glared at Marshal Miller.

"How did you ever become a business man, Youngblood? I told you what to do, you don't want me to tell you again…Trust me on that."

Carter ground his teeth and turned to his men. "All right, mount up." He looked back at Fiona. "This isn't over, Marshal."

"Who's goin' to ride double, Mister Youngblood?" asked Skinny.

"I don't give a damn. Bring me my horse."

Ness led Carter's steeldust stallion over and held him while the paunchy man mounted. He jerked the reins from his foreman's hand, viciously kicked the Saddlebred in the ribs and rode off toward the west.

McBride watched him ride off and turned to the others. "Alder, you double up with Skinny and lets git."

"Awe, Ness, why…"

"Shut your mouth and do what I said."

The three men mounted and rode after Youngblood.

Fiona watched the men ride off, and then turned to the Webers. "What on earth possessed you boys to do such a foolhardy thing?"

Charlie and Donny both began to cry.

"It's a terrible thing to shoot somebody…I should know."

"I didn't go to, Marshal," said Charlie through his tears. "The bank taken the place after momma and daddy died..." He looked over at Donny. "I'm the oldest an'...an' I jest didn't know what to do."

"Well, what's done is done."

"What are you agonna do with us, Marshal?" asked Charlie.

Fiona took a breath. "I'll take you to Jacksboro, the county seat. Sheriff Flynn's a good friend. He'll see you'll get a fair trial."

"They're agonna hang us...ain't they, Marshal Miller?" said Donny tuning up the tears again.

She pulled both the young boys to her and gave them a hug. "No, boys, you won't hang. You're under age, they'll get the money back and the shooting was accidental...no one got killed. But, you did wrong and broke the law...You'll have to pay the piper. Do you understand?"

The boys nodded and sniffed back their tears.

"Now, you both look a bit gaunted, when did you eat last?"

They glanced at each other.

"We had a little fried fat back yesterd'y mornin'," said Charlie as he looked down at his feet and then at Donny. "Leastwise I did."

"Well, go gather up some deadfall and I'll fix us something to eat. I have plenty in my saddlebags."

UNDERBRUSH NEAR CLEARING

"Knowed I smelt somethin' cookin'," said Bo Standish as he glanced back over his shoulder at his brothers crouched down behind some trees. "That's them awright...Got a woman with 'em."

The other two crept forward and peered through the branches of a juniper at Fiona and the boys eating around the campfire.

"Boy hidie, these beans with bacon are shore good, Marshal."

"Eat all you want, Donny…I can fix them two ways. Beans with bacon or bacon with beans…A Texas Ranger friend of mine likes the beans with bacon better."

Donny looked up. "Huh? I don't git…Oh!" He laughed. "That's funny…Didja hear what the Marshal said, Charlie? She said…"

"I heard her." Charlie looked off into the distance and felt of the pistol in his pocket.

Fiona's smile faded as she got to her feet. "We'll be leaving when ya'll are through and we clean up the tinwear." She picked up the sack of bank money, walked over where Spot was tethered and commenced tying it to her saddlehorn along with the gunbelts of Youngblood's crew.

"I'd be real still there, sister. Keep yer hands on that saddle an' don't turn around," said Cougar as he stepped out of the brush behind her. "Git them irons, Carson…an' hand me that sack…Bo, bring them kids over by the split tail."

Carson moved over and removed both Peacemakers from her crossdraw holsters, and then handed the bag to Cougar. "Looky here, looky here, she carries two shooters. Must fancy herself as some kinda lady gunhawk…Haw!" He stuffed the ivory-handled Colts under his gunbelt.

Carson noticed the badge pinned to her bustier. "Hey, now…She's wearing a Deputy US Marshal's badge. We got ourselves a lady law."

"A lady law? Whoever heard of such a thang?" said Bo as he shoved the boys over beside her.

Cougar opens the flour sack and peers inside. "Wooee! All this here money an' we didn't have to do nothin' but take it from a woman an' a couple a kids."

"Lemme see that money, Cougar," asked Carson.

He peered inside the sack. "Damnation at the greenbacks."

"Cougar, Carson and Bo...Guess that makes you the Standish brothers," said Fiona.

"Hey, Cougar, we must be gittin' a reputation," exclaimed Bo.

"Not really...I just happen to be carrying paper on you boys for breaking out of the penitentiary up at McAlister in the Nations," said Fiona.

Cougar laughed. "Don't matter none, lady, on account we're gonna have to kill you, long with these two snot noses."

Charlie subtly bumped Fiona with his elbow when Bo came over to look at the money too. He turned slightly so she could see the butt of the pistol in his back pocket.

Fiona shoved Charlie into Donny knocking both to the ground as she snatched the Colt Lightning from his pocket, dove to the dirt and rolled over, firing as she did.

Her first shot hit Cougar just above his eyebrows, punching a pencil-sized hole in his forehead. The big outlaw's head snapped back as his knees buckled and he dropped to the ground like a rotten apple falling from the tree.

Bo dropped the sack, bumped into Carson as both of them jerked their pistols and began firing wildly in her direction. She scrambled upright with the bullets kicking up dirt at her feet and one shot whipping through the side of her thigh length coat.

Fiona calmly aimed the double-action revolver from the hip at the two panicked outlaws, snapping off two more rounds—and then the quiet became palpable. The gray clouds of pungent gunsmoke slowly drifted away from the clearing on the morning breeze leaving the bodies of the three brigands scattered about the campsite in their grotesque positions of death.

Bo Standish's left foot drummed against the ground in his final death throes.

She looked over at the Webers. "You boys all right?"

They both got to their feet with eyes big as saucers and nodded.

Fiona stepped over to Carson's body, removed her Colts from his belt, replaced them in her holsters, and then picked up the money sack from where it fell next to Bo.

"You boys finish eating?"

They both nodded again.

"Then pick up the tinwear, go down to the creek and wash it off."

CHAPTER FIVE
EASTERN JACK COUNTY
RANCH ROAD

Carter Youngblood held up his hand as he reined his steel-dust stallion to a halt just west of a bend in the road.

"What are we stopping for, Mister Youngblood," asked Ness.

"You'll see," he said as he dismounted.

Skinny Conway slid off the back of Alder's horse. "Damn, glad we're stoppin' fer a bit. Ridin' on the back of yer horse eat a feller's crotch plum up." He walked around in a circle limbering up his legs.

"Cain't believe that damn woman got the best of us," said Ness.

"It's not over," said Carter.

"She even taken our guns…that's plumb embarrassin'," said Alder.

Youngblood stepped back to his soogan tied behind his cantle, reached inside the center of the rolled up blanket and tarp and pulled out a sawed-off double barreled shotgun, broken down in two pieces.

He snapped the barrels into the receiver and tightened the large single screw on the bottom of the forestock. Youngblood reached into his inside coat pocket, removed two brass ten gauge double-ought rounds, slipped them into the chambers and snapped the barrels back up in place with an audible click.

"What're you gonna do, Boss?" asked Skinny

"When they come around that bend up there, I'm goin' to take out that meddling marshal…then those damn kids."

"Alder, you take the horses down yonder out of sight and tie them up," said Youngblood.

"I didn't buy into killin' no peace officer. Them kids is one thang, but a marshal?…We're askin' fer a whole peck of trouble."

"I don't give a rat's ass what you think, Skinny. You're in for a penny, you're in for a dollar…Now, shut your face, I've got more rounds in my coat…Understand me," Youngblood hissed. "Ya'll get quiet, I can hear them coming. Take cover in that brush." He pointed to the other side of the narrow ranch road while he crouched down on his side, both barrels of the Greener cocked and ready.

***

As Fiona and the boys rounded the bend in the road, she reined up, drew her Winchester from its boot and laid it across her thighs. She pulled one of her Colts from its holster with her right hand.

"What is it, Marshal?" asked Charlie as he stopped right beside her.

"I don't know. Something's just not right. Hair on the back of my neck is standing up…Easy, now, we go slow."

She nudged Spot forward at a slow walk with the boys riding double at her side, her eyes carefully scanning the road and trees ahead.

Youngblood stepped out from behind a thick clump of cedar only twenty feet in front of them—the shotgun aimed at Fiona. "Well, fancy meeting you here, Marshal."

"No! Mister Youngblood, don't shoot," screamed Charlie as he hard reined his horse to the left in front of Spot.

The merchant squeezed the trigger to one of the barrels, discharging twelve deadly pellets at close range. Most of them struck Charlie in the chest blowing both him and Donny from the back of the horse to the ground.

Fiona snapped off two rounds from her Colt both hitting Youngblood in the center of the chest, not a half inch apart.

He fired off his second barrel into the dirt as he crumpled to the ground.

She fired one round from the .45-70 Winchester in her left hand, striking Ness McBride in the forehead. The big round blew the entire back of his head off. He dropped like a puppet with its strings cut.

She swiveled her Peacemaker to Alder Axline, drilling him in the center of his chest with an audible thump.

Her four shots, three from her Colt and one from the Winchester sounded almost as one, but there were three bodies laying in the road in front of her. She could see Skinny kneeling in the tall grass off to the side. It was obvious he was praying.

"On your feet," she ordered.

The cowboy did as he was told. "I ain't got no gun Marshal, you taken 'em…I never shot nothin' but snakes in my life anyways. I told Mister Youngblood I couldn't. 'Spect he was a gonna shoot me next."

"I forgot I took ya'lls guns, except for that coach gun he must have had hidden out." She pointed at Youngblood whose dead hands still held the sawed-off ten gauge. "Didn't notice that the other two weren't armed…Heat of the moment, I suppose."

Donny moaned from over at the side of the road. Fiona dismounted and rushed over to him as he dragged himself out from underneath his brother's bloody body. He was covered in blood also, but most of it was Charlie's. He had sustained two minor wounds in his left arm and shoulder from the pellets.

Fiona slid to her knees and helped the teenager move away from the carnage of his brother. "Are you hit, Donny?"

He nodded. "Shoulder an' arm, I think, Marshal." He looked over at his brother. "But, Charlie…"

She held him in her arms, comforting him as he cried. They both turned as they heard a rider approaching at a hard gallop.

Sheriff Flynn slid his blue roan Morgan gelding to a stop in the middle of the road, dismounting before the horse had finished drawing elevens in the dirt with his back feet. His .45 was in his hand as he quickly took in the scene—it came to rest on Skinny. "I heard shots...My God."

"It's about time you showed up, Mason...Now that the dance is over...Oh, and it's, all right." She indicated Skinny. "He didn't participate in the ambush," said Fiona.

"Well, he was standin'. Better to be safe than sorry...How're the boys?" he said as he looked at the massive amount of blood on Donny.

Fiona looked over at Charlie and shook her head. "Need to get Donny to a doctor. He's got a couple of double oughts in his arm."

Flynn turned to Skinny. "Go round up the horses, we got to haul 'em back to town."

"Yessir."

The cowboy went first to catch the horse Charlie and Donny were riding as it spooked when the boys were hit.

"I seen him go back down the road. I'll fetch 'im, he's mine anyways. He'll come to me...They's three more tied up in that grove of post oak over yonder." He pointed off the road a little way down in a swag.

The sheriff whipped off his bandana, wrapped it around Donny's arm and tied it off. "That oughta stop the bleedin' till we git back to town."

The boy looked over at Charlie. "They kilt him, Sheriff, they kilt my brother dead...I tol' him somethin' bad was gonna happen...I tol' him." He buried his face in Flynn's chest, his body racked with sobs.

"We'll have to send someone back out this way. There are three more bodies back up the way at a small creek."

"Three more bodies?"

67

Fiona nodded. "The Standish brothers apparently found out about the bank robbery somehow and were after the boys too. They tried to take the money back at our camp…It was their last mistake."

"The Standish brothers? How did you know who they were?"

"Got paper on them from Fort Smith last week after they broke out of the penitentiary up at McAlister."

Flynn shook his head. "Yep, they clabbered the milk when they stumbled on you…an' here I thought you needed some help."

"Did you catch the rustlers?"

He grinned. "Lot easier to track fifty or so beeves than a couple of kids horsebackin'…Plus the rustlers weren't too bright."

"How so?"

"They resisted arrest."

"Ah, true…Let's step over that way. We need to talk."

"Lead on, m'lady."

***

They walked down the road almost twenty yards, out of earshot of Donny and Skinny as he was walking his horse back up the road.

"What's on your mind?" asked Flynn.

"The boy…What do we do with him?"

"Meaning?"

"His older brother made him go along. It's my belief he was against the robbery from the start…You know what will happen if the state handles his case."

Mason glanced over his shoulder at Donny sitting next to his brother's body, weeping. "Yeah, they'll put him in the pen with all those hardcases. If he's not a criminal now, he sure will be when he gets out…Plus you know what they'll do to a young good looking kid like him in there."

"My thoughts exactly…Uh…Do you think your sister and her husband could take another wayward child?"

He looked up at her steel-gray eyes. "Only one way to find out."

"What do we put in the report?"

Flynn scratched the stubble on his chin. "Well, I suppose we could say he ran off when his brother got shot…while you were dealing with the bad guys…We just don't have to say he came back."

WILSON RANCH
COOKE COUNTY, TEXAS

Fiona, Mason and a very nervous Donny Weber pulled rein in front of the picket fence in front of the large dog-run style white house with a wrap-around porch.

A young girl with all the appearance of a nine year old in a pixie-style haircut burst out the screen door followed closely by a yellow and white Amstaff Terrier. The little girl was wearing boy's bib overalls and was barefoot.

"Fiona and Flynn!" She flung open the spring-loaded gate just as the two law officers dismounted and sprang into a hug with the tall woman.

"Lucy, so nice to see you. I see little Garin is not so little anymore, he's really grown." She bent over and petted the muscular dog while the little girl hugged Flynn.

She turned loose of Mason and pointed at Donny while surreptitiously winking at Fiona with a slight nod.

Mason's sister, Mary Lou followed by her husband, Cletus Wilson, came out the front door and headed for the fence.

"Mason! Didn't know you and Fiona were dropping by…and looks like you have someone with you. Ya'll come on in, I'll make some sandwiches…Got a big pitcher of ice tea brewed up…I think I smell a story coming."

"Never could hide much from you, Sis," said Flynn.

Forty-five minutes later and after several slices of Mary Lou's Dutch chocolate layer cake, Fiona finished, "…and that's the story. Donny here needs a family and…"

"Oh, hush, Fiona, you don't have to say anymore, you know he's welcome." Mary Lou got up, went around the table and hugged an embarrassed Donny. "Of course I'm going to have to put some meat on your bones. Gracious, you're thin as a rail." She wiped the buttermilk mustache from his face with a napkin.

Donny ducked his head and grinned. "Yessum."

"I see you didn't bring a bag or anything with you."

He looked up into Mary Lou's sky blue eyes. "No, ma'am, Marshal Miller bought me what I got on. Said what I had wadn't fit fer nothin' but the burn pile."

Mary Lou glanced over at Cletus. "Well, we'll go in to town tomorrow and take care of that situation…Lucy, why don't you take Donny out and show him the barn. Ya'll can get acquainted while we visit some more."

"Yes, ma'am," said the golden eyed little girl.

She grabbed Donny's hand. "Come on, they're going to talk grown-up stuff."

They watched the two children leave out the back door at the end of the dog run that ran the length of the house and run toward the barn.

"Lucy has become quite the actress, hasn't she," said Fiona.

Mary Lou giggled. "Yes, I think she figured she had to when she started school with other children her age…uh, I should say size."

"Are you going to tell Donny?" asked Flynn.

Mary Lou and Cletus exchanged glances.

"I think we'll let Lucy decide if and when, don't you, Cletus."

"Oh, absolutely. I still get a blank look when she starts explaining things…Not sure who adopted who."

"I suspect Lucy will take her time. She knows Donny has been through a very trying period. I could tell she knew all about him by the time we dismounted," said Fiona.

Flynn looked over at her. "How?"

"She winked and nodded at me when I introduced him."

"How do you think he'll react when he finally learns that that his new sister, Lucy, is over two hundred years old and that her spaceship crashed over outside of Aurora last April?"

"Would love to be a fly on the wall," said Fiona.

The End

About the Author

Ken Farmer didn't write his first full novel until he was sixty-nine years of age. He often wonders what the hell took him so long. At age seventy-five… currently working on novel number eighteen.

Ken spent thirty years raising cattle and quarter horses in Texas and forty-five years as a professional actor (after a stint in the Marine Corps). Those years gave him a background for storytelling… as he has been known to say, "always been a bit of a bull---t artist, so writing novels kind of came naturally once it occurred to me I could put my stories down on paper."

Ken's writing style has been likened to a combination of Louis L'Amour and Terry C. Johnston with an occasional Hitchcockian twist… that's a mouthful.

In addition to his love for writing fiction, he likes to teach acting, voice-over and writing workshops. His favorite expression is: "Just tell the damn story."

Writing has become Ken's second life: he has been a Marine, played collegiate football, been a Texas wildcatter, cattle and horse rancher, professional film and TV actor and now...a novelist. Who knew?

Contact: www.kenfarmer-author.net
www.timbercreekpress.net
Ken's Amazon page:
www.amazon.com/Ken-Farmer/e/B0057OT3YI
For new release announcements and other news go to my Face Book page.
www.facebook.com/KenFarmerAuthor/

Acknowledgements

Many thanks go to Lt. Colonel Clyde DeLoach USMC (Ret.) for his help in beta and proof reading Lady Marshal and to Tell Cotten for inviting me to join the Wanted Group.

HAPPY TRAILS

What's Right

By

Duane Boehm

What's Right

Deputy Gideon Johann slunk into the Boulder, Colorado jail an hour late for work. Not that he had any illusions of going undetected in the small building, but he wasn't any too proud of his tardiness. Sheriff Howell sat at his desk flicking his finger into his mustache in an attempt to remove a biscuit crumb while closely eyeing his deputy.

"Glad to see you could join us," Sheriff Howell said.

"I couldn't get to sleep last night and then I overslept," Gideon said.

"You look like you could use a cup of coffee and I could use a fresh cup. That pot smells a tad burned. Why don't you make us a fresh pot and then let's have a little talk?" Sheriff Howell said.

"Sure," Gideon said as he grabbed the coffee pot and walked out back into the alley to dump it. He came back in and made the fresh pot. Standing impatiently by the stove, he fidgeted as he waited for the coffee to cook and to get his conversation with the sheriff over and done. After what seemed like ages, he retrieved the sheriff's cup and one for himself and filled them. He carried them over to the sheriff's desk and took a seat.

Sheriff Howell took a sip of coffee and savored the taste a moment as he looked his deputy straight in the eyes. He liked Gideon a lot. Not only was the young man a fine lawman, he was a good person too, but something seemed broken inside Gideon that the sheriff wondered might be unrepairable. "You make a fine cup of coffee," he said before setting down the cup. "Gideon, you look like hell and smell like an empty bottle of whiskey. You've been here almost six months and you may be the best deputy I've ever hired, but I don't like where things are headed. What's going on?"

Gideon took a drink of coffee before habitually rubbing the scar on his cheekbone. "I've been having a lot of trouble getting to sleep lately. Usually a couple of sips of whiskey will do the trick. Last night it took a whole lot of whiskey," he said.

"I see. Do you want to talk about it?" the sheriff asked.

"Nothing much to talk about. Just can't sleep," Gideon lied.

"Gideon, you know as well as I do that being a good lawman is all about studying human nature and you've never fooled me. The first time you walked in here looking for a job, I could see that you were a troubled young man. Don't you think it's time we talked about it?" Sheriff Howell asked.

"Not much to talk about. I have trouble getting to sleep. Sure I have regrets from my past, but who doesn't?" Gideon said.

"None of my regrets keep me up at night," the sheriff said.

"Listen, you've been very good to me since I've been here and I truly appreciate all you've done for me, but you're not going to get me to talk about my troubles," Gideon said.

Sheriff Howell studied Gideon over the top of his coffee cup as he took a sip. He let out a sigh as he set down the cup. "Very well. Have things your way, but I don't see how you or anybody else benefits from your guilty conscience. Seems like a waste of time to me. Don't make it a habit of coming in late," he said.

"Yes, sir. I won't...," Gideon said.

Thelma Hues walked into the jail, banging the door when she shut it. Sheriff Howell could see from the moment he glanced up at her that something was wrong. She looked as if she had been crying and her color appeared ashen.

"Thelma, what's the matter?" the sheriff asked.

"Hallie Tolan and I take turns having coffee every morning at one another's house. Today was her turn, and when I walked over to her home, I found her beaten and stabbed to death. Sheriff, it was gruesome. I'll never get that sight out of my mind," Thelma said and started crying.

The sheriff walked over to the distressed woman and led her to his desk where Gideon vacated his seat for her. Sheriff Howell sat back down and waited for Thelma to compose herself. After a couple of minutes of sobbing, Thelma pulled a handkerchief from her bag and dabbed at her eyes.

"Did you see Thadius?" Sheriff asked.

"No, he was nowhere to be found. You know he killed her. I've told her for years to get away from him before just this thing happened. He's beat her more times than I can recall," Thelma said.

"I suspect you are right. Throwing him in jail sure never taught him a lesson. Thelma, you can go on home. Gideon and I will walk over there and take care of things," the sheriff said.

Thelma seemed on the verge of tears again. She quickly jumped up from her seat and scurried out of the jail.

"Let's go have a look," Sheriff Howell said as he got to his feet and retrieved his hat from a peg in the wall.

"I don't think I know a Thadius Tolan. Who is he?" Gideon asked as he followed the sheriff out the door of the jail.

"I'm sure you've seen him around town. He's a handyman. Big burly fellow with a limp. I have locked him up two or three times for beating Hallie, but it never did any good," the sheriff said.

"I know who you're talking about now. I always thought he looked as if he were looking for a fight," Gideon said.

"That sounds like him," Sheriff Howell said as he walked swiftly down the street on the pleasant late spring morning.

They found Hallie's corpse stretched out on the kitchen floor like a doll that had been tossed aside. Her face looked badly battered, one of her arms bent at an unnatural angle, and a butcher knife still protruded from her chest.

Gideon turned his head away from the body. "God have mercy on her. I've never seen a woman in such shape. What kind of person would do that?" he asked.

"Somebody that can't control their rage. Thadius did this - no doubt about it. I have to testify in court this week. You need to go get Farting Jack and track down Thadius. There's a rumor, and I believe it very well could be true, that he used to be a part of Quantrill's Raiders. You and Jack need to stay on your toes. Those boys knew how to fight and they didn't care about the rules," the sheriff said.

"I don't need Farting Jack. I'm a pretty fair tracker myself," Gideon protested.

"Yes, you are, but Jack is better and you get better every time you go out with him. And I don't like to send a man out by himself. Too many things can go wrong and then you'd be in a fix. Farting Jack makes good company anyways," Sheriff Howell said.

"Especially if you like the smell of shit," Gideon said, managing to grin in spite of the circumstance. He didn't want the sheriff doubting his resolve to track the killer on his own, but truth be told, he felt damn glad to have Farting Jack along for the trip. Nobody could track like Jack and the old trapper would have your back come hell or high water.

"Go ahead and get moving. I'll take care of things here," the sheriff said.

Gideon headed towards the door before stopping abruptly. He turned back towards the sheriff. "If Thadius Tolan gives me an opportunity, I'm going to make him pay dearly for what he's done here," he said.

"I wouldn't have it any other way. Just don't go getting yourself killed. I still have designs on making something out of you," Sheriff Howell said.

After walking to the livery stable to retrieve his horse, Gideon rode to the little shack outside of town that belonged to Farting Jack Dolan. The one room cabin wasn't much for looks but it served the mountain man well when he wasn't off trapping. Gideon had gotten to know Jack well by staying there for a short time when he first came to town.

"Farting Jack Dolan, is your sorry ass home?" Gideon yelled as he climbed off his horse.

The door to the cabin opened and Jack stepped outside dressed as always from head to toe in buckskin. "Well, if it isn't little Gideon Johann. I'd think the smoke from my chimney would've told even a simple thing like you that I'm home. Did you come for some schooling?" he asked.

Turning serious, Gideon said, "Thadius Tolan murdered his wife. Sheriff Howell wanted me and you to track him down."

The news seemed to take the air out of Jack's sails and his shoulders sagged. "That worthless piece of horse dung. I whupped him in the Thirsty Man Saloon one time. He started in on me for being loud and having some fun, but I ended it. Come on in while I gather my things," he said dejectedly.

After gathering his guns and some supplies, Jack saddled his horse and rode to town with Gideon. They first stopped at the jail. Gideon retrieved four boxes of .44 caliber Henry rimfire cartridges. Both his Winchester 1866 and his old Remington 1858 Army revolver that he had carried during the war used the ammo after he had a gunsmith convert the handgun. Sheriff Howell was at the jail and handed his deputy a sack of jerky and hardtack on the way out the door.

Farting Jack and Gideon rode to the Tolan home. Thadius had fashioned a stall in an old shed on the property and Gideon looked in it.

"The horse is gone," Gideon called out from inside the building.

"Yeah, I found tracks behind the shed," Jack replied.

Walking out of the shed and around back to Jack, Gideon said, "Well, let's see where he's headed."

"That would seem to be the prudent thing to do since we're supposed to track him down," Jack said. As he swung his leg over his horse, Jack ripped a rumbling fart. "Whoa, that was a good one."

"Have you ever gone to a doctor about your problem?" Gideon asked as he climbed onto his horse.

"What problem? Everybody farts. Just means my innards are clear and open. If a fellow spends too much time with a doctor, they'll eventually kill you," Jack said as he heeled his horse into moving.

Shaking his head, Gideon started riding.

The tracks led east down a side road to the edge of town and then headed cross-country in the same direction.

"Looks like Thadius is planning to stay off the roads," Farting Jack said.

"At least he's headed east into the plains instead of the mountains. Lot less chance of us getting ambushed and a whole lot easier to track," Gideon said.

"All true, but I hate the flat land. It all looks the same to me. I feel like a fish out of water," Jack said.

"How'd Sheriff Howell ever rope you into tracking for him?" Gideon asked.

"I was in the saloon one day in the fall before trapping season started having me a beer when word got out that a little girl was lost. It was late enough in the year where the nights were pretty cold so I went to the sheriff and volunteered to help find the child. I had her tracked down in a couple of hours and I made the mistake of impressing

Sheriff Howell. He's been pestering me ever since," Jack said.

"I see. So you don't like doing this?" Gideon asked.

"I'm a mountain man. We're loners by nature. If I wanted to be a wet nurse to a snotty nose kid I would have been born a woman," Jack said.

"I'll remember that the next time I risk my life to save yours," Gideon said.

"I've expressed my gratitude on numerous occasions for your past deeds. Don't go getting all sensitive on me. If I can't rant a little, what's the use in talking?" Jack said.

Grinning, Gideon nodded his head.

The two men spent the rest of the day following Thadius's trail. Tracking the hoof prints didn't take much effort. Most of the land stretched flat for miles covered in tall prairie grass that the murderer's horse had smashed to the ground. The only time that they had to work at staying on course was when they came across land that open range cattle had grazed and trampled. Thadius made a point of giving a wide berth to any of the sodbuster farms along the way. Towards dusk, with their butts aching in the saddle and their bellies growling, they came upon a small stream with good water and made camp for the night.

In the morning, Farting Jack roused Gideon out of his bedroll before there was enough light even to see anything but shadows. Gideon considered himself in charge and didn't appreciate Jack waking him, but held his tongue to keep from riling the mountain man. After some coffee and hardtack, the men resumed tracking. As the day wore on, the tracks began to head in a southeasterly direction.

"He's headed towards the Kansas Pacific Railway. If he boards a train, we're liable to never find him," Gideon said.

"I assure you that unless Thadius commits a robbery, he doesn't have money for fare. I doubt he'd part with his horse anyway. He probably plans to follow the line to Kansas. I imagine he has people there," Jack said.

"You seem to know a lot about Tolan," Gideon remarked.

"Don't know anything that I can state as fact except that Thadius was known to always be broke. I had heard that he rode with Quantrill's Raiders, and if so, I'm just speculating that he knows people in Kansas. Simple reasoning, my boy," Jack said.

Gideon liked Jack a lot, but there were some days where he liked him a whole lot better than others. Today wasn't one of them. "Let's make some time," Gideon said and put his horse into a lope.

Late in the afternoon, a small town appeared on the horizon. Thadius Tolan's tracks led straight to it. As Gideon and Jack neared the village, they could see the rails of the Kansas Pacific Railway. A sign read 'Deer Trail, Colorado'. Deer Trail wasn't much of a town, but what there was of it, looked all newly built. The town had come into existence the previous year after the railroad had located a station there.

"Do you think there's a chance he's still here?" Gideon asked as they rode down the main street.

"I doubt it unless he has a reason for being here. I judge we've gained maybe three or four hours on him. He probably kept on moving," Jack said.

Stopping in front of what served as a poor man's saloon, Gideon and Jack walked into the dark, smoky building. A few men were sitting at tables and a couple more stood at the bar. Gideon and Jack walked up to the bartender and each ordered a beer. The man filled two mugs and set them down without saying so much as a word.

"We tracked a fellow to this town. He's a husky man with a limp. Any chance he came in here?" Gideon asked as he paid the bartender.

"I serve beer and whiskey, not information. You might want to ask our constable. He's standing right behind you," the bartender said.

Gideon and Jack turned to see a shotgun pointed at them by a man with a badge.

"You boys put your hands in the air nice and slow. I don't want to bloody up our saloon. I'm Constable Ross," the man said.

The two men complied with the officer's demand.

"We're the law out of Boulder, Colorado. We tracked a man here by the name of Thadius Tolan that killed his wife. I have my badge in my pocket," Gideon said.

"A badge doesn't mean much. I've known plenty of men that work both sides of the law. Two men robbed the mercantile in Agate and killed the constable on the way out of town. One was old with a gray beard and the other one was a young buck. Sounds like you two to me," Constable Ross said.

"I don't know where Agate is, but we came from the northwest," Gideon protested.

Looking at the bartender, the constable said, "Wally, grab their guns for me."

The bartender stretched over the bar and pulled Gideon and Jack's revolvers from their holsters.

"This is a mistake. You need to telegraph Sheriff Howell in Boulder. He'll vouch for us and the reason we're here," Gideon said.

"We'll see. A man that fits the description you described did pass through town this morning. I'm going to lock you up until this is straightened out. Of course, if word gets back to Agate that I have you two, they're liable to come hang you tonight. Sandy was a right popular constable," Ross said.

Farting Jack lowered his hand and tugged on his beard couple of times. "Sheriff Howell and I go way back. Back to when your momma still wiped your butt for you. If you let something happen to us, I swear you'll be signing your own death warrant. Sheriff Howell will come here himself and kill you as sure as there'll be a sunset tonight," he said.

"Get your hand back up and march out the door," Constable Ross ordered.

The jail consisted of one cell and an office area big enough for a desk and a stove. Constable Ross locked them up and departed.

"Do you think he'll telegraph the sheriff?" Gideon asked as he sat down on one of the two cots.

"I think so. I could see in his eyes that I put some fear into him. I'm not sure he's got the balls to hold off a lynching party though," Jack said.

"That would be a real pisser to survive fighting in that damn war only to be hanged by some farmers and townsfolk that probably couldn't hit the broad side of a barn with a scattergun," Gideon said.

An hour later, Constable Ross brought in two plates of food and passed them through the meal hole. "I telegraphed your sheriff," he said.

"Much obliged. Can't you get a witness from that town? I'm telling you that we are not your killers. Our killer is getting away while we sit here," Gideon said.

"I will in the morning. Too late in the day to go now," Ross said.

Jack's threat had apparently gotten the constable's attention. Constable Ross spent the rest of the evening sitting in the jail. At nine o'clock, he turned the wick down on the oil lamp, set his shotgun across his lap, leaned back in his chair, and closed his eyes.

No more than fifteen minutes had gone by when the sound of running horses carried into the jail. The constable left the wick turned down and walked to the door, slinging it open. In front of him sat ten riders on their horses.

"Constable, we hear that you have Sandy's killers. We've come for them," a man called out.

From the darkness, Ross said, "This will all be resolved in the morning. Nobody is taking them tonight."

"Sandy was our friend and yours too. Just go on home. We don't want to hurt you, but we aim to serve justice," the man warned.

"You know I can't do that. If you harm me, you won't be any different than the men that killed Sandy," Ross said.

The leader of the vigilantes let out a sigh so loud that Ross could hear it from inside the doorway. "You know we can't leave. Everybody back home knows what we came to do."

"Send one of your eye witnesses over tomorrow," Ross pleaded.

"Sully saw them. He's with us," the man called out.

"Sully can come in and have a look then," the constable said.

All of the men started to climb down from their horses. Constable Ross pulled the hammers back on both barrels of his shotgun as they did.

"Anybody's foot touches the ground besides Sully's is going to get blown back to Agate courtesy of my scattergun," Ross said.

The men eased themselves back into the saddle as Sully walked towards the jail. Ross moved out of the doorway to let the man through and then bolted the door shut. Walking over to the desk, he turned the wick up on the lamp.

"Have a look at them. Are those the men that killed Sandy?" Ross asked.

Sully looked at Gideon and Jack and then back at the constable.

"I think that's them," Sully said in voice that lacked any semblance of conviction.

"You better be sure. I'd hate to show up to the gates of Heaven with the wrongful deaths of two innocent men on my list of transgressions. And that could happen real soon if you were to be hanged for murder," Ross said.

Looking into the cell again, Sully said, "I made a mistake. The old one looked fatter than this one and the younger one was taller than your man here."

"Okay, now go outside and make sure that you convince your buddies that you know what you're talking about. Otherwise, you, me, and some of those others are going to probably die," the constable said.

The talk seemed to motivate Sully. He walked outside, and in a booming voice, told the other riders that the constable had arrested the wrong men. Constable Ross still expected trouble and stood at the door with his shotgun held chest high if needed. The leader of the vigilantes apologized and rode off without saying another word.

Ross unlocked the cell door and then retrieved Gideon and Jack's revolvers from his drawer. As he handed them to each man, he said, "You're welcome to sleep in here tonight. It's kind of pointless to leave now. Sorry for the inconvenience I caused you."

"You made sure you got to the truth. That's the main thing," Gideon said.

"The main thing is that we didn't get out necks stretched," Jack said.

"True," Gideon said. "I think we'll take you up on your offer and just sleep here. We can't track in the dark."

"Your man bought a few supplies and then headed out of town going east. That's all I know. Well, I'm headed home. If I don't see you in the morning, I'll let your sheriff know that all is well," Constable Ross said before shaking each man's hand.

After the constable had left, Gideon said, "I guess he had more mettle in him than I expected. He had me worried."

Jack expelled a nauseous fart that chased the deputy from the cell. "You can thank me. I told you I put fear into him when I told him Sheriff Howell would kill him," he said as he fanned the air with his hand. "Whoa, that was a really good one."

"You might also poison me before the night is through. Thank God the cell door is open," Gideon said as he waited for the air to clear.

The next morning, the two men arose early and had breakfast at the little diner that opened at the crack of dawn. They rode out of town before Constable Ross showed up at the jail. Farting Jack spent a good half-hour searching for Thadius's horse track on the edge of town before he finally found it. The wife murderer's path ran parallel to the tracks at close to a quarter mile distance.

Gideon and Jack pushed their animals as hard as they dared throughout the day, altering the horses' gaits to provide them opportunities to catch their breaths and rest. The land was mostly flat and easy riding, and allowed the two men to cover a lot of miles. Towards sunset, they came upon a small creek lined with trees and plenty of good grass and decided to make camp for the night. A town could be seen in the distance, but with the events of yesterday still fresh in their minds, they decided it best to avoid the place.

Just before bedding down for the night, Gideon asked, "Do you think we gained any on Thadius today?"

"I expect we did, but not enough to make up for what we lost yesterday. We won't catch him now until he stops," Jack said.

"That's what I fear. He'll probably hole up with a pack of old Quantrill Raiders and we'll have our hands full," Gideon said.

"No need to worry about what hasn't happened yet. We'll get him," Jack said as he crawled into his bedroll.

"I suppose," Gideon said as he smoothed out his bedding.

Not fifteen minutes had gone by before Jack heard Gideon rummaging through a saddlebag and then the distinct sound of a cork popping out of a bottle. The mountain man raised his head to see the deputy take a couple of long pulls on a bottle of whiskey.

"Having troubles getting to sleep?" Jack asked.

"Yeah, my demons are chasing me tonight," Gideon replied.

Most nights when Gideon closed his eyes to sleep, he would see the little dead boy with the vacant stare gazing back at him. The vision had been haunting him since near the end of the war when he helplessly watched the child die. He carried the burden with him like a ball and chain fettered to him for life.

"Gideon, we've had that talk before and I don't suppose you'll listen to me tonight any more than you have before, but I'm telling you that you're going to grow old before your time if you don't stop it," Jack said.

"I know. If I could stop, I surely would," Gideon said.

"Talk about it. There's nothing like a good confession to clear the soul," Jack said.

"Can't do it. It's my burden to bear," Gideon said.

"If I thought it would do any good I'd slap you around until I either knocked some sense into you or a turd out of you," Jack said.

Taking a big breath before blowing up his cheeks as he exhaled loudly, Gideon said, "I wish it were that easy. Goodnight, Jack."

"Goodnight, Gideon."

Drifting off to sleep, Gideon dreamed of fishing with his best friend, Ethan Oakes, when the two were just old enough to go out unchaperoned. He could hear somebody digging through the belongings and he thought the sound came from Ethan looking for sandwiches until realizing that the noise was real. Opening his eyes just enough to see, Gideon spied a young girl in a flour sack dress and no shoes rummaging through his saddlebags. She gnawed on one of his hardtack biscuits as she worked.

Gideon rolled onto his side and made a swipe at the girl's leg, but she heard him move and deftly jumped out of the way. As he tried to climb out of his bedroll, the girl grabbed his saddle by the horn, heaved it his way, and pinned Gideon to the ground.

Farting Jack awoke from all the commotion. He jumped out of his bed, pulling his revolver from its holster and cocking the weapon. From the light of the fire, he saw the young girl. She hesitated a moment at the sound of the gun cocking and then picked up a chunk of stacked firewood, letting it fly toward Jack. The wood caught Jack on the shin, causing him to hop around on one leg and cuss up a storm.

"Get that crazy little vixen," Jack shouted out in pain.

Throwing the saddle to the side, Gideon freed himself from the bedroll. He made a dash for the girl. She gracefully stepped to the side like a matador before leaping over the fire. As she ran past Jack, she shoved the hobbling mountain man to the ground.

"Damn, Jack. She ran right past you," Gideon yelled as he gave pursuit.

"We ought to just shoot her. I could catch lightning easier," Jack hollered as he got to his feet.

The girl sprinted into the creek bed and started racing downstream. Gideon followed, gaining ground on her as he ran. Just as he closed in and opened his arms to swoop her up, the girl tripped. She fell head first into the water and let out a scream of pain. Gideon managed to run up onto the bank to keep from trampling the child. He reached down to pull her from the water, and as he did, the girl flipped onto her back and sunk her nails into the sleeve of his shirt like a mad bobcat and tried to bite his hand. Jerking his arm from her grasp, Gideon grabbed both of the girl's arms and yanked her from the water. As he lifted her to her feet, he spun her around and put her in a bear hug with his one arm around her neck and the other pinning her arms to her side.

He quickly threw his leg over her legs to prevent her from kicking.

"Calm down. Nobody is going to hurt you. We'll feed you if you're hungry, but you are not going to rob us," Gideon said.

"Let go of me, you big oaf," the girl yelled as she tried to pivot her head enough to bite Gideon.

"If you bite me, I'm going to chew off your ear," Gideon threatened.

Jack caught up to Gideon and the girl.

"What do you want me to do?" Jack asked.

"I don't know - tell a bedtime story. Have you ever wrestled a bobcat?" Gideon asked.

Hopping over the stream, Jack approached them. "Maybe you should have held her under water until the fight was all out of her," he said.

"Jack," Gideon admonished. "She's just a girl and I don't want to do her harm. I just want her to calm down."

Gideon could feel the girl start to relax as the fight seemed to go all out of her. She started crying.

"I think you broke my ankle," she sobbed.

"You tripped. I didn't have anything to do with your falling," Gideon said. "I'm going to let go of you, and if you run, we won't chase you. The wolves and coyotes can fight for what little meat is on your bones."

As Gideon released the girl, she attempted to stand, but let out a yelp and collapsed onto her butt.

"I should have shot her when I had the chance. Would have saved us a lot of grief," Jack said.

"Old man, the next time I throw chunk a wood at you I'll aim for your head," the girl warned.

"She probably was raised by wolves as mean as she is," Jack remarked.

Gideon squatted down beside the girl. "I'm going to carry you back to the fire so that you can dry off and we can look at your ankle. Okay?" he coaxed.

Sniffling, the girl nodded her head.

Scooping the child into his arms, Gideon carried her back to the camp. Once there, he gently set her down and retrieved a blanket. Farting Jack threw wood into the fire until he had a roaring blaze.

"We'll turn our backs. You can shed your dress and wrap up in the blanket. No need to stay in wet clothes," Gideon said.

The girl waited until Gideon and Jack turned away and did as she was told.

"You can turn around," she said.

"What's your name?" Gideon asked as he laid the dress across the woodpile to dry.

"Lily Mae," the girl answered.

"Well, Lily Mae, I'm going to cook you some salt pork and Jack is going to look at your ankle. He's a better doctor than I am," Gideon said.

For all his bluster, Jack tenderly examined the girl. He gently felt the joint and rotated her ankle to check the range of motion. Lily Mae's eyes welled with tears as he worked, but she held her tongue and offered no resistance.

"It doesn't appear to be broken. I think it's a bad sprain," Jack announced as he stood up and walked to his saddlebags. "I carry a tincture of willow bark. That should help with the pain and swelling."

The pork sizzled in the pan and as Gideon flipped the meat, he said, "Tell me how you ended up out here."

Lily Mae looked at Gideon a moment as if she were trying to decide whether to tell him the truth. "There are ten of us children and the farm wasn't big enough for Pa to feed us all. I was the oldest girl and Pa thought a girl was mostly useless so he left me in town. The people there put me on a train to go out west to a new home. I ran away today when the train stopped at that town over there," she said.

"Why did you do that?" Gideon asked.

"I heard things about what happens to girls. I'm twelve years old and I ain't ready to marry a man," Lily Mae said.

Jack handed the girl a bottle. "Take a swig of this. It tastes bad, but it'll help you," he said.

After taking a drink of the medicine, Lily Mae's face contorted into an awful expression and Jack handed her his canteen to wash the taste away.

"Thank you," Lily Mae said.

Gideon forked the pork into a plate and handed it along with a fork and knife to Lily Mae. Not bothering to let the meat cool, she cut a bite, plopped it into her mouth, and chased it with water from Jack's canteen to keep from burning her mouth.

"Didn't anybody provide you with some shoes?" Gideon asked as he watched Lily Mae devour the pork.

"They bought me a pair before putting me on the train, but they were too small and hurt my feet something terrible. I gave them to a girl that could wear them," Lily Mae replied.

Waiting until Lily Mae finished the meal, Gideon walked over to the dress and felt the material. "Your dress is dry," he said and handed it to her. "You can sleep in my bedroll. Do I have your word that you won't try to kill us in our sleep?"

"I promise, but what about the old man? He might knock me in the head after you fall to sleep," Lily Mae said.

"His name is Jack and mine's Gideon. I doubt he would have wasted his medicine on you if he planned on killing you."

Jack tugged on his beard and rolled his eyes. "I think we should tie up the little vixen. It'd be right embarrassing to die at the hands of a child," he said.

"I trust her. And besides, I'm pretty sure she'd try to kill you first and that would give me time to save myself," Gideon said.

"Gideon Johann, you only think that you're a funny man," Jack said.

After Lily Mae slipped back into her dress, she attempted to walk to the bedroll but found that she couldn't bear any weight on her foot. Jack rolled his eyes again and picked up the child. He gently placed her on the bedroll.

"Do you want me to tuck you in too?" Jack asked gruffly.

Lily Mae gave the mountain man a look of scorn, but the corners of her mouth turned up slightly, betraying the smallest of smiles.

Gideon retrieved his slicker and spread it on the ground. Using it and the spare blanket, he fashioned his bed. With the night getting late and the rush of all the excitement long worn off, everybody soon fell asleep.

As the dawn arrived the next day, Jack arose and started adding wood to the fire until he had a good blaze burning. Gideon soon joined the trapper while Lily Mae slept. In sleep, the child looked more like an angel than the wildcat from the previous night.

Jack walked a few feet away from the camp and motioned for Gideon to join him.

"What are we going to do with her?" Jack asked when Gideon joined him.

"I figured we'd take her to that town over there in the distance and turn her over to the sheriff. He can put her on a train to wherever she was supposed to go in the first place," Gideon said.

"I don't know about that. I've heard some bad things about those orphan trains and where the children end up. I'd hate to see her be some old man's wife or a prostitute," Jack said.

"Really? You that threatened to shoot her last night is now worried about her?" Gideon asked.

"You know darn well I never intended to shoot her. I admire the girl's spunk and I just wanted to put a little fear

93

into her to make her behave. Don't play dumb with me," Jack said.

"Well, what do you suggest that we do with her?" Gideon asked.

"The Widow French, back in Boulder, has taken in a couple of strays and made proper ladies out of them. I bet she'd take in another," Jack said.

"She's not a dog or cat. You mean to tell me that you want to take her with us to capture Thadius Tolan and then haul her all the way back to Boulder?" Gideon inquired with skepticism.

"You're the one in charge. You decide what we do with her. It will be on your conscience and not mine," Jack said.

Gideon grinned at Jack. "Well, so much for your reputation as an old, ornery, narcissistic mountain man. You'll probably be starting you up an orphanage one of these days," he teased.

"There's not much reward in being your friend. People like you made me a loner," Jack groused before walking back to the fire.

"Rise and shine," Gideon called out back at the campsite.

Lilly Mae's eyes opened as big as saucers and her mouth dropped open in panic until the events of the previous night came back to her. She started to crawl out of the bedroll, and as she moved her foot, her face scrunched up in pain.

Jack walked over to the girl. "Let me have a look," he said as he squatted down. "It's sure black and blue and swollen. "You really turned your ankle. I'll give you another dose of medicine."

Wrinkling up her nose at the thought of the taste of the tincture, Lily Mae then asked, "What's going to happen to me?"

Walking back with the medicine and his canteen, Jack said, "The way I see it, you have three choices. We can leave you here and you can go back to the wolf pack you came from, we can hand you over to the sheriff in that town over yonder, or you can go back to Boulder with us. There's a lady there that has taken in a couple of girls like yourself. I imagine she'd take in one more. They say she's strict and wouldn't tolerate a sassy mouth like yours, but she also has a heart of gold and would give you plenty of love and make you into a proper lady."

Taking the bottle of medicine from Jack, Lily Mae took a swallow and shuddered all over. She quickly guzzled water from the canteen until she washed the taste from her mouth. "I guess I don't have too many choices. Boulder it will be," she said.

The girl still couldn't bear weight on her ankle and sat useless as Gideon and Jack made breakfast and broke camp. When they were ready to ride, Gideon climbed aboard his horse and Jack hoisted the girl up behind the deputy's saddle cantle. With the touch of Gideon's heels to his horse's ribs, he, Jack, and Lily Mae set out for another day of tracking the killer.

Thadius had made a wide berth of the town where Lily Mae had snuck away from the train. He then had resumed following the railroad line from a distance.

The temperature had cooled considerably during the night and allowed Gideon and Jack to travel at a brisk pace without fear of overheating their horses. They paused at noon for a quick lunch of hardtack and jerky before resuming their ride.

If Lily Mae felt any pain from her ankle injury, she never complained. She kept her arms securely wrapped around Gideon's waist and balanced herself well as they rode. Occasionally, the girl would ask Gideon a question about his life and seemed to know when not to prior any further. She talked a little about her life on the farm and then grew silent for a long stretch.

About an hour before sunset, a town came into view much larger than any they had seen in a while. Thadius's tracks took a turn straight for the village. At the edge of town, a sign read 'Welcome to Kit Carson, Colorado'. Several saloons, gambling houses, and dance halls lined the main street and a few soldiers milled about the place.

"This is quite a little town," Gideon said as they rode down the street taking in the sights.

"A man could have some fun here if we weren't on business and babysitting," Jack said and looked at Lily Mae.

Lily Mae stuck out her tongue and said, "You're too old for fun. It would probably kill you."

Gideon chuckled. "Let's not make a spectacle of ourselves," he said.

Jack abruptly pulled his horse to a stop. "Gideon, I believe that is Thadius's horse tied right there in front of that saloon. I know he rode a spotted and I think I recognize those markings," he said.

The two men tied their horses to a hitching rail and Gideon carried Lily Mae to a bench in front of a mercantile. He disappeared into the store and returned a few minutes later with a bag of licorice.

"You sit here and eat your candy. Stay out of trouble and I mean it," Gideon said sternly.

"Thank you. I'll be good," Lily Mae replied in a voice that seemed to be genuinely moved by the gift.

"I guess we'll walk in the saloon and see what we find," Gideon said to Jack.

"Sounds good," the mountain man replied.

Walking into the saloon, they spotted Thadius at the end of an L-shaped bar directly facing them. He was laughing and drinking beer with another man when he saw Jack and Gideon. The grin quickly left his face as he recognized them. He ducked behind the bar, pulling the other man down with him.

"We've got two of them to deal with," Gideon said.

Thadius and his companion popped up over the bar with their pistols drawn. Gideon dove left and Jack to the right as two shots screamed their direction. One of the bullets took out the front window and the other thudded into the doorframe. Drawing their revolvers, Gideon and Jack jumped up ready to return fire, but their quarry had taken cover again behind the bar. A door at the end of the bar led to the back of the saloon. From his squatting position, Thadius launched himself into the door with his shoulder, knocking it off its hinges as he did so. Jack fired a shot as the second man disappeared into the back of the saloon, further damaging the doorframe.

"If he tarried a tick longer, I'd had that second man," Jack lamented.

"If wishes were horses …," Gideon said.

"At least I fired instead of just standing there," Jack said as they moved towards the back of the saloon.

The broken doorway led to a storage room stacked with whiskey barrels, crates of liquor, and beer kegs. At the end of the room, a door led outside. Gideon and Jack ran through the room and into the alley. On the other side of the lane, the back door to a feed store swung wide open.

"You go around to the front and I'll go through the store," Gideon ordered.

Gideon peeked around the edge of the doorway and scanned the inside of the store. A store clerk and a couple of customers were staring his way as if expecting trouble, but Thadius and his accomplice were not in sight. Gideon eased into the doorway and cautiously took a step. From the end of the counter, Thadius leaned out with his gun. Gideon dove behind feed sacks stacked nearly head high just as shots rang out. Bullets tore into the sacks, sending a shower of oats dropping to the floor in a pitter-patter cascade. The clerk and his customers ran for the door, clomping across the wooden floor like a herd of stampeding buffalo. Once they made it outside, the place became peacefully quiet with only the soothing sound of the oats hitting the floor.

"Thadius you need to surrender before you get hurt," Gideon called out.

"Seems to me that you're the one in a pickle," Thadius yelled before sending another shot into the feedbags.

Gideon snuck a look around the side of the bags. He didn't see anyone and he wished he knew where Jack and Thadius's friend were. Switching his revolver to his left hand to avoid exposing his body in order to shoot, he pointed the gun towards the front and waited. Thadius peeked around the counter and Gideon fired. The shot missed the mark and sent a chunk of wood flying through the air from above the killer's head.

"Damn it. I need to learn to shoot left handed," Gideon mumbled to himself.

From the front doorway, Jack yelled, "Drop your gun."

A barrage of shots echoed inside the wooden building. Fearing the worst, Gideon took off in a run towards the front. As he raced forward, he could see Jack taking cover from outside the front door. Just before reaching the counter, Gideon dove to the floor and slid past the counter. He surveyed the situation before coming to a stop. Thadius was crumpled into a heap and his accomplice was squatted against the wall firing towards Jack. Gideon fired two shots into the man as his target swung his arm to take aim at the deputy. A bullet smacked into the floor near Gideon's head, forcing him to squeeze off two more shots into the man. The assailant seemed undeterred and fired again, showering wood splinters into Gideon's chest. Jack swung around the doorframe into the room and emptied his remaining three bullets into the man as Gideon fired his last shot. The man finally slumped over onto the floor.

"It's about time you showed up," Gideon hollered.

"I got here as fast as I could. You were just scared and thought it took a long time," Jack said as he checked the two men for a pulse. "They're both dead."

Gideon gave the mountain man a dirty look as he reloaded his gun. Before he finished, the town's sheriff and two deputies barged into the feed store with shotguns trained upon the two men.

"Put your hands in the air," the sheriff barked.

One of deputies grabbed Gideon's still open gun from his hands. Gideon and Jack complied with the order. The other deputy confiscated Jack's revolver before checking on the dead men.

"They're both dead. One of them is Alonso Miller. He has more holes in him than a sieve. I don't recognize the other," the deputy said.

"I'm Deputy Gideon Johann from Boulder, Colorado. My badge is in my pocket," Gideon said.

The sheriff gave a slight nod of his head and Gideon reached into his shirt and produced the badge.

"That still doesn't give you any jurisdiction in my town or the right to shoot up the place," the sheriff said.

Jack cleared his throat. "I can explain everything. If you would first be so kind as to let us return to the front of the mercantile, my daughter is waiting there. I fear if left unattended that she may cause you more mischief than what has already gone on here," he said.

The sheriff eyed the two men suspiciously. "You can put your hands down, but if you try anything while we're walking, we're going to put more holes in you than you did Alonso."

Gideon glanced over at Jack as if the mountain man had lost his mind.

The group of men walked back to the mercantile where Lily Mae still sat eating her licorice.

"Okay, what's your story?" the sheriff asked.

Jack made eye contact with Lily Mae and winked. "I was taking my daughter, Lily Mae, back to her mother in Kansas. The child is a wretched little waif that I can't control. I hope her mother can shape her up. Anyway, Gideon decided to ride with me to visit an old girlfriend. The other dead man's name is Thadius Tolan. He killed his wife back in Boulder. We stopped at this here saloon, and when we walked in, Thadius recognized the deputy and I assume thought he came here to arrest him. You can ask everyone inside that he shot at us as soon as we walked in the door. Naturally, we didn't take kindly to being shot at and pursued our enemies. They got the short end of things, but I assure you that we weren't looking for trouble," he said.

The sheriff squinted his eyes skeptically and looked at Gideon. "Is that true?" he asked.

Gideon rubbed his scar. "It is," he replied.

Turning back to Jack, the sheriff said, "It doesn't say much for you that you can't make a child behave."

"I must confess that you are correct. I'm too kindhearted for my own good. I should get me a switch and apply it judiciously to her backside, but I just can't bring myself to do it," Jack said.

"You should at least put her in a pair of shoes," the sheriff said.

"She has shoes. Look at her ankle. It's badly sprained. She can't get her shoe on and there's no point in wearing only one. That girl is the fastest thing you ever saw. Most nights she catches us a rabbit for supper. She runs right past them, scoops them up by the ears, and then pounds their head into the ground until they stop kicking. I think she enjoys it. She saves us considerable on bullets. The other night she stepped in a gopher hole. If she'd been a horse I probably would have had to shoot her," Jack said.

The sheriff looked over at Lily Mae. The girl tugged off a bite of licorice and smiled devilishly at the lawman.

100

Turning his attention back to Gideon and Jack, the sheriff said, "I'm not sure how much of what I've just heard is fact or fiction, but I believe enough of it to think that you were in the right. I know Alonso was no angel. I suggest the three of you get on out of my town and never come back."

One of the deputies handed Gideon and Jack their guns.

"Thank you, Sheriff," Gideon said.

Gideon wasted no time mounting his horse. Jack quickly lifted Lily Mae onto the saddle and they began riding back in the direction that they had come.

"Hey, you're riding the wrong direction. Kansas is east," the sheriff hollered.

Jack looked back over his shoulder and replied, "After getting shot at, I need to go home and change my clothes - if you know what I mean."

Gideon put his hand over his mouth to suppress laughing.

The sheriff looked at his deputies and said, "I probably should have arrested them, but I didn't want to deal with the girl. I was afraid the part his story about her was true. She looked like the daughter of the devil himself. Anyway, anybody that rids this town of Alonso Miller can't be all bad."

At the edge of town, Gideon looked over at Jack and said, "Where did you come up with all that? That was some impressive lying."

"I have an intellect that someone like you could never appreciate," Jack said in a haughty voice.

"That just means that you're good at lying and I'm not," Gideon responded.

With Boulder on their minds, Gideon and Jack pushed for home. They traveled as fast as they thought the horses could stand without wearing down the animals. On their last night out, they made camp about twenty-five miles from home.

Lily Mae had resumed walking with the aid of a stick that Jack had fashioned into a crude cane. She had even volunteered to cook supper after Jack had gone off hunting and returned with two rabbits. After the meal, the two men stretched out using their saddles as backrests and patted their stomachs while bragging on Lily Mae's cooking until the usually boisterous girl blushed.

As Gideon sat by the fire thinking about their return to Boulder, he could feel his spirit start to sag. He loved living there and being a deputy for Sheriff Howell, but the vision of the dead boy had become so frequent that he knew that the time had come to once again try to outrun his demons. With a little luck, the boy wouldn't find him for a while.

Looking over at Jack, Gideon said, "I'm resigning my position when we get back to Boulder. It's time for me to move on."

Jack looked at Gideon, pulling his head back and raising his eyebrows. "Gideon, you don't want to do that. You could make something of yourself in Boulder. Don't tell anybody that I said so, but we make a pretty good pair," he said.

"I didn't say that I wanted to do it, but my demons have caught up with me here. I've got to keep moving to stay ahead of them," Gideon said as he pulled his whiskey bottle from his saddlebag. He already knew he'd have a hard time sleeping that night and decided to get an early start on medicating himself. Uncorking the bottle, he took a long pull on it and passed it to Jack.

Lily Mae keenly watched the two men drinking from the bottle. "Pa says that whiskey is the devil's drink," she said.

Gideon cocked his head and looked over at Lily Mae. "That may be true, but I wouldn't put much stock in the words of a man that abandoned his daughter. If you were my child, I'd rob a bank or a stagecoach before I gave you away. I think you're right special," he said.

The girl blushed again and looked away into the darkness.

Jack took a drink from the bottle and wiped his mouth with his sleeve. "For once in my life I have to agree with Gideon. You have spunk, child. That will take you far. I suspect that Widow French will make you into one fine little lady," he said before passing the bottle back to Gideon.

"I need to work the stiffness out of my ankle before we go to bed," Lily Mae said and stood with the help of the cane.

Jack tried to talk to Gideon some more about staying in Boulder, but the deputy waved his hand in the air to banish further talk. By the time that Lily Mae returned to the campsite, Gideon felt warm and mellow. His demons would stay at bay that night. He crawled into his bed without saying another word and the other two did likewise.

The next morning, Gideon beat Jack out of bed for the first time ever and had the coffee brewing before the mountain man even stirred. He roused Jack and Lily Mae out of bed and rushed them through breakfast. His need to wander again overwhelmed his melancholy about leaving Boulder. Whiskey might allow him to sleep, but running kept him alive.

They reached Boulder in mid-afternoon and rode straight to the jail. Sheriff Howell sat out front talking to a resident of the town. He eyed the girl riding behind Gideon suspiciously as he stood to greet them.

"What's the word?" the sheriff asked.

"Thadius is dead. We almost got ourselves arrested in Kit Carson in the bargain," Gideon said.

"Good job. Saves us having a trial and a hanging. What's the story with the girl?" Sheriff Howell asked.

Jack raised himself in the stirrups. "Bill, you know Widow French pretty well, don't you? This is Lily Mae and she needs a home," he said.

The sheriff pushed his hat back off his forehead and studied Jack. The old mountain man was about the last person he would have thought would be worried over an orphan. Not that he considered Jack hardhearted, but other people's business was never the trapper's concern. "I know her," he said before giving Gideon a look.

"We found her on the trail and she needed a home," Gideon said.

"Why didn't you leave her in Kit Carson? She really isn't Boulder's problem," Sheriff Howell said.

"She can hear you. Show a little respect," Gideon said in a tone that he had never before taken with the sheriff. "You're the one that's always saying that there's the law and then there's what's right. This is one of those what's right situations."

Sheriff Howell grinned at Gideon. He admired the young man's pluck and just plain liked him as a person. "My apologies to Lily Mae. You and Jack have a point. I'll take her to meet the widow right now."

Gideon managed to climb out of the saddle with Lily Mae still behind the cantle. He reached into his pocket and pulled out a Double Eagle twenty-dollar gold piece that he handed to Lily Mae. "Buy yourself some nice clothes and some shoes that fit," he said with a wink.

Lily Mae reached over and pulled Gideon's hat off his head. She leaned over and kissed him on the forehead. "Thank you," she said.

Farting Jack wore a fringe leather pouch on a rawhide string around his neck. He climbed off his horse and handed it to the girl. "I'm not rich like Gideon, but it has a little money in it and it's something you can keep your things in," he said.

The girl thanked him and gave him a kiss.

"You'll need to lead my horse to the widow's place. Lily Mae turned her ankle and can't walk much," Gideon said to the sheriff. "We need to talk when you get back anyway."

"Will I ever get to see either of you again?" Lily Mae asked.

Jack patted the girl's leg. "I'll check on you from time to time. Don't you worry about that. I want to see if the widow can make a lady out of a vixen," he said.

Gideon smiled at Lily Mae. "We will see," he said.

The sheriff grabbed the reins to Gideon's horse and walked away with Lily Mae. Jack waited until they disappeared down a side street before ripping a roaring fart.

"I've been about ready to explode ever since that girl started riding with us," Jack said. "Whoa, that was a good one."

The End

About the author

Duane Boehm grew up on a farm outside of Petersburg, Illinois. The two passions he developed early in life were the love of playing guitar and reading books. He eventually moved to a mini-farm outside of Murfreesboro, Tennessee with his wife and replaced planting corn with trees and raising dogs. For a number of years he worked as an IT consultant and eventually became inspired to begin his journey as a novelist.

To date, Duane has written seven Bestselling novels in the *Gideon Johann Western Series*.

You can find Duane's books on Amazon:
http://www.amazon.com/Duane-Boehm/e/B00GV0HDQ2/ref=dp_byline_cont_pop_ebooks_1

To learn of future novels by Duane Boehm, like his FaceBook page:
https://www.facebook.com/DuaneBoehmAuthor/
or join his mailing list: http://eepurl.com/Jg0yD

DAMSEL IN DISTRESS

A Jess Williams Western
Western
A Short Story

By

Robert J. Thomas

CHAPTER ONE

Jess ducked down behind the woodpile again as two more slugs tore at the bark in the stack of wood. He shoved a few fresh rounds into his Winchester. He moved again along the woodpile to another spot, raised his rifle and fired at the old shack that Russell Bell was firing from. The slug whizzed through the glassless window and slammed into the wall.

"You can't get me, bounty hunter," Bell shouted in a high-pitched voice. "No one's gonna take me in again!"

"Oh, you're going, but won't be slappin' those lips together when you do."

"I done kilt the last two bounty hunters who tried," he bragged.

"How much food did you find in that old rickety shack?"

Bell looked around and saw the empty shelves. "Plenty of food in here, and water too," he lied.

"That shack looks like it's been empty longer than you've been lyin'."

"Go to hell, bounty hunter."

Jess peeked through the small opening in the woodpile where he could see the cabin. Bell's saddled horse was tethered to the side of it. Jess saw the saddlebags still on the horse, which meant they were either empty of supplies or he had simply forgotten to take them inside the shack. Jess levered another round into the Winchester and leaned it up against the pile.

He opened his own saddlebag that he had pulled off Gray. He realized he was a little hungry himself so he pulled out a can of peaches and opened them. Bell fired twice and there was no response, which worried him. There was enough cover on the other side of the woodpile to allow Jess to move to another location so Bell ran around to all the windows and searched frantically for him. He moved back to the window he had been firing from.

"You still out there, bounty hunter?" he asked nervously. Jess swallowed the first piece of peach and licked the juice off his fingers.

"Yeah, but I'm busy eating some delicious peaches," he said.

"You's a lyin' bounty hunter!"

Jess finished the last of the peaches, drank the juice from the can and pitched it over the woodpile toward the shack. Bell saw it and cursed. He had no food left except for a few small pieces of jerky, a half-filled canteen of water and he was already starving. He licked his lips and his stomach growled as he looked at the can on the ground.

"I got plenty of food, just no peaches," he shouted.

"I got another can right here," declared Jess. "Just thinkin' on whether I'll eat it now or save it for later."

Bell licked his lips again. "I'll trade you a can of beans for that can of peaches," he said.

"I already have a can of beans."

"How 'bout I throw in an apple?"

"An apple sounds mighty good right about now."

"It's a big one. Nice and red too."

"You really want those peaches, don't you?"

"I like peaches."

"Throw the apple over here first."

"Oh no, bounty hunter, you gotta throw that can of peaches over here first."

"How do I know I can trust you?"

"You can't, but if you want this apple, you gotta give me the peaches first."

"Well, seeing as I got all this other food with me, I guess I can take the chance," said Jess as he pitched the can of peaches up in the air.

It landed right where he had hoped for, three feet from the front door. He picked up the Winchester and pushed the barrel through the small opening. It was just large enough to be able to look down the barrel and he could see the can by the door.

He watched and waited and then the barrel of a rifle appeared in the doorway. Bell was trying to move the can closer to him without exposing himself. The can rolled one way and then the other, but it wouldn't move closer to the door opening. Bell extended the rifle farther out and Jess fired. The slug careened off the rifle and Bell jerked it back inside.

"Son...of...a...bitch!" he howled as he felt his left hand, which was numb from the shock. Jess levered another round into the Winchester and fired at the can of peaches. It exploded and the peaches flew everywhere.

"That wasn't very neighborly of you, bounty hunter," he blurted as he moved his fingers around to get the feeling back in them. "You ain't gettin' this apple now."

"We ain't exactly neighbors. Besides I doubt you even have an apple," Jess said as he levered another round into the Winchester.

Bell checked his rifle and realized he only had several rounds left in it. He checked his pockets. He had no rifle cartridges left and only three extra bullets for his pistol in the bullet loops on his holster. He cursed himself for not stopping in the last town he rode around to buy some food supplies and ammunition with the last of the money he had taken off an old man before stabbing him in the heart.

He crawled on his hands and knees and peered through the side window to see his horse still standing there. He decided he had no choice but to make a run for it. He crawled to the edge of the door and stood up with his back to the wall. He moved the rifle to his left hand, pulled his pistol out and cocked it.

"Hey, bounty hunter."

"What?"

"Got any more of them peaches?"

"Not with me, but I have another can in my saddlebags."

"But I didn't see your horses."

"That's because I left them over in those trees behind me."

Bell edged a look around the doorway and saw the trees were about two hundred feet from the woodpile. He figured if he could get to his horse and keep out of sight behind the shack, he might get far enough away to escape a slug from a rifle. And the bounty hunter would have to run two hundred feet on foot before he could get to his horses, which in his muddled mind, was a fair play. Especially considering he had no food or extra ammunition to keep up a prolonged standoff.

"Hey, bounty hunter?"

"What?"

"How much am I worth?"

"Three hundred."

"That's all?"

"Yep."

"That don't seem like a lot of money for a man's life."

"That's funny coming from you, since you stabbed that old man in the heart for a measly fifty dollars."

"He was old and had one foot in the grave already," cackled Bell as he gathered the courage to make a run for it.

"I'd say you got one foot in the grave too," Jess told him as he took a bite off a piece of beef jerky and chewed it.

Bell suddenly appeared in the doorway, firing his pistol as fast as he could as he ran for his horse. Jess saw his rapid movement and stuck the piece of jerky between his teeth. Bell fired all five rounds before he got on his horse.

Jess stayed down until he heard the pistol hammer fall on an empty chamber. He rose up and took aim at Bell, but before he could pull the trigger, Bell was out of sight behind the shack. Jess stood up and took another bite from the jerky and stuffed the rest of it into his back pocket.

111

He put his Winchester down on the woodpile, moved over to his buffalo rifle and chambered a custom-loaded three hundred seventy-five grain fifty-caliber cartridge into it. He rested the rifle on top of the woodpile, raised the sights and waited for Bell to come into view again.

When he did, Jess checked the wind and made an adjustment for elevation as he chewed the jerky. He stopped chewing and slowly squeezed back on the trigger until the rifle bucked and boomed, spewing out flames, smoke and lead.

He looked up from the rifle and saw Bell's arms fly up in the air as the slug slammed into his right side, tearing a hole in his left lung before bouncing off a rib bone and exiting out his front. He fell from the saddle and tumbled a few times before skidding to a halt in the dirt on his back. Jess set the Sharps buffalo rifle down, snatched up his Winchester and began long-striding it straight for Bell, whose arms were flailing around in the air.

By the time he reached him, Bell was breathing raggedly and coughing up blood. He saw Jess approaching and looked around for his rifle, but it was too far away. He started to reach for his pistol, but remembered it was empty. Jess stood over him now, chewing the jerky with his rifle pointed at Bell's head. Bell blinked several times and focused his eyes. Suddenly, he recognized who it was.

"You didn't tell me it was you," he wheezed.

"You never asked."

"I might have surrendered if I knew it was you behind that woodpile."

"I don't accept surrenders," Jess said as he raised his eyebrows and moved the barrel until it rested on his forehead. "You should know that if you know me."

Bell's eyes went cross-eyed as he laughed slightly. "So, you're just gonna kill me?"

"Yep. Just like you killed that old man for his money."

"That makes you the same as me," he wheezed as he struggled to breathe.

"We ain't nothin' alike," whispered Jess as he pulled the trigger.

Bell's head bounced off the ground once and slowly fell to the side. Jess looked up and saw Bell's horse a few hundred feet away eating grass. He retrieved it and used the rope he found on the saddle to haul the dead body up over the horse and tie it down tightly. He walked the horse to the woodpile and picked up his things before moving to where his two horses, Gray and Sharps, waited in the trees.

After eating a can of cold beans, Jess led his horses out of the trees with Bell's horse tied to his packhorse Sharps. He found the trail leading to the town of Elk Ridge, Texas, where he would turn Bell's corpse in to the law for the bounty.

CHAPTER TWO

Jess had his horse Gray at a slow walk as he ate some cold beans while sitting in the saddle. His packhorse followed faithfully behind as always. Bell's legs and head bounced around as his horse walked behind Sharps. Jess was taking a sip from his canteen when he caught some movement out of the corner of his eye.

He halted his horses and instinctively jerked out his Winchester. He was about to lever a round into it when he saw it was his good friend Shadow, a huge timber wolf with a grayish coat and bright green eyes. The wolf seemed to show up unannounced from time to time, stay with him for a while and then disappear whenever he felt like it. Shadow ran up to him and started barking. Jess looked down at him.

"Hey, boy, how've you been?" he asked. "I ain't seen you in over a week now. Where did you run off to?"

Shadow barked again and started running back the way he'd come. He stopped after traveling fifty feet, turned around and started barking again. Jess slid from the saddle and called the wolf over. Shadow ran back to him and rubbed up against his legs.

"You hungry and can't find a rabbit? Is that what this is?" Shadow barked and ran back the way he'd come again, turned around and kept barking and pawing at the ground.

"I know you're trying to tell me something, but I'm just not sure what it is," Jess said. Shadow ran back to him and went to Bell's corpse. He clamped his teeth on one of the boots and tried to yank the body off the horse.

"What are you doing, Shadow?" queried Jess as he walked over to him. Shadow kept yanking on the boot and the ropes began to strain. Jess reached down and scratched the wolf's ears and he licked Jess's hands.

"I gotta take this stinker to Elk Ridge to turn in for the bounty. If you want to come with me, that's okay, but you gotta quit trying to pull him off his horse."

Shadow barked again, grabbed the boot and continued to try to pull the body off. Jess stood back with his hands on his hips wondering what it was all about. The wolf was an exceptionally smart animal who had saved his life more than once. He had proven his intelligence many times over and Jess had to take whatever he was trying to do as something serious. He sighed, walked to the horse and started cutting the ropes with his bowie knife.

"I'm not sure what this is all about, Shadow, but I'll go along with it, just like you've helped me," he said as he cut the last of the ropes. Shadow pulled the corpse onto the ground.

He barked and ran back the way he'd come again. He turned and waited for Jess to unsaddle Bell's horse and let it go free. He looked down at Bell's body. The right boot had fallen in a small shallow hole in the ground left by a large rock someone had removed.

"Well, looks like you have that one foot in the grave already. I'm sure it won't take long for Lucifer to reach up and drag you down where you belong," he said as he climbed up in the saddle and nudged Gray into a walk toward Shadow, his packhorse Sharps following behind.

Shadow took off running and Jess followed him, watching the trail ahead for any trouble. After about two hours of riding, Jess reined up his horses when he saw a fancy-looking white carriage way off in the distance. He extended his spyglass and peered through it. Shadow kept running toward the carriage.

Jess spotted what looked like one body on the ground near it, but he saw no one else. The carriage had no horses hitched to it. He put the spyglass away, slid out his Winchester and started slowly for the carriage, watching and waiting for any surprise.

As he got closer, he could see Shadow's tail wagging out from behind the carriage. He moved Gray to the left so he could see what was on the other side of the carriage. When he did, he saw the dead body of a man on the ground and a woman in a fancy dress leaning up against the rear wheel of the carriage petting Shadow. He stopped and watched for a minute and saw a rifle on the ground by the woman's side.

"What the heck did you find, Shadow?" he said as he kneed Gray forward at a slow walk.

Shadow turned to Jess and barked several times. The woman turned her head to see him approaching on horseback with another horse following behind. Jess reached her and Shadow was licking the woman's face. He slipped effortlessly from the saddle and walked over to the woman, who watched him with keen interest.

"Are you here to finish me off or rescue me?" she asked in a weakened voice.

"Well, Shadow brought me here so I guess I'm here to help," he said.

"Who is Shadow?"

"That wolf who seems to have taken a liking to you."

"I didn't know he had a name," she said as she grabbed Shadow's massive head and kissed him on his nose. "Thank you, Shadow. Sorry about shooting at you."

"You tried to shoot him?" asked Jess as he squatted down to check the man on the ground.

"Yes, when I first saw him approaching. I figured he was here to kill me for a meal, so I fired the last round in the rifle to scare him off, but he just ran back some and sat there watching me for the longest time. Then, he started walking toward me with his head down and I thought I was a goner since I couldn't get up to reach the bullets in the carriage. I just said a prayer, closed my eyes and waited for what I thought was certain death. But all of a sudden, I felt him licking my face. He stayed with me for a few hours,

116

but then he jumped up and took off. I thought I'd just die of thirst out here."

"Who is this man?" Jess asked as he stood up.

"That's my poor husband," she said as tears filled her eyes. "They shot him down like a dog. He wasn't even putting up a fight, but our driver just shot him."

"How bad are you hurt?"

She wiped the tears from her eyes. "Well, they didn't shoot me," she said. "They just beat me up so badly I couldn't stand any longer. I think one of my ribs is cracked and my stomach hurts like the dickens."

Jess took one of his canteens and knelt down beside her and let her drink from it. He picked up her rifle, stood up and started shoving rounds into it until it was fully loaded. He put it down next to her again.

"Don't hesitate to use that if they come back," he said as he looked around the area.

He walked to his horses, pulled out the spyglass and scanned the area in all directions. He looked at the tracks leaving the carriage. He counted five sets, three carrying riders and two without a rider.

"How long ago did they leave?" he asked.

"It's been seven, maybe eight hours or more," she estimated. "I passed out several times so I lost track of the hours."

"Why'd they take the team that was pulling the carriage?"

"Those two horses were worth a lot of money," she explained. "My husband was coming out west to start a breeding ranch for horses. Our driver Vern knew the value of them. They also took all the cash my husband brought with him. He had fifty thousand dollars in a valise under the seat of the carriage. Our driver was the only one who knew about that and he was in on it. He stopped the carriage when the other two men rode up to us. We trusted him. He's worked for my husband going on ten years."

Jess cradled his Winchester in his arms as he stood there thinking. She saw all the weapons he wore: the two cut-down shotguns tucked into the back of his holster, the shotgun in the sling on his back, the Colt Peacemaker tucked into the front of his holster forward of his left hip and the unique shiny pistol that rode in a very strange-looking holster on his right leg.

"Who are you? Or maybe I should ask, *what* are you?"

He looked down at her. "My name is Jess Williams, and I'm a bounty hunter by trade. And you?"

"Elizabeth Schoen, but most folks call me Liz."

"Nice to meet you, Liz, although I wish it was under better circumstances."

"I agree. So, being a bounty hunter is why you wear so many weapons?"

"Yes."

"Are you good at what you do?"

"Yes."

"So, what now?" she asked.

"Can you stand up?"

"Maybe, but I'd rather not try just yet."

Jess looked up at the large orange orb heading downward.

"We have two hours of daylight left, so we'll stay by the carriage for the night and see if you can ride tomorrow," he said as he slid his Winchester back into the scabbard on Gray. "I'll cook us some grub and put up a lean-to for you to sleep under so you don't have to climb into the carriage. You'll stay dry in case it rains, although I don't believe it will."

"Thank you so much, Mr. Williams," she said.

He looked over his shoulder at her and saw Shadow curled up next to her. "Thank Shadow," he said smiling. "If it weren't for him finding me, I would have kept riding for Elk Ridge with a dead body to turn in to the law there."

"How much money would you have been paid?" she asked.

"Three hundred."

"I can make sure you get reimbursed for that once I can get to a bank," she said. "My husband was a very rich man."

Jess took out some canvas and quickly fixed a lean-to over her. He took out a blanket and covered the body of her husband for the night. After cooking beans and salt pork, along with some pan bread with raisins in it, he cleaned up and made coffee. He handed her the peppermint stick from the bag of Arbuckles' and then rolled his bedroll out under the carriage after placing his cans with strings around their perimeter. When he finally crawled into his bedroll, he looked over at Shadow watching him. He waited a few seconds, but Shadow put his head back down and closed his eyes as he lay next to Elizabeth.

"Traitor," muttered Jess. Shadow lifted his head, whimpered softly, and then put his head down and went back to sleep.

CHAPTER THREE

In the morning, after cooking some breakfast and getting everything ready, Jess studied the body of her dead husband. Liz was sitting up now and looking at the dwindling fire.

"I don't have a shovel and my packhorse can't carry his body and you all the way to Elk Ridge."

"We can't just leave him like that," she said. "The coyotes and vultures with get after him after we leave. Isn't there anything else you can do?"

He looked at the body and sighed. "I can dig a shallow grave with a flat rock or a board I could rip off the carriage and then cover him with enough rocks to keep the critters at bay for a day or so."

"Use the board they pried up on the seat to get at the money in the valise," she suggested.

Jess went into the carriage and got the board. He used the corner of it and started scraping at the ground. Shadow walked over and began digging with his huge paws. Between the two of them, they had a shallow hole dug in short order. Jess rolled the body into the hole and began searching for rocks. Shadow began picking up rocks in his teeth and depositing them on the grave. When they finished, Jess took out his handkerchief and wiped the sweat from his brow.

"Shadow sure is an intelligent animal," she said. "When we get to town, I'll have some men come out and collect his body and have him buried properly."

"Let's see if we can get you up on my packhorse," he said as he reached down and locked arms with her.

He hauled her up on her feet and she leaned heavily against him. He felt her large breasts against his chest and he glanced down at them without thinking. She noticed it and smiled strangely at him.

"Sorry, but I had to get my legs under me," she said as she moved away slightly. He nodded and helped her get her foot in the stirrup and boosted her up in the saddle. He looked at her fancy shoes and shook his head.

"How much riding have you done before?" he asked.

"I've been riding for years," she said. "Remember, my late husband raised horses. I'll be fine with these shoes."

"I could give you my boots if you'd like."

"That's not necessary."

Jess climbed up in the saddle. "Elk Ridge is the closest town so we'll head there," he explained. "Sharps doesn't need to be led. He'll follow Gray wherever he goes. Leave the reins wrapped around the saddle horn and just hold on."

"Okay," she said as she rubbed the horse's neck. "These are fine animals."

"Yes they are. They were trained to run long distances for long periods of time, but we'll take it slow going for now." She nodded and Jess nudged Gray into a walk heading to the trail that would lead into town.

When they rode in, most of the townsfolk stopped and stared at the unlikely threesome: Jess with all his weapons, the huge wolf and a woman who looked like she'd just come from a ballroom somewhere with her fancy dress and shoes. Jess headed for the jail and when the marshal, Allan Babbitt walked out, he recognized both of them.

"Mrs. Schoen, where are your husband and that fancy carriage of yours?" he asked.

"We were robbed after we left here," she explained. "Mr. Williams came to my rescue after Shadow found me."

"Who the heck is Shadow?"

"The wolf sitting right there," she said as she pointed.

"Where is your husband?"

"I'm afraid our driver killed him," she said. "I need some men to go and get his body and retrieve my carriage."

"Why didn't you drive the carriage back here?"

"They took the two horses pulling it," she explained.

"You know, the livery owner was bragging on how he bought some fine horses yesterday for pennies on the dollar," said the marshal.

"I'll want to buy them back," she said.

"I'll take care of all of that for you," he said as he looked over at Jess.

"Try not killin' anyone in town while you're here, Williams," said the marshal.

"I'll do my best, Marshal, but I can't promise anything."

"Why would you say that, Marshal?" asked Liz. He just shook his head and turned toward the undertaker's parlor. She looked over at Jess.

"Why did he say that to you?" she asked. He pursed his lips and smiled.

"I have a lot of people who would like to see me dead," he said as he shrugged his shoulders. "Let's get you to the hotel in town so you can clean up and let a doctor examine you." She nodded and they headed for the large two-story hotel at the end of Main Street.

Liz demanded the two largest rooms in the hotel that were joined by an inside door. Jess paid the bill and she told him to keep a record of what he spent and she would reimburse him once she was able to go to the bank and have money wired to her.

Jess took a much-needed nap while she saw the doctor and took a bath. Jess woke to a light tap on the door separating their rooms. He got off the bed and opened it with his pistol in his right hand behind his leg. She handed him a list of things to purchase and he holstered his gun and looked at the list. Shadow stood behind her.

"You need all this?" he asked.

"Yes, and do you always answer the door with a gun in your hand?"

"Most of the time, yeah."

"Well, it's only me in this room."

"I don't take chances."

"Please go and get those items on the list and quickly."

"I'm not sure I know what some of these things are," he said as he read the list.

"Don't worry, the woman at the woman's apparel store will know exactly what to give you," she said as she shooed him away with a hand gesture.

He narrowed his eyes and frowned at her.

"What?" she asked.

"Oh, nothing," he said as he closed the door, walked out of his room and into the hallway. She stood at the door and huffed.

"That was rude," she said. Shadow made a whimpering sound.

"Woman knows how to tell people what to do for sure," Jess whispered to himself as he headed down the stairs and out to the street.

He went to the women's apparel shop and handed the list to the woman behind the counter. She scrunched up her face as she read the list before looking back up at him. He stood there with a confused look on his face.

"How many women is all this stuff for?"

"One."

"Only one?"

"It's for Mrs. Schoen."

The woman took in a large breath and exhaled. "That explains it then," she said sarcastically.

She moved around the store and collected all kinds of things in small bottles and jars, along with some clothes and other things he had never seen before. She put it all in a box, put the clothes on hangers and wrapped them in some heavy cloth material. He paid the bill, picked up the box and threw the clothes over his shoulder. When he walked outside, he saw a young boy kicking a rock around in the street.

"Hey, kid," Jess called out. The boy spun around on his heels.

"What?"

"You wanna make a dollar?"

"Absolutely."

"Come and carry this box of stuff for me."

The boy picked up the rock and ran over and stuck his hand out. "Money first," he said. Jess set the box down on the boardwalk, fished around in his pocket for a silver dollar and handed it to the boy.

"Gee thanks," he said as he threw the rock over his shoulder and picked up the box. "I can buy me a real ball now."

Jess started to walk along the boardwalk with the clothes over his shoulder. He noticed a man leaning up against a post outside a saloon, watching him with keen interest. He was smoking a quirley, which he finished and threw out into the street. He stepped off the boardwalk and headed directly for Jess.

The man's spurs jingled as they raked against the ground. He was of medium build, nicely dressed and wore a Navy Colt that rested in a fancy embossed holster. Jess shifted the clothes to his left hand and kept his right hand free as he slipped his hammer strap off, which caused the man to smile knowingly as he stopped in the middle of the street.

"Is that really Jess Williams?" he asked.

"Who wants to know?" said Jess.

"Fran Birkin," he said. "I'm surprised you never heard of me."

"I've heard the name before. Just never laid eyes on you yet. They say you've been on quite a killing spree lately, trying to build your reputation, I reckon."

"Well, I wouldn't call it a killing spree," Birkin countered. "Every man I killed accepted the challenge fair and square."

"Even the ones you goaded into drawing on you?"

"I did call a few of them yeller, if that's what you mean."

"Yeah, that's what I meant."

"So, the question is, are *you* yeller?"

CHAPTER FOUR

Jess turned to the boy, put the clothes on the box and told him to move away, which he quickly did. A few of the townsfolk noticed and stopped to watch. Jess caught movement on the second floor of the hotel and saw Liz looking out the window. He flashed a smile at her before stepping off the boardwalk and moving to the middle of the street.

"I think you know the answer to your question, but the real question is, are you ready to end your killing spree today?" Jess asked him.

"They said you had grit," said Birkin. "I guess I won't have to goad you."

"No, but I will give you fair warning. If you jerk for that iron, you *will* die today."

"You sound so sure of yourself. How'd you get to be so cocky?"

"I wouldn't call it cocky; it's just that a good man knows his abilities and I learned mine from putting a long list of men just like you in their graves."

"Yeah, but you've never seen me skin this thing out of leather," he bragged as he tapped the butt of his pistol with his right index finger.

"And I could say the same about you."

"Not really. I was there when you put down Nevada Jackson. I knew I couldn't beat you back then, but I've been practicing every day since and I think I can take you."

"So did Nevada, and I've gotten better since then too."

"Why don't we find out," said Birkin as he lowered his right hand down to the butt of his pistol. They locked eyes for what seemed like an eternity, but in reality, it was only a few seconds.

Birkin's right hand moved in a blur and he cocked the hammer back on his pistol by the time the cylinder cleared

126

the holster, but he jerk-fired the pistol when two slugs whumped hard into his chest like battering rams.

The slug from his pistol tore a hole through the front of his holster and ended up in the dirt. Birkin looked at his smoking holster, then at the two holes in his chest as his eyes rolled up in the back of his head before falling facedown in the dirt, dead. Dust rolled up from his body as a pool of blood formed. The dusty street sucked it up as quickly as it drained out.

Jess looked up at the window where Liz stood with her hands over her mouth. She quickly closed the curtains as he replaced the spent shells in his pistol. Marshal Babbitt came striding toward him with his right hand on the butt of his pistol. He looked down at the dead body.

"What did I tell you?" he wailed angrily as he waved his hands around. "I told you not to kill anybody and now look what's happened. You done killed somebody and you ain't been in town more than a few hours."

"It weren't his doin'," said the boy, who was standing there still holding all the things. "That man pushed him into it."

"Oh, shut up, Louis," groused Birkin.

"Don't yell at the boy," argued Jess as he holstered his pistol. "He's just telling the truth. Ask anyone else standing around who saw it."

"Aw, hell, I believe Louis," he said with frustration on his face. "I just didn't want to have to fill out the paperwork and arrange for two burials, what with Mr. Schoen gettin' himself killed." The marshal walked away cursing under his breath as he did. Jess smiled at Louis and picked up the clothes from the box.

"You just earned a five-dollar gold piece for telling the truth," Jess told him as they started walking toward the hotel.

"That's just great," Louis said with a wide smile. "How'd you do it though?"

"Do what?"

"Make your pistol appear like that? I don't even think I saw your hand move."

"I practice a lot," Jess said as he took a five-dollar gold piece and dropped it into the front pocket of the boy's shirt.

When they reached the room in the hotel, Jess placed his hand on his pistol after rapping on the door. Liz opened the door and frowned at his right hand, but smiled when she saw the clothes and the box of things.

"Please, come in and put it all on the bed," she said. "Unless you plan on shooting me too."

"That wasn't my fault," argued Jess. "Ask Louis or anybody else who witnessed it."

"I saw it for myself through the window," she admitted. "I've never seen anything like that before. I guess you *are* good at your job. Now, make sure you pay the boy for his services and put it against my bill."

Louis shoved his hand out palm up and shrugged his shoulders. "She said to pay me," he said grinning from ear to ear.

"I guess it's her money, so here you go," he said as he handed the boy a twenty-dollar gold eagle coin. They both looked at Liz, but she seemed not to care, so Louis ran out before she could say anything. Jess watched him turning the corner.

"Crafty little shit," he whispered as he turned around to see Liz standing there stark naked. He stood there wide-eyed and at a loss for words. He frowned when he saw the bruises on her stomach and sides. Shadow went to a corner and stuck his nose in it.

"What? You've never seen a woman naked before?" she asked.

"Well, yeah, but…I gotta close the door," he said as he went and quickly shut it. He turned around and she held one of the dresses up to her neck.

"How do you like this one?" she asked.

128

"Uh, it's fine." She put the dress down on the bed, reached over and picked up the other one. She put it up to her neck and looked down at it.

"How about this one?"

"Uh, they're both very pretty," he said as he clasped his hands together and rubbed them back and forth nervously. She put the dress down on the bed and moved over to him until her naked body was pressing against his. She felt the cold butt of his extra Colt Peacemaker against her stomach.

"You're not very good around women, are you?" she asked as she put her face closer to his and pressed against his body even more.

"Not really," he stammered. "And you just lost your husband yesterday."

"Yes, I did, didn't I?" she said in a soft voice. "I suppose I should at least wait until he's buried."

"At least," agreed Jess.

She took a step back and smiled at him. "So, is it just that you don't like what you see?"

He looked at her naked body and smiled. "No, it's not that," he said. "You're a very beautiful woman and would make a fine catch for any man. But I think you should wait a while, at least until you're done grieving for the loss of your husband."

"Yes, I suppose there's that," she said as she turned and walked back to the bed and sat down. "Would you please have the hotel send me up a steak cooked rare with some potatoes and carrots?"

"Sure, I'll arrange for a waiter to bring it up to you," he said as he headed for the door.

"You know, it's odd," she said. "You faced that gunman down in the street without any problem. You looked as cool and calm as could be. But facing me with no clothes on, well, you looked like a scared child."

"Yeah, that seems to happen a lot," he admitted. "Maybe I should bring your meal up to your room, now that I think on it."

"That's very sweet of you. Make sure you tip the wait staff for me," she said.

"All of them?"

"Of course," she said as she crossed her legs and smiled. He went out the door, closed it and stood there for a long minute.

"Hell of a woman, but a strange one indeed," he whispered to himself.

CHAPTER FIVE

By the end of the day, some men had brought the carriage back to town, along with Mr. Schoen's body. Arrangements were made for a burial the next day. The owner of the livery put the carriage inside and repaired the seat where Jess had used the board to help dig a hole. Jess stabled his horses and when he finished brushing them down, he walked over to the owner, who was wiping the dust off the carriage.

"Where are the two horses you bought off those men the other day?" he asked.

"Oh, those two fine animals over there," he said, pointing. "Great horseflesh. I'm not sure I want to sell them yet."

"Mrs. Schoen wants to buy them back from you."

"Well, I got a good deal purchasing them, but if I were inclined to sell, I'd have to ask at least what they're worth."

"They belong to her," advised Jess. "They're considered stolen or even rustled in the eyes of the law."

The man scrunched up his face in disappointment. "Well, I only paid fifty dollars for the both of them, but they gotta be worth a few hundred each. I suppose I'd have to be happy with just getting my money back. I don't want to be called a horse thief, not in my business."

Jess saw the distress on the man's face and then he looked over to where the hotel was, even though he couldn't see it from inside the livery. He thought about tipping Louis and the entire staff in the hotel café and Mrs. Schoen's willingness to throw her dead husband's money around like there was no end to it. He turned back to the man and smiled.

"Four hundred dollars it is then," he said as he counted out the money and handed it to him. The man smiled widely and pocketed the money.

"You're a very generous man, Mr. Williams," he said.

"Mrs. Schoen is the one paying you, not me," he said. "Now, what can you tell me about the three men who sold them to you?"

He gave a detailed description of the men as he walked outside and showed the three sets of tracks leaving his livery. They went along the side of the building and off in a direction where there was no trail.

"I thought it odd they went that way, 'cause there ain't anything in that direction for at least a hundred miles," he said as he showed Jess the tracks. Jess knelt down and examined them closely before standing up.

"Is there an artist in town who could do a drawing of the men from your description?"

"The man who runs the newspaper shop can do it."

"Go over there and have him make two copies of each and deliver them to the marshal at the jail," Jess told him as he handed the man a five-dollar gold piece to give to the man at the newspaper shop. The livery owner headed for the shop and Jess headed for the jail to see Babbitt.

When he walked in, Babbitt looked up at him. "Please tell me I don't have to arrange for another burial," he said frowning.

"No, I haven't killed anybody else," Jess said smiling. "But the day ain't over with yet."

"That's not funny, Mr. Williams," he scolded him.

"Listen, I have someone drawing up some sketches of the three men who killed Mr. Schoen and beat up his wife," he said. "He's supposed to deliver them here."

"That would be Hatch over at the newspaper office. He's really good at drawing and painting. He did that one on my wall over there."

Jess looked at it and smiled. "That's really nice," he said.

The marshal looked out his window and grunted. "Here comes Hatch now," he said.

Hatch was a frail-looking man with a rumpled suit that was two sizes too big for him. He walked in, nodded at the marshal and shook hands with Jess. He held a large pad of paper tucked under his arm.

"It's a pleasure meetin' you, Mr. Williams," he said. "Would you do me the honor of posing for a painting?"

"Why would you want to do that?"

"Because you're famous," he said as he put the three sketches on the desk. "All you have to do is stand up for me."

Jess stood up and Hatch went to scribbling on his pad of paper. After a bit, he motioned for Jess to turn around. He continued to scribble quickly and when he finished, he showed it to Jess, who smiled as he looked at it.

"You really are good," he said. "You got all the detail in it."

"I'll use this to make the painting," he said. "I don't suppose you'd pose with your gun in your hand, would you?"

"Not really," Jess said as he handed the pad back to Hatch.

"Can't blame a man for trying," he said as he walked out. The marshal was looking through wanted posters and found two that matched the sketches.

"I thought I'd seen those two before," he said as he handed them to Jess. "That's Leon Curtis and Bernie Norton. They're wanted dead or alive for the sum of one thousand dollars each for the murder of a bank manager up in Kansas City, Kansas, a few months ago. They must have high-tailed it down here to Texas, hoping no one would recognize them here."

Jess folded up the posters and put them into his pocket. He looked at the other sketch that had to be the driver who worked for Mr. Schoen.

"Nothing on this one?" Jess asked as he showed the other one to the marshal.

"Naw, only seen him once when he passed through here with Mr. and Mrs. Schoen," he said.

"Thanks, Marshal," said Jess as he took the sketch and headed for the hotel.

CHAPTER SIX

Vern Juda sat on the ground poking the fire with a piece of wood. The three men had already eaten their morning meal and were just sitting around doing nothing. Leon Curtis was pushing sand around with a branch. Bernie Norton was counting the cash in the valise for the tenth time.

Juda looked at him and shook his head. "You think it's going to grow if you keep counting it over and over again?" he asked.

Norton glanced up from the money and huffed. "Now you made me forget where I was," he blustered. "I've never had my hands on so much money before."

"Just divide it into three piles and give us our share," said Curtis. "How long are we gonna have to hide out in this arroyo?"

"Another week or so and they'll stop lookin' for us," said Norton. "Then we'll head across the Big Muddy, split up and go our separate ways."

"That'll be just fine with me," said Juda.

"You're just mad that I beat that woman up some," said Norton.

"Yes I am, because you didn't need to do that," said Juda.

"I got tired of listening to her complain," argued Norton. "I should've put a bullet into that smart mouth on her."

"You two shut up and give me my share," said Curtis. Norton counted out three piles of money and handed Curtis and Juda their shares.

"Happy now?" asked Norton as he started counting his share. Juda sat there shaking his head at him, but said nothing more about it.

***

135

Jess rapped on the door of Liz's room. When she answered it, she was dressed fancy and had painted her face with the stuff Jess had bought at the women's apparel shop. Her lips were a dark red color that highlighted her powdery white skin.

"Come in, Mr. Williams," she said. He walked in to find a small table with all kinds of food on it, small snacks of cookies, chocolate, breads, cheeses, pickles, crackers and a dozen other things he had never seen before.

"Are you hungry?" she asked as she waved her hand at the table.

"I've never seen some of this stuff," he said. He picked up a round doughy thing and popped it into his mouth. He nodded his head as he chewed it and swallowed.

"That was delicious," he said. "Makes me want to have some coffee to go with it."

"Coffee is on the bureau," she said as she waved her hand over to it.

He crossed the room and poured some coffee into a cup and sipped it. He handed her the wanted posters on Curtis and Norton, along with the sketch of her driver, Juda. She looked them over and frowned.

"This is the man who beat me up," she said as she held up the one on Norton. Jess nodded since he was eating another one of the little pastries. When he swallowed, he smiled at her.

"He's wanted dead or alive for one thousand and so is the other man by the name of Leon Curtis."

"Does that mean you're going after them?"

"Yes."

"And will you kill them both?"

"Yes."

"And what about the driver Vern?"

"He's not actually wanted yet, but I imagine the marshal will put in a request to put him on the dead or alive list."

Shadow skulked over to where Jess was and sniffed his fingers. He looked down at him and rubbed his head. "You want some of this?" he asked.

Shadow pressed against his legs and Jess started throwing the little pastries at him. He grabbed every one of them in midair, swallowing them as fast as Jess pitched them. Liz watched and then cleared her throat loudly. Jess and Shadow both looked at her.

"I don't think that sweet stuff is good for him," she lectured.

"Well then, why don't you order several raw steaks up to the room for him?"

"I will, but in the meantime, when are you going after these men?"

"First thing tomorrow morning," he said. "You seem to be doing fine right here for now. You can go to the bank and have them wire you some of your husband's money. I'll pay your bill downstairs before I leave tomorrow and you can reimburse me later."

She nodded and handed the papers back to him. "Will you have supper with me tonight in the café downstairs?"

"Sure, might as well get a good meal before I head out tomorrow," he said. "I'm going to go to my room, clean my weapons and pack a few things in my saddlebags."

Jess headed for the door separating their rooms and Shadow followed him. When Jess opened the door, the wolf ran ahead of him. Jess looked over his shoulder at Liz, who looked somewhat unhappy.

"I guess you don't need to order up them steaks," he told her. "Shadow must figure you're doing fine on your own too."

"Or maybe he's upset because I told you to stop feeding him those pastries," she said huffily. Jess opened his left hand to reveal several of the little round ones.

"You mean these?" he asked as Shadow barked in the background. She strolled over and slammed the door. Jess turned around and pitched the pastries to the wolf.

"Like I said, hell of a woman, but strange," he muttered.

"I heard that," she said sharply from the other side of the door.

"See what I mean?" he whispered to Shadow, who tilted his head.

CHAPTER SEVEN

Jess met Liz for supper in the café of the hotel. She had two waiters standing by their table, waiting for any requests that she might think of. She ordered champagne and they ate steaks, carrots and potatoes. She had sent one of the waiters to the livery to retrieve her fine silverware and special steak knives. Jess examined the steak knife and smiled as he put it down and pulled out his bowie knife. She put her silverware down and narrowed her eyes at him.

"What's wrong with my steak knives?" she asked.

"They're dull."

"I haven't had them sharpened lately is all."

"I know. They're dull. This bowie knife is sharp enough to shave a man."

"You're embarrassing me," she said as she glanced around the café.

Jess looked around and smiled at everyone. "They're not looking this way because of this knife."

"And just what does that mean?"

"Well, you have these two waiters standing by our table in case you want anything and you've asked for a dozen extra things so far and we haven't even cut into our steaks yet."

"I'm sorry, but I have standards," she huffed. "I'm used to having things a certain way."

"I'm not complaining. I'm just telling you why people are staring at us. Most folks around here just order their food, eat and leave. They don't have three or four waiters taking care of them or standing around waiting to see if they want something."

"They're being paid to do that," she argued.

"I know, and I'll bet they're happy about that. I'm only telling you people ain't lookin' over here because of this," he said as he held the gleaming knife up.

"Oh, just eat," she said as she cut into her steak.

He shrugged his shoulders and cut into his steak effortlessly, while she continued to saw through hers. She reached over and picked up his steak knife and handed it to one of the waiters who was standing at attention by their table.

"Would you please sharpen this for me?" she asked.

"Yes, ma'am," he said as he took off with the knife. They finished the meal and Jess paid the bill. He escorted her up to her room.

"Would you like to come in for a drink?" she asked.

"Thank you, but I have to get my things ready and go to the general store," he said. "And I have to get something for Shadow to eat."

"Will I see you in the morning?"

"I doubt that," he said. "I'll be in the saddle before you open your eyes in the morning."

She nodded, pecked him on the cheek and he closed the door. He stood there for a long moment thinking about her. She was a beautiful woman and he knew she wanted him to stay, but he spun on his heels and headed down the steps.

The next morning found Jess and Shadow riding northeast along some rough terrain. It was slow going. Tracking the three men was difficult at times. Whenever he lost the tracks, he kept looking around until he found them again.

He halted his horses and peered through his spyglass. He couldn't see the arroyo from where he sat atop his horse, but the slight sliver of smoke rising in the air was a dead giveaway. He put the spyglass away and looked up at the sun. He calculated he had only an hour or so before dusk would settle in. The tracks he had been following all along continued straight toward the smoke that seemed to be coming out of the ground.

"Gotta be a deep arroyo up ahead," he muttered to himself. He looked down at Shadow and put his finger to

140

his lips. "We have to be quiet, boy. We'll sneak up on them before the sun comes up tomorrow."

He wagged his tail and Jess turned the horses to his right, heading for some cover that would be provided by some thick bushes. He fed Shadow another chunk of ham and he ate cold beans and biscuits. He leaned against the saddle and fell off to sleep sitting up with his hat over his eyes, his pistol on his lap and Shadow curled up next to him.

***

The sun hadn't quite come out yet and Jess was on his stomach looking down the barrel of one of his Sharps buffalo rifles that was pointed directly at the thin column of smoke wafting up in the cold damp air. He had walked to a slight rise so that he could get a glimpse of the arroyo, but it wasn't enough for him to see the three men down inside it. He did see one of the horses when he lifted his head up high.

The sun rose just enough to start burning off the morning mist. Shadow was down on all fours next to Jess, his bright green eyes fixed on the edge of the arroyo. Jess lifted the sights and turned his head to Shadow.

"I need you to startle those men and maybe flush them out of there," he said. "Can you do that for me?" Shadow made a low groaning sound and stood up. He used his nose to knock Jess's hat off and then started walking toward the arroyo with his ears pinned back and his head low.

"I guess that meant yes," Jess said as he put his hat back on.

Juda, Curtis and Norton were still asleep in their bedrolls. Shadow made his way to the edge of the arroyo and looked down at the three men. He started growling softly at first, and then he got louder and louder. Juda was the first to open his eyes to see the huge timber wolf

141

revealing his fangs and growling. As soon as he realized what it was, his eyes went wide with fear.

"Ooh," he wailed as he struggled to get out of his bedroll.

The other two men woke and saw it. Now the three of them were scrambling to get out of their bedrolls. Juda tripped over his boots and fell as he tried to get his pistol out of his holster. Norton was wrestling with his blanket and Shadow was barking and growling wildly now.

The three men were in a panic. Jess could only see their horses at the one end of the arroyo. They were bobbing their heads up and down and stomping at the ground. Juda finally got up and got his pistol out, but Shadow turned and bolted into a dead run before he got off the first shot that went aimlessly in the air.

"What the hell was that?" screeched Norton as he finally got his balance and pulled his pistol out of his holster.

"A damn timber wolf. I think he' been chewing on loco weed or something," hollered Juda as he ran to a shallower part of the arroyo to fire his pistol again.

Shadow was too far away now. Juda fired twice as Norton picked up his rifle and levered a round into it. He ran to the shallow side and leveled his rifle at the retreating wolf, but before he pulled the trigger, the custom-loaded fifty-caliber slug punched through his ribcage and exited out the other side.

Norton fell to the ground and let out his death rattle as the icy fingers of death wrapped around his body. Juda and Curtis frantically looked around to see where the shot had come from, but they were so discombobulated now, they didn't see the black smoke off in the distance.

Jess picked up the other buffalo rifle that was already loaded and tried to pick out Curtis from Juda. When he did, he squeezed back on the trigger until the rifle bucked and boomed heavily against his shoulder, sending the slug burning through the air. It traveled through Curtis's neck.

He instinctively grabbed it with both hands after dropping his rifle. He stumbled over the dead body of Norton and fell facedown on top of it.

Juda was in a frenzied panic now, ducking down in the arroyo and holding his hands over his ears. His pistol was still in his right hand, which was shaking so badly, he could hardly hold onto it. Jess stood up, chambered another round into one of the buffalo rifles and started long-striding toward the shallow end of the arroyo.

As Jess got closer, he saw Juda's head appear first. He slowed his walk down and aimed the rifle straight at him. Juda finally saw him approaching. He threw his gun away and raised his hands in the air frantically.

"Don't shoot! Don't shoot!" he implored.

Jess moved the rifle to his left hand and slicked his pistol out as Shadow came running up beside him. They walked down into the deep arroyo. Shadow skulked up to Juda and bared his fangs at him. He pulled his hands and arms in tighter to his chest and started shaking with fear.

"Keep that beast away from me," he cried. Jess called Shadow off. He walked back to him and stood by his side.

"You must be Vern Juda, the driver who killed your boss, Mr. Schoen," said Jess as he toed the other two bodies to make sure they were dead.

Juda stood there shaking. "Now hold on, mister. That's not what really happened."

CHAPTER EIGHT

Jess led the way with Juda tied up on his horse. The bodies of Curtis and Norton were draped across the saddles of the other two horses. When they reached the livery at the end of Main Street, Jess helped Juda out of the saddle. He took him inside and the owner looked surprised.

"That looks like the man who drove that fancy carriage in the back," he said.

"It is," said Jess as he tied Juda to one of the heavy posts. "I've got two stinkers outside and I need you to go and fetch the marshal for me."

"Sure thing," he said as he walked out and headed down the street. Jess looked down at Shadow and scratched his head.

"If he tries to get away, you can have him for supper," he told the wolf, who looked up at Juda and growled. Jess reached into his back pocket and pulled out some jerky and took a bite of it. He was chewing on another piece when Marshal Babbitt walked in with the livery owner.

"Did you get all of them?" he asked.

"The other two are outside, but they ain't going anywhere," he said.

"So why did you let this one live?" asked Babbitt.

"Because he has an interesting story to tell you before you lock him up," said Jess as he looked at Juda. After five minutes of Juda's blabbering as he explained what he had told Jess earlier, the marshal was shaking his head in disbelief. Jess looked down at Shadow.

"You stay here and watch him," Jess said as he nodded at Juda.

Shadow got down on all fours a few feet away from him. Jess and Babbitt headed for the hotel. When they walked in, Liz was sitting in the café eating and drinking champagne. Babbitt took off his hat and sat down across from her. Jess stood next to the table.

"Are you two joining me for some late lunch?" she asked.

"Not exactly," said Babbitt. "Mr. Williams killed the three men who robbed you and killed your husband. I understand you identified the other two men as Leon Curtis and Bernie Norton?"

"Why yes," she said slowly. "Jess showed me a picture of them and the one called Norton is the one who beat me up."

"So, you say that your driver, this Vern Juda, had the other two men stop the carriage out on the trail and the three of them took the money and killed your husband. Do I have it right?"

She looked up at Jess. "You killed the driver too?" she asked.

"Yeah, he forced me to kill him," Jess lied.

She looked back at Babbitt. "Yes, that's exactly how it happened," she said cagily as her right hand moved from the table to the purse by her side.

"You see, Mrs. Schoen, I find that kind of funny, seeing as how the undertaker showed me the slug he took out of your husband. He said it didn't penetrate far into the body after bouncing off a rib. Kind of like what a small derringer would do.

"The two men, along with your driver, all carried 45-caliber pistols and should have done a lot more damage if one of them had shot him. So I'm just wondering, how long did he suffer before he finally passed on after you shot him?" Liz's right hand started to come out of her purse, but the cold steel end of Jess's gun barrel pressed lightly against her temple.

"I've never been forced to kill a woman before, but I will if I have to," he said as he leaned over and removed the little two-shot derringer from her right hand. "You didn't think you could shoot your way out of here with this, did you?"

"I...I don't know," she stammered as she put her hands on her lap. "And to answer your question, he didn't suffer long enough for me. He was a mean scrooge of a man. 'You can't have this, Liz, and you can't have that.' Why do you need a bigger house and more furniture? Then he decides to bring me out here to this savage land to live? I tried to reason with him, but he wouldn't listen, so I bribed the driver to stage the robbery and blame his death on them."

"I got one question," said Jess.

"What?" she blurted angrily.

"If you staged this whole thing, why did they beat you up so badly? I saw the bruises myself and they were real."

"That one man kept telling me to shut up and when I didn't, he started punching me until the driver pulled him off. That part wasn't supposed to happen."

Babbitt started chuckling and she glared at him hatefully.

"Why do you find this funny?" she demanded.

"You hired two ruthless killers like Curtis and Norton and you're surprised that it didn't go well for you? Actually, you're lucky to be alive."

Jess handed the derringer to Babbitt and holstered his pistol after picking up Liz's purse and emptying it on the table. A large wad of bills fell out of it, along with several other items that Jess had purchased for her at the general store.

"Does this mean I'm going to jail?" she asked hopefully.

"Ain't no law says I can't lock up a woman," said Babbitt.

"Can I at least finish my meal?"

Babbitt smiled at Jess and then he leaned forward across the table toward Liz.

"You can finish it, 'cause it's the last good meal you'll be gettin' for quite some time, I suspect," he said firmly. "I feed my prisoners three squares a day, but it ain't steaks and champagne."

"But I have money now. I can pay you to have special meals delivered to the jail, or maybe you could just keep me in the room upstairs and I can take my meals up there."

"All your money has been confiscated, including the fifty thousand dollars those three men took," said Babbitt as he shoved the money and things back into her purse and set it on the chair next to him. "Best you eat that steak quickly, ma'am." She began cutting the steak, but her fancy silver knife was dull.

Jess folded his arms at his chest. "I'd let you borrow my bowie knife, but it wouldn't look very proper, according to you," he said.

"Oh shut up," she mumbled as she shoved the piece of steak into her mouth.

CHAPTER NINE

The next morning, Jess finished saddling his horses at the livery and took them to the general store to supply up before leaving the town of Elk Ridge. After packing his saddlebags, he walked his horses over to the jail and found Marshal Babbitt getting ready to pour some coffee into his cup.

"Mornin', Mr. Williams," he said. "Could I interest you in a cup of coffee?"

"Wouldn't hurt to have one more before I hit the trail," he said as he looked through the small barred window of the heavy door going back to the cells.

He shook his head when he saw Liz sitting on the cot with a gag tied around her mouth. Vern Juda was on his cot with cotton sticking out of his ears.

"Wouldn't shut up, I reckon?"

Babbitt turned around with two cups of coffee in his hands. He handed one to Jess and sat down behind his desk.

"I can see how that woman talked herself into that beatin' she took," he said as he set his cup down. "I was married to a woman for five years and she was quite a talker, but that woman in my jail talked about two years' worth before I put that gag on her." Jess took a sip of the coffee and his mouth puckered up.

"I know," said Babbitt. "Can't afford good coffee. I buy the cheapest beans and crush them with a rock before I boil 'em."

"I believe you," Jess said as he set the cup down on the desk. Babbitt reached into his desk and pulled out a wanted poster and shoved it across the desk to him. Jess picked it up and read it.

"One bad hombre," he said as he continued to look at the picture.

"I thought you might be interested in that one," Babbitt said.

Jess folded it and stuffed it into his pocket. "He's officially at the top of my hunt list."

"I understand you paid for most of the expenses that Mrs. Schoen ran up in town," Babbitt said. "I can reimburse you out of the money she had on her if you'd like." Jess glanced over at the coffee pot on the stove and smiled.

"I have plenty of money, Marshal," he said. "Why don't you use it to buy a new pot and some good coffee?"

"That's mighty generous of you, Mr. Williams."

"So, what do you think the judge will do with her?"

"Not sure, but a beautiful woman like that is like a cat. They always fall on their feet again."

"Well, I have to hit the trail," said Jess as he stood up and shook hands with him. "Still plenty of bad men out there who need to be put down."

"You want me to open the door up so you can say goodbye?" asked Babbitt as he smiled and raised his eyebrows.

Jess glanced at the door and shook his head. "Naw, I don't have that much time," he said as he walked out.

Shadow was curled up on the boardwalk outside and he got up and stretched. Jess swung up on Gray, tipped his hat at Babbitt and turned his horses around. Jess's packhorse Sharps followed behind Gray and Shadow walked alongside Sharps.

Babbitt watched them until they turned the corner out of sight. "He's one interesting fellow indeed," he said as he turned and walked back into his office.

The End

Read the Entire Series of Jess Williams Westerns (Listed in Order)...

COLD JUSTICE
GOD'S GUN
DARK CLOUD
REDEMPTION
TROUBLE IN NAVARRO
BLACK HEART
THE JOURNEY
THE TRANSPORT
PAINTED LADIES
RANGE WAR
CROSSROADS
DEATH BY LEAD
DUNDEE
A CHRISTMAS MIRACLE
OLD GUNS
WILD CAT
HADES
FOOL'S GOLD
DEVIL'S DUE
THE KID
GOLD FEVER
LONE WOLF
SISTER'S KEEPER
MEDICINE MAN
SHANE
CHASING EVIL

*COMING SOON… THE NEXT BOOK IN THE JESS
WILLIAMS WESTERN SERIES*

*ALSO LOOK FOR "WANTED, A WESTERN STORY
COLLECTION" BY ROBERT J. THOMAS AND SIX
OTHER WESTERN AUTHORS. "THE SHEPHERD" IS A
SHORT STORY BY ROBERT J. THOMAS IN THE
COLLECTION FEATURING JESS WILLIAMS.*

You can find Robert's books on Amazon:

https://www.amazon.com/Robert-J.-Thomas/e/B001K91KPO/ref=ntt_dp_epwbk_0

THUNDERING HOOVES

By
Brad Dennison

CHAPTER ONE

Lura and I had three young children, and we were building a small ranch in California. She was the love of my life and I would have been happy to grow old with her at my side. But a bullet meant for me found her instead, and she died in my arms.

The love I had for Lura was stronger than I thought was possible, and when you suffer the kind of hurt I felt when I watched her die and had to bury her, you just wanted to fold up and die yourself.

But the children were young and I had to be strong for them and not let myself cave in to the hurt.

To ease the aching in my heart, I brought the children north to a valley in Montana Territory that I had found years earlier. I say *I* brought them, but it wouldn't have been possible without the help of Zack Johnson and my brother Joe. And Aunt Ginny came along. Lura's aunt. She was a blessing from God in that she helped with the children. I couldn't have gotten though those years without her.

We put up a cabin first, and later on, a full-size ranch house. We brought two hundred head with us, and they fattened up on the lush grass of that Montana valley.

We claimed not only the valley as ours, but also thirty square miles of rangeland east of the valley. When I say *claimed*, I'm using the term loosely. Montana was a territory back then, and we were in a mighty remote section of it. There was no government office to report to, no paperwork to fill out. To claim the land, we just said it was ours, and we defended our claim any way we had to. With our guns if necessary.

The years passed, and the children grew. Other ranches came to Montana territory, but our herd multiplied and our ranch became one of the biggest.

It was 1869, and spring was a little late coming to the mountains. I stepped onto the front porch to greet the morning, like I usually did, and the grass growing out beside the barn and down off to the river was silvery with frost.

I had a blue speckled cup in one hand, and the cup was filled with coffee. The coffee was hot and thick and bitter. Just the way I liked it.

My twin revolvers were at my hips. Remingtons. I had come to Montana for the first time back in '58, carrying Colt Dragoons. But they were old and near wearing out when I got them. A couple of years ago we took a herd down to the railheads in Kansas, and we did better than we had expected. I used some of the money to buy me these new Remingtons.

The holster and gun belt had been built especially for me by a leathersmith in Texas, back in my Ranger days. He was an older Mexican man, and a couple of yahoos with too much whiskey in them decided they didn't like Mexicans and were going to shoot up his shop. I stopped them, and he made me the gun belt as a way of saying thanks. The belt had two holsters that each were attached and dropped a couple of inches from the belt itself, so I could reach the pistols a little easier. The leather was black and shiny.

I sipped at my coffee and watched the red and pink rays of the morning sun decorate a feathery smattering of clouds in the sky. I held my coffee in my left hand always, so my right could be free to grab a gun.

Zack Johnson told me it was because I had been shot at one time too many. Such a thing can make a man jittery. But I had seen Zack get shot at more than once and such a thing didn't seem to bother him. My brother Matt said once that maybe it bothered me more.

I hadn't seen Matt in a lot of years. I thought of him often. I thought of my brother Joe, too. He had ridden off maybe five years ago, getting a little itch to travel like he sometimes did. We hadn't heard from him since.

When my coffee was done, I set the empty cup on the railing of the porch. Aunt Ginny would take care of it later. I had a full day ahead of me, and it would be starting in a few minutes.

My Sharps rifle was beside me, leaning against the porch railing, and my soogan was at my feet. I grabbed them both, and I walked out to the corral. Our wrangler was there, saddling some horses.

"'Mornin', Fred," I said.

"'Mornin'. I took the liberty of pickin' out some horses for you all."

I nodded. "I suppose I can take the buckskin, over there."

I was looking at a buckskin gelding that was in the corral.

Fred looked at me. I suppose he heard the lack of enthusiasm in my voice.

He said, "This will be your first time mustanging without Bravo."

I nodded again. The horse had died the previous fall, just before the first snow.

Fred said, "Ain't never seen a horse like that 'un before."

I shook my head. "Doubt we'll ever see another, either."

I was taking Zack, Hunter and Bodine with me. And the new man, Percy Parks. Fred would stay at the ranch headquarters and be in charge until we got back.

I knew they were still in the bunkhouse, having a final cup of coffee or a cigarette before they mounted up.

I saddled the buckskin myself. I wasn't one to stand around while the men who worked for me did the work. When the horse was saddled, I tied my soogan to the cantle, tucked the Sharps into the saddle boot, and then mounted up.

The buckskin let me know that he wasn't too pleased about being saddled this early in the morning. He bucked a bit and gave us both a little workout. He humped and jumped and spun around in a circle a couple of times.

As wild a horse as Bravo had been, he never fought me in the morning. I could saddle him and mount up, and he would be ready to go. As long as it was me who was riding him. He wouldn't let anyone else into the saddle.

I swung into the saddle and said, "I'm gonna ride out and have a look at things. Scout the territory. Tell the men to meet me out there. I'll be at the canyon north of the valley."

Fred nodded his head. A silent man, Fred was. Most men I had met in the West were. Aside from my brother Matt, most men of the frontier were not talkative. They were more than comfortable with the silence of a campfire, and the sound of the wind in the trees or coyotes in the distance.

I was about to ride out, then I noticed a little hombre standing on the porch. He was in canvas pants, riding boots, and a wide-brimmed felt hat, and he stood barely four feet tall. My son, Josh.

I rode over to the porch.

I said, "'Mornin', pardner."

He looked at me and nodded. He looked sad. His lower lip was sticking out a little, but he was trying to be a man and not let the sadness show. Ten years old, and already well on his way to being a man to ride the river with.

I said, "Are you gonna be all right here while I'm gone?"

He nodded again.

I said, "What's wrong, Josh?"

"It's just," he kicked the toe of his boot against the floor of the porch. "It's just..."

I waited. I remember being ten. An age when you want

157

so bad to be a man, but are still a kid.

He said, "When'll I be old enough to ride along with you, Pa?"

"Soon," I said. "The way you're growing, it won't be long."

He nodded a third time.

I said, "I'll be back in two or three days."

He nodded one more time, so I nodded back, and turned my horse away.

Then I swung the horse back around so I could face Josh again. I said, "I need you to do me a favor while I'm gone."

Josh looked at me with big eyes. A little boy, trying so hard to be a man.

I said, "Fred's gonna be running the ranch. Watching over the remuda and the grounds. But he also has to keep Aunt Ginny, Jack and Bree safe. It's a lot for one man to handle. I'd sure feel better if I knew he could count on you to back him up."

Josh blinked with surprise. He hadn't been expecting that. He said, "Sure can, Pa."

"You're a good man. You and Fred take care of things, and I'll be seeing you in two or three days."

Josh was smiling but trying not to look boyishly enthusiastic. He said, "Bring us back some good mustangs, Pa."

I said, "I'll do that."

CHAPTER TWO

In those days, we were the only inhabitants of the valley. The nearest settlement was Bozeman, which was a six-hour ride by horseback from the house. Took a little longer by wagon. When I rode through the valley, I felt like I was riding through land that was as God intended it to be.

I remember back in Texas, a Mexican padre by the name of Father Timoteo once talking about the concept of God's peace. He said peace isn't really about the absence of war. It's not about a cease fire. He said there's already a term for that—it's called *cease fire*. He said when they talk about God's peace, it's about peace in that things are the way they are meant to be. He was talking about a balance, like what you often find in nature. I couldn't help but wonder if places like this valley and the ridges around it and the mountains north of it were like what the padre was talking about.

I left the valley at the northern side, riding up a small ridge. The trees grew far apart and there was no underbrush. It wasn't like the thicker forests back east. The woods near the farm where I grew up in Pennsylvania were filled with bushes and such, and the trees grew close together. A man couldn't have gotten a horse through country like that without getting knocked out of the saddle by a low-hanging branch, or the horse getting all tangled up in a thicket.

I topped the ridge and then headed on to a box canyon that was beyond the valley. The canyon wasn't large. A few hundred acres with good grass at the canyon floor, and we used it more than once as a natural corral. There was a ledge at one side that rose up a little, so that if you stood on it, you looked over the whole canyon. I thought it might be a good spot for a line cabin, one day.

As I rode toward the canyon, I saw two sets of tracks.

One made me elated, and the other gave me cause for concern.

The first set of tracks was made by unshod hooves, and they were running together. A small herd of mustangs. Their trail was meandering in the general direction of the canyon, which would make our lives easier. The second set were of horses both shod and otherwise. This meant there were other riders in these ridges.

I don't like to be one of them folks who is naturally suspicious of others, but my home in the valley was far from civilization. From what I knew, ours was the only ranch between here and Canada. If we saw riders, they were usually Indians or white renegades. Most Indians in those days were either being rounded up and confined to reservations, or were at war with the Army, so I had to presume any Indians I saw were looking for trouble. And any white renegades were looking for trouble or they wouldn't be renegades.

I would normally never leave the ranch house with only one man to guard it, but we had seen no riders in months.

The tracks made by the riders were moving in a direction from east to west and not going toward the valley, but I thought I would follow them for a bit and see just where they were going.

Looked to me like five horses, and I could see by the tracks that three of them were shod. There were folks who believed Indians rode only unshod horses, and all white men rode horses with shoes, but I had found that was not always the case. Especially this far from civilization.

I figured the trail I was following was made the day before. Maybe toward late afternoon.

I followed them through a low area, not quite a gulley, between two short ridges, and then through a pass between larger mountains. In the distance, I could see a mountain to the west that was a little jagged looking, and it was showing white near the summit.

After a few miles, I found where they had reined up and rested their horses. I saw the remains of cigarettes on the ground.

I decided to head to the canyon where I was going to meet the men. It was near nine in the morning, judging by the sun. I figured they would be there waiting for me.

I figure the canyon at one time had two entrances. At the far side was a wall of rocks and debris, and it looked like long ago there had been a landslide that filled in the other entrance.

I hadn't ridden far when I heard a commotion from off to one side. Sounded like a growling, a roaring and a thrashing, all at the same time. The land rose up to a wooded ridge, and it was coming from up there.

I pulled my rifle and turned my horse up the ridge.

Partway up, the land leveled off to a rocky ledge, and then dropped down a little to form a gully that was maybe ten feet deep at the far end. In that gully was a horse, and he was facing off against a mountain lion.

We have mountain lions here in these mountains, and this was a big 'un. I would guess he weighed in at near a hundred and fifty pounds.

The horse was a magnificent stallion. Chocolate brown, with a black mane and a couple black stockings. He was tall for a wild mustang. Many were barely fourteen hands, but this one was over sixteen.

The cat's ears were back and it was clawing at the horse. The horse was rearing up and attacking with its front hooves.

I had never seen such a thing. I sat and stared in wonder. My horse tried to turn away, but I held the reins tight.

The cat's claws caught one foreleg, opening up three red slashes.

The stallion then stumbled in a small section of loose gravel and went down, and the cat was on top of him.

The cat was going to kill him, I realized.

I still had my rifle in my hand. I let go of the reins and brought the rifle to my shoulder. That was when my own horse reared up and I found myself separated from the saddle.

I hit the ground hard, and my horse took off in a dusty gallop.

I got to my feet a little slowly. My ribs were hurting in back. I think I must have landed on a scattering of small stones. One shoulder felt a little wrenched, too.

Down below, in the gully, the fight was still going on. The stallion kicked the cat away, but then as the horse tried to scramble to his feet, the cat landed on his back.

I had to get off a shot. I didn't think the horse could last too much longer.

I brought the rifle to my shoulder again. The horse and cat were moving and it was going to be a tricky shot. I didn't want to shoot the horse by mistake.

The stallion kicked the cat away again, and that was my chance.

I snapped off a shot and I caught the cat just below the shoulder. My rifle was a fifty caliber, and it could bring down a buffalo. The cat was knocked away to one side, and it rolled to its feet.

There was a gaping hole an inch below the shoulder, but it was on its feet. The bullet hadn't been as dead-center as I had wanted it. Blood was dripping down onto its fur.

There is a belief that when something is shot, it dies. Not necessarily. I once saw a deer take a bullet to the neck, a shot that should have finished it off, but it ran for a mile before it dropped. I saw a man do that kind of thing once, too. He took a bullet to the chest in a gunfight. He ran to his horse, climbed into the saddle and rode off. He was found a few miles down the road. He had apparently died in the saddle and fell to the dirt.

The cat turned and looked at me. Animals don't always recognize gun shots and understand where the direction of

162

the attack came from, but this cat was looking directly at me. It bared its fangs, and then took a step toward me.

A Sharps was a single-shot rifle. I had a handful of cartridges in my vest pocket, but I wasn't sure I would have time to dig them out.

I tossed the rifle aside, and the cat leaped up onto the edge of the gulley, not thirty feet from me. He began crouching and wiggling as he got ready to jump at me. I knew I would have to make the shot of my life, and I would get only one chance.

The cat jumped, and I drew and fired. The bullet caught the cat in the head, and he landed in the dirt, sliding to a stop five feet from me. I saw a gaping hole between the eyes.

I was blessed with an almost unnatural skill with a gun. I was fast and could make seemingly impossible shots. Even still, I knew this shot was pure dumb luck, or the will of God. Whatever it was, the cat was dead and I was still breathing.

I was glad no one else was around to see that shot. Folks were talking about me in saloons and bunkhouses, from these parts all the way to the Mexican border, and I didn't like it. Some called me the Gunman of the Rio Grande in Texas, and I didn't want to do anything to add fuel to it. I was one who preferred to go through life quietly, stepping lightly, not drawing any attention to myself.

I looked down to the gulley. The stallion was on his feet. He was bleeding from the three slices in one front leg, and the cat had raked him across the neck and back but good.

I stepped to the edge of the gulley. The stallion stood and looked at me. I don't know if he knew I saved his life or what he was thinking. The old Shoshone shaman Many Lives had said to me once that animals are much more aware of what goes on around them than people realize.

After a minute or so, the stallion ran out of the gulley. He had a long-legged gait and was soon gone from sight.

I found myself thinking that this was a horse that could have stood alongside Bravo.

I reloaded my Sharps and then began tracking the buckskin. I hoped it hadn't run off too far. I didn't relish the thought of walking all the way to the little canyon where Zack and the men would be waiting for me.

CHAPTER THREE

I found the men in the canyon. They had built a fire and
had coffee going. I was on the buckskin, and I swung out of
the saddle and fetched my tin cup from my saddle bags. I
was moving a little slow because of the fall I had taken
when my horse had reared up.

I grabbed the kettle, using a bandana so I wouldn't burn
my fingers, and I filled my cup. I told Zack and the boys
about the tracks I had seen.

Zack said, "Yeah, we seen them tracks, too."

"Wonder who they are," Hunter said.

"Likely not anyone up to any good." Zack took a sip of
his own coffee. "Want me to ride back to the house?"

Zack wore only one revolver, but the man surely knew
how to use it. He had ridden alongside me in the Rangers,
years ago. One of the best fighting men I had ever known.

I said, "I'd be obliged. Bodine, I'd like you to go with
him."

He nodded. "We'll keep your family safe."

Bodine was a Cherokee from the Nations. He dressed
like a cowhand, like many of the Indians from the Nations
did. I had hired him a few years ago. He wore his gun like
he knew how to use it, and he was quiet and kept to himself
like many a man who are troubled by something in his past.
I asked no questions, because in the West in those days, we
didn't ask probing questions. A man's business was his
own. But Bodine did his work well and rode for the brand,
which was all I could ask of any man.

I told them of the battle I had seen between the horse
and the mountain lion.

"Odd thing that is," Hunter said. "You seldom see a cat
attack a larger animal like that."

"Unless the cat is rabid," Bodine said.

I shook my head. "Didn't move like a rabid animal."

165

After we all finished our coffee, Zack and Bodine mounted up and headed back to the ranch.

Hunter, Percy and I were out here to do some mustanging, so we decided to get to it.

Percy was a former slave from Georgia. He was about thirty, and had that rawboned type of strength of a man accustomed to hard work. He wore batwing chaps and had a bandana that fell across his shirt like a big triangle. Spurs jingled at his heels, and though he wasn't a gunman, he was an accurate shot with a pistol. Like Bodine and the others, he rode for the brand.

We trailed the herd and caught up with them the next day. By the end of the second day, we had six mustangs in the canyon.

We had a fire burning, and I was standing at the outer edge of the firelight, looking off into the darkness. I had a cup of coffee in my left hand, and my right was near my right-hand gun.

Hunter walked over. He was a tall man, and not just tall but big. And like many big men I had seen, he stepped along with a lightness of foot and could move surprisingly fast.

I said, "Something's out there."

He nodded. "The horses are uneasy. You think it's wolves?"

I shook my head. "It's unusual for them to come close to a fire."

"Maybe them riders whose tracks you saw."

I nodded. "Maybe. Keep a rifle close at hand."

Hunter went back to the fire, and that was when I heard a voice call out. "Hello, the fire!"

The customary way of approaching a campfire.

Hunter had a rifle in his hand, and he jacked a cartridge into the chamber. Percy was doing the same.

I said, "Come on in, but nice and slow."

"We don't want no trouble, mister."

I said, "Neither do we. Come on in nice and slow."

A man came into view. He was afoot and was leading a horse. There were two other men with him. They had been on the trail a while. While some men in more civilized parts wore beards as a fashion statement, these three had beards that were just from a lack of shaving. They smelled of campfire smoke, grease and sweat.

The lead one was squinting, and sometimes when a man squints, his upper lip curls up. Some men just develop a perpetual squint from years of riding in the sunlight.

He said, "My name's Callahan. That coffee smells might good, mister."

I said, "Help yourself."

I didn't have a gun in my hand, and maybe that made Callahan and his men feel confident. It shouldn't have. Zack once said that a gun in my holster was as good as a gun cocked and ready in the hands of another man. I took a sip of my coffee and let my right hand brush the front of the holster while I watched the three men walk toward the fire.

I wasn't forgetting that I had seen the tracks of five riders.

I went over to Hunter and looked him in the eye. He nodded, catching my meaning. Sometimes when you've ridden with a man long enough, you each know what the other's thinking. He held his rifle with both hands, ready to bring it up for a shot if he had to, and he stood looking off into the darkness, watching for the other two.

Callahan pulled a cup from his saddle bags and filled it from the kettle.

He said, "There's no need to be jumpy. Ain't no one else out there."

That's when I said, "I saw the tracks of five riders, a couple of days ago."

He shook his head. "Weren't us. Only three of us."

"I hope so," Hunter said. "For your sake. That there is

167

Johnny McCabe."

Callahan blinked and looked at me. "Johnny McCabe?"

I nodded.

Hunter said, "If any shooting starts, he'll take you down even though he hasn't drawn his gun, yet. He'll take out one of your men, too. And Percy, over there, will take the third one. That'll leave just the two men out there, and three of us."

The man said, "We really don't want no trouble."

"Neither do we," Percy said.

Hunter added, "But we're sure good at givin' it, if'n we have to."

Callahan said, "You got some horses in this canyon."

I nodded. "Been doing some mustanging."

"That's what we're out here to do. We're looking at maybe starting up a little outfit. Maybe run some cattle. There's a lot of grass in this part of the territory."

"That's funny," Percy said. "You look more like rawhiders."

The man grinned. "You do what you have to, to earn a dollar. We've done all sorts of things, rawhidin' among 'em."

"It's that way with many men," I said. "You do what you have to, to survive."

One of the other two said, "You really Johnny McCabe? You really as fast with them guns as they say?"

Hunter said, "You don't want to find out."

When their coffee was done, Callahan said, "We'd best be riding on."

I nodded. "It's getting late."

Maybe Callahan was hinting at wanting to share our camp. I was never too good at picking up hints. Now, my brother Matt, he could play the game of hints and such all night long. But me, I preferred things out in the open. Plain and simple. And I wasn't gonna invite them to share our fire. I didn't trust them a'tall.

You learn fast on the frontier to trust your gut. My pa had always said to trust your gut, and so had men I knew in the Texas Rangers. Many Lives had said it, too.

Callahan and his men mounted up and rode off into the night.

I said to Hunter and Percy, "We'll keep one man on guard tonight. I'll take the first shift. You two had best sleep light, and keep your guns handy."

CHAPTER FOUR

By the following night, we had four more wild mustangs in the canyon. As the sun was drifting low in the sky, I sat in the saddle at the edge of the canyon, looking at the horses as they grazed. One rolled on his back in the grass.

Percy was beside me.

I said, "I think we've done fine. We can head back to the ranch in the morning."

"You gonna break 'em the way you always do?"

I nodded. "Shoshone style."

As darkness pushed away the daylight, Hunter built a big campfire. Wolves were howling out there in the darkness, but I was doubtful they would come near a big fire.

The horses were picketed off a little ways, and Hunter opened a can of beans and dumped them into a skillet. We all had a big hunger. Hard work can do that to you. But I found myself hankering to get back to the ranch and Aunt Ginny's cooking.

When the beans were hot, Hunter dropped them onto a plate and handed them to me, and I sat in the grass and began eating.

As I shoveled them in, I noticed it had gotten quiet. No crickets. I looked over at Hunter and Percy, and they had noticed, too.

In the wild, if crickets stop chirping at night, or grasshoppers by day, it often means something is there that shouldn't be.

I set the plate of beans down in the grass. I hated to, because my belly still felt mighty empty. I reached one hand toward my right-hand gun and began walking toward the edge of the firelight.

The horses we had picketed were looking up and off into the darkness. They knew something was out there.

Hunter reached for a rifle, and that was when there was a gunshot from out beyond the camp.

The bullet hit Percy square in the chest, and he went down.

I drew my gun and dropped down on the grass so I was laying face-down, my pistol ready for a shot.

Hunter had his rifle up and was firing.

Shots were being fired toward us. One kicked up a chunk of sod near me. I could see the flash of the gunshot, and I fired back.

One bullet caught Hunter and spun him around. I saw a shape in the darkness, and I snapped off a shot. I couldn't tell if I had gotten him or not.

Hunter was down on one knee, but he was holding his Winchester at his hip and still firing.

Three men charged the camp, and Hunter took one of them down. I got the second.

I pushed myself to my feet, thinking I would run out beyond the circle of firelight. Once in the darkness, I would present less of a target. That was my mistake. A bullet caught my left shoulder.

I was staggered by the impact of the shot, but I knew if I remained on my feet I might take a second bullet, so I let myself go down.

That was when three men came running into the camp. One of them was Callahan, and he had a revolver trained on me.

Hunter's rifle was empty, and one of the other men aimed a rifle at him and said, "Toss that there gun away."

Hunter did. He was still on one knee, and with one hand he pressed down on a wound on his leg.

Callahan said, "Drop that pistol."

I did. It was empty, anyway.

He said, "Drop the other."

I reached around with my right hand to my left-hand holster, pulled the gun out and let it fall to the grass.

A hole was torn in my shirt at my left shoulder and blood was running down my sleeve. I reached over with my right hand to clamp it over the wound and stop the bleeding.

I said, "What is it you men want? We have no money."

"We'll take them horses," Callahan said. "And your supplies and guns."

"You're on the run."

He nodded. "We gotta make it to the northern border. For that, we need fresh horses to switch off with. We can travel a lot faster that way."

He cocked his pistol and aimed it at my face. "Sorry to do this. I guess I get to be the one folks will know as the man who killed Johnny McCabe."

We heard a thundering sound that was growing louder. I recognized it as a drumming of hooves on sod, and at first I thought it was a small stampede. Callahan looked toward the sound, and the great chocolate-colored stallion came charging into camp.

He tore into Callahan, who went down with a muffled cry. His gun fired off toward the sky.

The horse reared up and came crashing down on him, digging in his hooves.

The other two men were standing and staring.

The horse then left Callahan and charged at the second man. He got off a shot, but if it hit the horse, I couldn't tell. The horse tore into him and the man flopped under the hooves like a rag doll.

The third man was holding a Winchester, and he brought it up for a shot at the horse. My revolver was on the sod at my feet, so I dropped to one knee, snatching the gun in the same motion. I brought it out to arm's length, cocking it as I did so, and fired.

Like I said, I seemed to have an almost unnatural ability with a gun. I always had. Getting off this shot was nothing more than trick shooting to me, and I had no doubt my bullet would find its target. The man's head snapped back and down he went.

The horse then stood and looked at me. I didn't think there were any bullet wounds, but the cuts and scratches from the cat were plain in the firelight.

After a moment, the horse turned and trotted off.

I looked back at Hunter. I said, "You all right?"

He nodded. "I don't think the bullet broke anything. But that horse. I ain't never seen anything like that."

I had to admit, neither had I.

CHAPTER FIVE

The horses we had picketed had bolted when the gunfire started, but they didn't run far. I managed to get two of them saddled, and Hunter and I didn't wait for morning to start back to the ranch.

I had a bandana tied tight around my shoulder and under my arm and was hoping it would hold back most of the bleeding until Granny Tate could fix me up. I didn't think the bullet had caught any bones, and I didn't think it had caught any major blood vessels or I would bleed out long before Hunter and I got back to the ranch house.

Hunter was in about the same shape, with a strip of cloth from his soogan tied around his leg.

Once we got back to the ranch, Fred went and fetched Granny Tate and she dug the bullet out of my shoulder.

She said, "I never seen a man get as shot up as many times as you have been, and still live."

Hunter was wounded no worse than I was. The bullet was caught in his thigh muscle. Granny dug it out, and he would be hobbling about with a cane for a few weeks.

We lost the mustangs. When Zack and Bodine rode out to the canyon to bring back Percy's body, they found the horses had run off.

We buried Percy out back. I felt real bad about losing him. He had been a good man.

I told everyone about the tall, dark stallion whose life I had saved, and who had then saved Hunter's and mine. I told them how he had sounded like thunder as he charged into the men.

Ginny said, "If it was anyone else, I would think you were making it all up."

***

Three days later, I slept a little later than usual. Trying to recover from a bullet wound can do that to you. Normally I was up before dawn, but I found the sun was in the sky as I came down the stairs.

My left shoulder was wrapped tight with a bandage, and my arm was in a sling. My shoulder had been a little numb feeling when the wound was fresh, but now my shoulder was stiff and hurt even if I laughed too hard or coughed.

Granny Tate said she thought there would be nearly a full recovery. I might find the shoulder would stiffen up when it rained, and I might not have the full range of motion. Time would tell, she said.

Even though my arm was in a sling, I managed to get my guns buckled about my hips.

I normally began my day with a cup of coffee out on the front porch and figured I would do the same today even though the sun was already up.

I went to the kitchen and while Ginny was pouring me a cup, Fred stepped in through the back door.

"Johnny," he said. "There's someone out front. I think he wants to see you."

I walked through the house to the front door. I stepped out onto the porch and found the tall stallion a few yards from the porch, just standing there and looking at me.

Ginny and Fred stepped onto the porch. Ginny said, "Well, I'll be."

The cuts the horse had gotten from the cat looked to have closed up and there didn't seem to be any infection.

I didn't realize Josh was standing beside me until he said, "Is that the stallion, Pa?"

I nodded. "It sure is."

I stepped down from the porch and walked up to the horse.

Ginny said, "Be careful, John."

I said to the horse, "I didn't expect to see you again, big fella."

175

The horse turned and started walking away. But he didn't head back the way he must have come, across a wooden bridge we had built across a stream beyond the barn. He trotted around the side of the house and then headed out back.

I followed him, to see where he was going.

The nature of this valley was that we had a couple hundred acres of good grass behind the house, and then the pastureland had a sort of natural fence of thicket on three sides. Fred and I let the remuda run free back there, knowing they wouldn't get far if they decided to run off.

A couple of mares were grazing, and they looked up as the stallion ran out to join them. Two bay geldings and a grulla were running about, enjoying the morning air, and they looked over at the new stallion.

Fred was beside me. He said, "Doesn't look like you came back from mustanging empty-handed after all."

I shook my head. "Apparently not."

I stood with Fred, Ginny and Josh. Jack and Bree came running out of the house.

Bree was five, with long dark braids and wearing a brown dress. Fred scooped her up so she could sit on his shoulders. I would have done it, but it would be awhile before I was carrying anyone on my shoulders.

Jack was nine, and he said, "Is the stallion gonna live here?"

I shrugged. "I don't really know, son."

We stood and watched as the stallion stared down the two bays and the grulla. Other horses in the remuda wandered over, but he reared up and they backed off. Then he went to the two mares and began chewing on some grass.

It looked to me like he was declaring himself the boss of his new herd.

"Pa," Bree said. "We should call him Thunder."

And so we did.

The End

About the Author

Brad was born in rural New England and grew up reading Louis L'Amour, Luke Short, A.B Guthrie, Jr., and even Edgar Rice Burroughs. He knew at 14 he wanted to write for a living, and refused to give up the goal even when the odds seemed overwhelmingly against it. Now, thanks to Amazon, his stories are available. He is a member of the Western Writers of America

Brad fell in love with the Old West at a very young age. It began with movies and old TV series like GUNSMOKE and BONANZA, and later expanded to western novels. This led to his study of western history. The pioneers, the Indians, the cattlemen, the gunfighters. His interest in history is not so much about wars and great leaders, but the people who lived on the land. And that's what he writes about. The people. He doesn't write about the old west as much as he writes about what it might have felt like to be there.

He loves contact from readers. He can be reached by email at mccabewesterns@gmail if you want to discuss his stories, or even just the American West in general.

You can find Brad's books on Amazon.
http://www.amazon.com/Brad-Dennison/e/B00FW3R6CU/ref=sr_tc_2_0?qid=1456457719&sr=1-2-ent

The Mirror II

By
Tell Cotten

PROLOGUE

Jacob owned a small ranch. It wasn't much, but it was *his*.

The spread wasn't big enough to make a living running cattle. So, he raised horses.

He was proud of his small herd, and it showed. His colts were always gentle, and each year he sold them up north in the bigger towns.

He was currently on his way home. He'd just sold a good string of horses, and his pockets were full of money.

Jacob was in his mid-fifties. A simple man, he minded his own business and was a hard worker.

Lewis, his young ranch hand, was with him. This was his first trip to the bigger towns, and his eager mind was still absorbing all the impressive sights he'd seen.

They were a half-day's ride from home when the sun started its descent. They had enough food, so Jacob decided they might as well camp out one more evening.

This delighted Lewis, and he hustled about gathering firewood. Meanwhile, Jacob unpacked their food and built a fire.

Their camp was in a little draw. Trees surrounded them, and they were also between two steep, brushy ridges.

"Tend to the horses, and I'll make some coffee," Jacob suggested.

"Yes, sir," Lewis replied.

He walked toward their horses, but a rifle shot erupted before he reached them. The gunfire was loud and unexpected. It came from the ridge, and Lewis heard a thumping sound as the bullet hit flesh.

There was a groan from behind. Lewis spun around, and Jacob collapsed into the campfire.

Lewis ran to him. Jacob was floundering about, and Lewis grabbed his arm and pulled him away from the flames. There was a fallen tree trunk nearby, and they fell behind it.

Another rifle shot split the air, and Lewis heard the whine of a bullet as it ricocheted through camp.

"Lewis! You all right?" Jacob gasped.

"I'm fine!" Lewis replied. "You?"

"Hit bad," Jacob's voice was grim. "They got us pinned down."

"What'll we do?" Lewis' voice was surprisingly strong.

"My rifle's on the other side of the campfire," Jacob replied. "I've got cartridges in my saddlebags. Can you crawl over and get them?"

"I'll try."

"Be careful."

Lewis nodded, and he hugged the ground as he made his way across camp.

His movements were spotted, and several rifle shots sounded out. Bullets peppered the ground around him, but Lewis never flinched as he grabbed the saddlebags. Next, he grabbed the rifle on his way back to the fallen tree trunk.

Jacob reached out and took the rifle. His hand was shaking and covered in blood, but he still managed to work the lever.

"What do we do?" Lewis asked, anxious to do something.

"Can you get to the horses?" Jacob grimaced.

"Without getting shot?" Lewis asked as he eyed the distance.

"Yes."

"I can try."

"Good boy," Jacob said. "I'll fire a few shots and keep them distracted. Climb on your horse and git, and take my horse with you. No sense leaving him here for *them*."

"What about you?"

"I'm done for," Jacob said plainly.

"I'm not leaving you," Lewis insisted.

"Not your choice to make, son. Now do as I tell you."

Lewis didn't like it, but Jacob was determined. He had grown very fond of the boy, and his only concern at this point was Lewis' safety.

"Tell Maggie the ranch is hers," Jacob continued. "She'll need help, and I'm counting on you."

Lewis had to fight back tears. He didn't reply; he just nodded.

"You'd best be off," Jacob sounded tired. "Ready?"

"Thanks for everything," Lewis managed.

"Luck, son," Jacob said. "Now go!"

Jacob fired two shots up the ridge, and Lewis started crawling. The men from the ridge returned the gunfire, but they were focused on Jacob.

Lewis reached the horses, climbed into the saddle, grabbed the reins to Jacob's horse, and slammed his spurs into his horse's sides. The horse leaped forward, and only then was he spotted.

Bullets rained down all around Lewis, but it only took him a few seconds to reach the safety of the trees. Bullets slammed into the nearby tree trunks, and Lewis thought he heard swearing from the ridge.

Lewis climbed toward higher ground, and he was careful to stay behind cover. He pulled up and looked back when he reached the top.

He spotted two men, making their way down the ridge toward Jacob.

One was tall, and the other one was shorter with a stocky build. The taller one looked athletic and limber, while the shorter one moved like an older person.

Lewis frowned his displeasure. He didn't want to leave, but he also wasn't one to disobey. So, he turned his horse to the south and encouraged him forward.

Rifle shots thundered out behind him, and Lewis said a silent prayer as he headed for town as fast as he could ride.

CHAPTER ONE
Same day; several miles to the west

Here we were again, bouncing across the vast state of Texas in a wagon.

We were eastbound, heading to Dallas.

My back ached from all the bouncing, and my longing for my horse was close to lust. However, no matter how I figured it, there was just no way to carry a mirror a-horseback. Hence the wagon.

The reason for our trip was a painful one.

Brian Clark and I were the proud owners of the fanciest hotel in Texas. It was also rumored that we had the largest mirror in Texas, and it hung in proud display behind our polished mahogany bar.

It was also the *heaviest* mirror in Texas. I knew from experience, because I helped carry the thing in.

Life was grand until a stray bullet shattered our beloved mirror. We took it hard, and Brian almost shed a tear as we swept up the broken glass. We ordered another one, and we were now on our way to pick it up.

My name is Lee Mattingly. I'm tall, thin, and ruggedly handsome. Last time I figured it, I was in my mid-thirties.

Most folks in Texas know who I am. And, almost everybody's opinion is that I need to have my neck lengthened by a rope.

I've often been described as a rough, mean gunfighter of the West. I've ridden with Ben Kinrich, Rondo Landon, and the Oltman brothers, and we've robbed stagecoaches, payrolls, banks, and even rustled a few cows.

Harsh as that sounds, I've never considered myself to be quite as bad as everyone's made me out to be. I've always had a different set of values than most outlaws, and I'm extremely loyal.

I've never killed anybody unless it was necessary, and I'll admit it's been necessary quite a few times these past few years. However, Ben always made sure all those folks we robbed were no good Northerners. That was real important to us, seeing how we were poor ol' Southerners fresh from the war.

Rondo Landon finally had enough. He walked away, and a few years later he finally convinced me that living honest had more perks than being an outlaw. So, I managed to receive a pardon by doing some work for the Texas Rangers, and I was now attempting to live an honest and straightforward life.

My companion, Brian Clark, was also an ex-outlaw. He was in his mid-fifties, and was a grizzled veteran.

Brian and I were alike in a lot of ways. He was loyal, and he had a gentle-like way about him. He was always careful; he never took any chances unless he had to.

The two of us had recently received a big sum of money, and we'd come by it honest too. Jessica Tussle had hired us to do a job, and we'd done it.

We were now partners, and we'd invested all our money into building the hotel. I handled the poker room, and Brian managed just about everything else.

A harsh bump interrupted my thoughts, and I grimaced as my body rocked back and forth in the wagon seat.

"You know what they should invent?" I asked Brian.

"What's that?" Brian glanced sideways at me.

"Mirrors that don't break."

"Be helpful," Brian nodded. "Especially for us."

I grunted emphatically in response, and we bounced along for another mile.

"You realize where we are?" Brian asked suddenly.

"Yes, I realize," I replied, my voice flat.

"I wonder how Maggie's getting along," Brian commented, and he looked wistful.

"I'm sure she's *just* fine."

"We don't know that," Brian argued.

I took in a deep breath and sighed.

"Are you suggesting we swing by town and see her?" I asked.

"Well, it's a thought."

"Last time we saw Maggie, she almost got us killed," I reminded.

"I know, but that's all cleared up now."

"Besides, we might not even be welcome," I continued.

Brian was silent as he thought on that.

"I think Maggie would be glad to see me," he finally declared. "After all, we go way back."

"She's *your* wife, so you would know," I shrugged.

"*Ex*-wife," Brian corrected.

"Whatever."

"It's not just Maggie," Brian continued. He hesitated, then added, "I'd like to see my boy too."

"The sheriff?" I raised an eyebrow.

Brian nodded.

"But he doesn't even know you're his father," I pointed out.

"I know that. I'd still like to see him."

I studied Brian a moment, and then I sighed again.

"What do you say?" Brian looked at me.

"Well, the thought of a meal cooked by someone else is appealing," I admitted.

"So no objections?"

"I guess not."

Brian grinned, and he changed our course a bit. Meanwhile, I reached down and adjusted my gun belt.

"What's the matter?" Brian noticed my movements.

"I'm getting that ol' feeling."

"What ol' feeling?"

"Feeling that something bad is about to happen."

"Quit being superstitious," Brian grunted. "What could go wrong?"

185

"With us? Plenty."

"You worry too much."

"Being worried has kept me alive a long time," I replied stubbornly.

Brian chuckled and glanced at the sun.

"We won't make it to town before dark," he said. "Want to stop early?"

"Might as well. I've bounced enough for one day," I replied.

Brian nodded, and we looked for a spot to camp.

CHAPTER TWO

The campsite we picked was a good one.

There was a creek nearby, plenty of firewood, and it was well sheltered with brush.

We unhitched our team of horses. Next, I gathered some wood, built a fire, and got the coffee on while Brian unpacked our bedrolls and made camp.

My favorite meal when traveling was salt pork. It was easy to cook, and was mighty tasty.

I cut and placed thick slices in a frying pan. It didn't take long to start sizzling, and my stomach growled in anticipation.

Brian joined me. The coffee began to boil, and I grinned, grabbed my cup, and reached for the coffee pot handle.

I was just about to pour some when a rifle shot bellowed out from afar. I was startled, and I dropped my cup in the fire.

"Hear that?" I frowned as I picked up a stick and dragged my cup from the coals.

"Sure did," Brian replied.

"What'd I tell you?" I looked at Brian. "Trouble."

"Too far to be shooting at us," he objected.

"No, but they're shooting at *something*."

"Probably just hunters," Brian suggested.

Before I could reply, more shots sounded out. Then there was silence, followed by another burst of gunfire.

"Either they're hunting to feed an army, or they're really bad shots," I commented.

Brian didn't reply, and the gunfire continued.

"There's three, perhaps four of them," I declared as we listened.

"Mebbe we should ride over there and take a look," Brian suggested.

"Ain't none of our business."

187

"But somebody could be in trouble."

"Or, they could be practicing."

"I'd sleep better if I knew," Brian replied. "Wouldn't you?"

I sighed and nodded reluctantly.

"I reckon I would," I admitted.

"Let's go then," Brian urged. "Be dark soon."

"What about the wagon?" I asked.

"We'll just leave it here."

"You sure about that?" I made a face.

"Why not. It's not going anywhere."

"We'll remember you said that."

Brian grunted and turned away. Meanwhile, I grabbed the pot of coffee and set it to the side of the coals. The salt pork was cooked, so I set the frying pan beside the coffee pot and covered it with a towel.

I took a long, lustful look at my supper, and then I followed after Brian.

CHAPTER THREE

Our saddles were in the wagon. We pulled them out and saddled two of our horses, and I tied our other two horses to the wagon. Then, we climbed on and took out.

"I don't like this," I complained as I followed after Brian.

"What don't you like?"

"Trouble has never had any problem finding us. We've never gone looking for it."

"We ain't looking for it now," Brian replied. "I just want to make sure everything is all right."

"You sound like Yancy."

Brian grunted, and we trotted on.

By now, all the shooting had stopped. There was only an eerie silence, and I felt uneasy.

A tall, steep ridge loomed in front of us. There were trees and brush scattered all around, providing plenty of cover.

"The shooting came from over there," Brian gestured toward the ridge.

"Sounded like," I nodded my agreement.

Brian nodded, and we trotted on in silence. It took us several minutes to reach the base of the ridge, and we pulled up amongst some trees.

Brian started to say something, but stopped. He cocked his head sideways and frowned.

"What is it?" I watched him.

"Thought I heard something," he replied. "To the north."

"I don't hear anything," I replied.

Brian listened a moment more, and then shrugged.

"Probably nothing," he said.

"That's what I've been saying all along," I grumbled.

Brian made a face at me, and then we looked around.

There was a worn path going upwards, and Brian eyed the top of the ridge.

"We could see a long ways from up there," he commented. "Probably see what's going on."

"Why don't *you* do that," I said.

"You ain't coming?" Brian looked at me.

"This wasn't my idea."

Brian sighed and dismounted.

"We should leave the horses here," he said.

I didn't reply, and Brian ignored me as he tied his horse to a branch. He trudged upwards, and I grumbled as I dismounted, tied my horse beside Brian's, and followed after him.

CHAPTER FOUR

Our legs felt heavy by the time we reached the top. Our shirts were drenched with sweat, and we gasped as we got our wind back.

"I'm getting too old for this," I complained.

"You're twenty years younger than I am," Brian pointed out.

"Boy, you really *are* getting old," I remarked.

Brian grunted, and I grinned as we hunkered down behind some bushes and looked the country over.

Below us was a small valley, nestled between two ridges. We could see a faint, red glow, and I narrowed my eyes as I studied it.

"I see a campfire," I commented.

"I see it too," Brian nodded.

"Odd there's no horses around."

"Or people," Brian added.

Suddenly, my eyes made out a form beside the campfire. It was a human form, and it wasn't moving.

"Uh-oh," I said softly.

"What is it?"

"I think there *is* somebody down there."

"I don't see anything."

"That's 'cause you're twenty years older than I am," I reminded.

Brian ignored my comment and asked, "Where is he?"

"By the campfire."

"And he ain't moving?"

"Hasn't yet."

"That ain't good."

"My thoughts exactly."

"Think somebody shot him?"

"Probably," I mused. "Unless he shot himself."

"Why would he do that?"

"I was being sarcastic."

"Oh," Brian said, then asked, "So now what?"

"Well, I figured you'd want to go down there."

"And you don't?"

"We've come this far. Might as well."

Brian frowned at me, but I ignored him as we stood, checked our Colts, and made our way down the ridge.

CHAPTER FIVE

It was dark by the time we reached the bottom. We were wary, and we were watchful as we approached the narrow valley.

Sure enough, there was a body stretched out beside the campfire. His shirt was soaked with blood, and he was face down, on his stomach.

Brian and I took one more look at our surroundings. Satisfied that we were alone, we approached the downed man.

I knelt beside him. I grabbed his shoulder and rolled him over, and I heard a soft groan.

"He's alive," I announced.

Brian nodded, but his face was grim as we studied his wounds. He had several gunshot wounds in his chest, and he also had a bullet in his gut.

There was no need to say anything. Brian and I had been around death for years, and we knew he was done for.

But, he wasn't dead *just* yet. He opened his eyes and blinked as he looked up at us.

"Easy there, old-timer," I said gently.

"Name's Jacob," he muttered, his voice weak.

I nodded and told him who we were.

"I was robbed," he said hoarsely.

"We sorta figured that," I replied.

"Took everything I had, 'cept my campfire."

"Hard to steal that," I said as I looked at the slow burning coals.

"They rode that way," he raised a blood covered hand and pointed north.

"How many?" I asked.

"Two."

"I think I heard them," Brian spoke up.

I nodded, and Jacob took in a shaky breath. He closed his eyes and leaned his head back. A few seconds passed, and he opened his eyes and stared at me with an intent and wild look.

"Maggie," he whispered. "Tell her I'm sorry."

"Maggie?" Brian was startled. "Maggie who?"

"My wife."

Brian's eyes grew wide.

"Maggie from town?" Brian asked.

"Yes."

"Maggie married *you*? When did this happen?"

"Few months ago," Jacob replied, and he grabbed my arm and grasped it tightly. "She'll be all alone. You'll help her, won't you?"

"Sure, old-timer," I tried to sound reassuring.

Brian was disturbed. He wanted answers, and he cleared his throat and looked down at Jacob.

"Are you sure your wife's name is Maggie?" He demanded.

Jacob didn't hear him. He released my arm, closed his eyes again, and drifted off.

"Did he just die?" Brian looked at me.

"Not yet," I shook my head. "But, I suspect he will soon."

"He must be delirious," Brian insisted.

"He seemed sane enough to me," I replied.

Brian frowned his irritation but didn't reply.

CHAPTER SIX

While Brian stood there looking bewildered, I tried to make Jacob as comfortable as possible. However, there really wasn't much I could do.

"He won't make it much longer," I said, stating the obvious.

"You suppose what he said was true, 'bout him and Maggie?" Brian wanted to know.

"Mebbe it was another Maggie," I suggested.

"You think so?"

"Not really. I was just trying to be helpful."

Brian snorted his disgust.

"How could Maggie do this to me?"

"I'm sure she married again *just* to spite you."

Brian missed my sarcasm, and his face turned mulish.

"I had hoped we might work out our differences someday," he admitted. "You know, after she had time to think things over."

"How much time does she need?" I raised an eyebrow. "She's had twenty years."

Brian started to reply, but stopped. He thought a moment, and then sighed.

"Well, it doesn't *seem* that long ago."

"Time flies."

Brian nodded sullenly, and it fell silent as we assessed our situation.

"We can't leave Jacob like this," I finally said.

Brian nodded his agreement and said, "You stay with him. I'll fetch the wagon."

"You don't want to stay here?" I objected.

"Not particularly."

"Why not?"

"I'm sorry Jacob got shot and all, but the man did steal my wife."

I studied Brian a moment and sighed.

"That's how you're going to take it?" I asked disapprovingly.

"Yes," Brian declared, then added, "I'll be back."

I nodded, and Brian turned and disappeared into the darkness.

CHAPTER SEVEN

I hunted up some more firewood and built the fire back up. Then, I sat across from Jacob and got comfortable.

Jacob was still asleep, and I was grateful for that. Being gut shot was painful, and I'd seen many a man during the war suffer greatly during his last hours. For Jacob's sake, I was hoping he wouldn't wake up.

An hour passed, and I began to wonder where Brian was. Then another hour passed, and I became worried.

I finally heard some movement from afar. I was confused, because it didn't sound like a wagon. I could only hear horses, and they were coming closer.

I drew my Colt and stood. I backed into the darkness and pulled the hammer back.

The horses stopped, and it was silent for several seconds. But then, I heard Brian's voice.

"Don't shoot! It's me."

"Took you long enough!" I replied as I eased the hammer down, holstered my Colt, and returned to the campfire.

Brian trotted on in, and he led my horse behind him. He looked flustered and irritated.

"Where's the wagon?" I asked, fearful of the answer.

"It's gone!"

"What do you mean, it's gone?" I narrowed my eyes.

"Like, it's not there anymore."

"Where'd it go?" I demanded.

"I don't know. I rode back to our camp, but everything – and I mean everything – is gone!"

"How 'bout the salt pork?"

"That's gone too."

I scowled, and it was silent as we thought on that.

"The fellers that bushwhacked Jacob must have stumbled across our camp," Brian finally said. "We weren't around, so they helped themselves."

"And we even cooked them supper," I muttered, then asked, "Find any tracks?"

"No, too dark," Brian said as he dismounted.

I grunted at that.

"They won't be hard to find in the morning," I declared.

"Don't suspect they will be," Brian agreed, and he looked down at Jacob. "How is he?"

"Still asleep."

"Has he mentioned Maggie again?"

"Nope."

Brian frowned, but he didn't say anything as we unsaddled the horses.

CHAPTER EIGHT

Brian and I settled around the campfire, and we were somber as we listened to Jacob's raspy breathing. We didn't talk much; instead we just thought our own thoughts.

An hour passed, and Brian finally looked over at me.

"I'm hungry," he said.

"So am I."

"I hope they enjoyed our supper."

"I'm sure they did. I'm a good cook."

Brian grunted, then asked, "What will we do in the morning?"

"Go get our wagon," I declared.

"What if Jacob is still alive?"

"Then you can stay here."

"And let you go after them alone?" Brian objected.

"Got any better ideas?"

It was silent, and then Brian said, "No."

"I doubt Jacob lasts 'til morning anyway," I said truthfully.

"We don't have a shovel to bury him," Brian pointed out.

"We don't have a shovel, or a wagon, or food, or bedrolls, or a blanket, or even a coffee pot," I said sourly.

Brian nodded. He started to reply, but Jacob stirred before he could. He gasped and tried to sit up, but then collapsed.

"Take it easy, old-timer," I said as we hurried to him.

He looked up at me through terror stricken eyes.

"Tinker man," he whispered.

"What?" I frowned in confusion.

"Tinker man," he repeated, and his voice was fading.

"What's he talking about?" Brian asked.

"*Now* I think he's delirious," I replied.

Jacob seemed frustrated. He swallowed, closed his eyes, and leaned his head back.

"Maggie," he whispered.

I patted his shoulder, and we watched as Jacob took several shuttering breaths. Then he smiled and exhaled. Several seconds passed, and his chest became still.

A heavy silence surrounded us. Brian and I studied him closely, but he never moved.

"Is he –?" Brian's voice trailed off.

"He is," I said somberly.

Brian nodded, and we were silent as we paid our last respects.

CHAPTER NINE

There wasn't much we could do until daylight. I placed a few more branches on the fire, and we sat across from Jacob and got comfortable.

We didn't talk for a while. But then, Brian cleared his throat and looked at me.

"Lee," he said, his voice somber.

"Yes?" I looked at him.

"We ain't leaving Jacob. He's going to get a decent burial."

"That's a nice thought, but we don't even have a shovel," I reminded.

"Come morning, I'll head to town while you stay here with Jacob," Brian continued. "I'll fetch the sheriff, and we'll come back with a wagon."

"That'll take time," I warned.

"I owe it to Maggie."

I looked at Brian, and we stared at each other a moment.

Brian was determined, and there was no use arguing with him. And, the more I thought about it, the more I agreed with him.

"All right," I finally said. "We'll do it your way."

Brian nodded emphatically, and our conversation played out.

CHAPTER TEN

As soon as it got daylight, Brian saddled his horse and led him in a circle to loosen him up.

"Be back quick as I can," he said.

Before I could reply, I spotted several riders pouring over the ridge.

"Hold on," I said, and I gestured upwards.

Brian turned and looked, and we watched as they came toward us. I counted six riders, and they rode with determination.

"This doesn't look good," I said.

"There's no need to worry," Brian replied. "We haven't done anything wrong."

"We didn't do anything wrong last time," I reminded.

Brian didn't reply, and we were silent as they approached us.

There was a tall, thin man out in front. There was a badge pinned on his shirt, and my eyes lit up with recognition.

"It's the deputy," I announced softly. Brian nodded, and I added, "I wonder where the sheriff is?"

"Not sure," Brian replied.

"I wish he was here," I replied, and then I turned my attention to the deputy.

He recognized us. His face turned dark, and I didn't like the way he glared at me.

Not that long ago, I had smashed two plates over his head as we escaped from jail. And, judging by his expression, he hadn't forgotten about it.

The deputy gestured at his men, and they spread out. I noticed they all held Colts, and they were pointed in our direction.

They formed a semi-circle in front of us, and it was silent while we looked back and forth.

"Morning," I finally said, and I tried to sound cheerful.

"Are we glad to see *you*," Brian added.

The deputy didn't reply. He studied Jacob's still form and looked back at us.

"First thing," he said in a low, somber voice. "Keep your hands where we can see them."

"There's no need for that," Brian replied.

"I'll decide what's necessary here," the deputy corrected, and he puffed his chest out and tried to look important.

"But I was just on my way to fetch you," Brian tried again.

"Sure you was," the deputy replied, and he gestured at Jacob. "He's dead, ain't he."

"He passed during the night," I confirmed.

"Why'd you do it?" He demanded.

"Do what?" I narrowed my eyes.

"Kill him."

"Hold on now," I replied. "We didn't do this."

"Then who did?"

I looked at Brian, and he explained all that happened. I thought it sounded logical, but the deputy didn't look convinced.

"Sounds far fetched," he said.

"But that's what happened," I insisted.

The deputy studied us, and it was silent for several seconds.

"Tell you what," he finally said. "We've got a witness back in town. We'll let him decide if you're guilty or not."

"A witness?" I frowned suspiciously.

"Sure. He managed to escape with the horses."

"Did he get a good look at the men who did this?" Brian asked.

"Said he did."

Brian and I glanced at each other.

203

"All right," I agreed. "We'll go see this witness. Then we can start tracking the folks that did this. I want my wagon back."

"We'll see," the deputy said. "But first, I want you to unbuckle your gun belts and step back. Real slow now."

I didn't like it. However, at the moment our options were limited. So, I sighed and reached for my belt buckle, as did Brian.

CHAPTER ELEVEN

While half of them covered us with their Colts, the others stepped forward. The deputy motioned me to put my hands behind my back, and he tied my wrists together. The knots were tight and harsh.

I expected the deputy to tie Brian's hands next. Instead, he turned to the horses.

"This ain't fair," I muttered softly.

The only person that heard me was Brian. And, despite our current situation, he couldn't help but grin briefly.

The deputy saddled my horse. He led him in a little circle to loosen him up, and then he gestured for me to get on.

It wasn't easy with my hands behind my back, and the deputy had to push me from behind as I swung on.

Brian moved toward his horse, but the deputy stopped him.

"You two ride double," he said.

"What for?" Brian scowled his protest.

"We need your horse to fetch Jacob home," the deputy explained.

That made sense, and Brian said no more as he moved to my horse.

It took a lot of effort to get Brian mounted. Once he was on, he wrapped his arms around my waist and held on tight.

"You're going to squeeze me in-two," I grumbled.

"If I fall off, you're coming with me," Brian replied. "We're in this together."

"That brings me a lot of comfort," I said sourly.

Being as gentle as possible, they picked up Jacob and laid him over Brian's saddle. They tied him down, and then they climbed on their horses.

The deputy grabbed the reins to my horse and led out. Everyone else fell in behind him, and we climbed the ridge in a trot.

Riding with my hands tied behind my back wasn't comfortable, especially with Brian hugging me. I bounced harshly in the saddle, and I actually yearned for our wagon.

"Where's the sheriff?" Brian asked after a while.

"He's gone on business," the deputy replied.

"When will he be back?" Brian asked.

"Few weeks."

"And he left you in charge?"

"That's right."

Brian didn't reply, and no more words were spoken.

CHAPTER TWELVE

By the time we reached town, my wrists throbbed and my shoulders ached.

Town was still a shabby gathering of some two-dozen buildings. There was a general store, a hotel, a doctor's office, a blacksmith shop, a few livery stables, and a small sheriff's office. At the end of town were some pole corrals for cattle.

We received several stares as we rode to the jail, and a crowd gathered as we pulled up. Folks studied Jacob, and their faces turned grim.

"What happened?" A short, skinny man asked.

"Jacob was murdered," the deputy announced, and a surprised murmur passed through the crowd.

"These the fellers that did it?" Skinny demanded.

"Perhaps," the deputy replied.

The crowd glared at us, and the hatred in their faces made me uneasy.

"Where's Lewis?" The deputy asked.

"He rode out to Maggie's," Skinny replied.

The deputy frowned, then said, "Well, go fetch him."

"Why waste the time?" Skinny demanded. "Let's string them up now!"

I don't like Skinny, I thought.

"Not yet," the deputy replied sternly. "I want Lewis to have a look at them. *Then* we'll hang them."

Skinny frowned his displeasure, but nobody objected.

"All right," Skinny agreed reluctantly. "I'll go after Lewis."

"'Preciate it," the deputy replied, then asked, "Would you mind taking Jacob down to the undertaker while I take care of the prisoners?"

"I can do that," Skinny replied.

He glared at us once more, and then he grabbed the reins and led the horse down the street. Meanwhile, the deputy dismounted and gestured for us to get down.

Brian slid off, and I was next. The deputy pushed us inside the jail, and he closed and bolted the door behind us.

The jail looked the same. There were still only two cells, and both were empty. The deputy placed us in the closest, and he untied me and slammed the door shut.

I started rubbing feeling back into my hands, and the deputy watched me with a smirk.

"I reckon you know the routine," he said.

"How long 'til Lewis gets here?" I asked.

"This afternoon sometime."

We nodded, and the deputy turned and walked back to the front room. He sat behind the desk, threw his feet up, leaned his head back, and promptly went to sleep.

I grunted as we watched him.

"Things ain't changed much," I commented.

Brian nodded as he glanced around our cell.

"Home, sweet home," he muttered.

CHAPTER THIRTEEN

There was nothing to do but wait. We stretched out on our bunks, and it only took Brian a few minutes to drift off to sleep.

Like before, Brian and the deputy snored in unison *and* in the same key. As for me, I just lay there trying to think.

The snoring finally got to me. I got up, walked to the window, and looked out.

My movements woke Brian. He sat up, blinked several times, and looked at me.

"See anything?" He asked.

"Not much," I shook my head and sighed. "I was thinking how nice it'd be if the real killers rode into town and confessed."

"You said the same thing last time," Brian reminded.

"One can only hope."

Brian grunted. He started to reply, but a knock at the door interrupted us.

The deputy woke with a snort. He bolted to his feet, rushed to the window, and glanced out. Then he unbolted and opened the door, and an older Spanish lady stepped in and handed him a basket covered with a towel.

She left, and the deputy closed and bolted the door behind her. Then, he walked over to us.

"Lunch," he said.

"I could eat," I admitted. "We missed supper *and* breakfast."

The deputy started to hand us the basket through the opening, but he stopped suddenly. He removed the towel and peered down. Then he grunted in satisfaction and handed us the basket.

"You're learning," I said wryly.

"I also don't forget," the deputy replied. "You might have fooled the sheriff last time, but not me. And, now that I have you again, you won't be escaping."

"Time will tell," I smiled.

The deputy grunted and returned to the front room. Meanwhile, I sat on the bunk and took a peek at our lunch. It was a modest meal of bread and beans, but it looked mighty good to me.

I grinned as I gave Brian his food.

"Tin plates," I commented.

"They *are* learning," Brian replied.

CHAPTER FOURTEEN

We savored our meal in silence. As I was taking my last bite, there was another knock at the door.

The deputy glanced out the window again. Then, he unbolted and opened the door, and Maggie and a young boy walked in. The deputy bolted the door behind them, and they walked to our cell.

Maggie was in her mid-fifties. She was small, a little round, and had gray hair. However, she was aging gracefully, and there was a hint of youth in her face.

As for the boy, I figured he was around fourteen or so.

I glanced at Brian. His eyes were stuck on Maggie, and a pained, distraught look crossed his face.

That same look was displayed on Maggie's face. However, her eyes grew wide when she saw us.

"Brian," she muttered, obviously surprised.

"Hello, Maggie," Brian said gently. "It's good to see you again."

Maggie was stunned, and several tense seconds passed. "Did you do this?" She finally asked.

"No, Maggie, we didn't."

Maggie didn't reply, and the deputy took advantage of the silence.

"Lewis," the deputy ushered the boy to the front of our cell. "I want you to look carefully now, and tell me if you recognize these men."

The room became silent while Lewis studied us. I smiled and tried to look innocent, but Brian just stared at Maggie.

"Yes," Lewis finally decided. "I think it's them."

I uttered a small, groaning sound. The deputy grunted his satisfaction, and Maggie's eyes narrowed.

"You're sure?" Maggie looked at the boy.

"Yes," he said thoughtfully. "I think so."

"That's good enough for me," the deputy grinned.

"Hold on now," I protested. "You must be mistaken."

"It was a tall, limber looking man and an older, shorter man," Lewis replied. "Just like you two."

"Limber? Me?" I scowled. I looked at Brian for help, but he was still watching Maggie.

"Did you know Jacob was my husband?" Maggie asked Brian.

"Not until yesterday," Brian replied.

"Did you kill Jacob because of me?"

A hurt expression crossed Brian's face.

"You know me better than that."

"Do I?" Maggie replied.

Brian didn't reply. They stared at each other some more, and then Maggie grabbed Lewis' hand and spun toward the door.

"Maggie," Brian called after her. "We didn't do it!"

I'm not sure she heard him, because she never looked back as she hurried out. The deputy closed the door behind her, grinned wolfishly at us, and sat behind the desk.

I turned to Brian, and his face was heavy and mulish.

"Will she be back?" I asked.

"I don't know," Brian shrugged. "Maggie's always been hard to figure."

I suddenly had a headache. I massaged my temples and turned away.

CHAPTER FIFTEEN

A somber silence filled our jail cell. There was no need to discuss the matter; we knew we were in big trouble.

Skinny showed up, and he and the deputy talked in hushed tones. Then Skinny left with a look of importance, probably to go find a rope.

I had a cigar in my pocket. I pulled it out, bit off the end, struck a match, lit it, and took a deep puff. Then I walked over to the window and exhaled.

"Enjoying one last smoke?" Brian asked from his bunk.

I grunted in response and looked out the window.

There was a wagon rolling into town. I didn't pay it much attention, but as it got closer it caught my eye.

I gasped in surprise, dropped my cigar, and clenched the bars covering the window.

"What's the matter with you?" Brian looked at me strangely.

"Our wagon," I muttered, still stunned.

"What about it?"

"It just pulled into town!"

"What?" Brian's mouth fell open.

He jumped to his feet and joined me at the window. He was too short to look out, so he took little hops.

"You sure it's our wagon?" He asked.

"I'm sure."

The wagon rolled to a stop across the street. There was a tall, limber man driving, and he jumped down with ease and tied the horses to the hitching rail.

"He really *is* limber," I said, then added, "I recognize two of those horses too."

Brian grunted, and I watched as Limber jumped back in the wagon. He stood on the seat and called out to everyone. I couldn't hear what he was saying, but a crowd quickly gathered.

213

A short, squatty man appeared from the back of the wagon. He was carrying a bedroll, and my eyes grew wide when I realized it was mine.

"What are they doing?" Brian asked impatiently.

"Not sure yet," I replied.

Squatty placed my bedroll in the street, and then he returned to the wagon. He disappeared inside, and when he returned he was carrying Brian's bedroll.

He made several trips, and I recognized most of the stuff he carried.

"Looks like they're going to have an auction," I observed.

"What are they selling?"

"Mostly our stuff."

Brian grunted again, but then his eyes grew wide.

"Tinker man!" He exclaimed.

"What?" I looked at Brian.

"That's what Jacob said," Brian reminded. "A tinker man, meaning horse trader!"

"Makes sense," I mused.

"We've got to do something!" Brian insisted.

I nodded my agreement and left the window. I walked to the front of our cell and looked at the front room.

The deputy was in his usual position. He was sitting behind the desk, his feet up, and was snoring.

"Deputy!" I yelled.

He woke with a start. He jumped to his feet, tripped, and fell across the desk. Then he straightened up and looked around the room.

An irritated look crossed his face as he turned to us.

"What do you want?"

"The real killers!" I exclaimed. "They just came into town!"

The deputy's expression turned sour.

"You don't say," he said, his voice flat.

214

"They're right across the street!" I tried again. "If you'll only look."

The deputy didn't reply. Instead, he walked over to the corner and picked up a bucket. He filled it with water from a barrel and walked over to our cell.

"I want you boys to be quiet," he said, his voice stern.

"But you've got to believe us!" I protested.

"One more word, and I'm going to douse you with this water," the deputy warned. "And once I start, I won't stop. I just filled that water barrel yesterday."

I opened my mouth to speak, but stopped. The deputy was watching me, and he held the bucket ready.

I glanced at Brian and looked back at the deputy. Then I closed my mouth and frowned.

The deputy chuckled gruffly. He set the bucket beside our cell and walked back to the front room.

He sat at the desk and closed his eyes. Meanwhile, I scowled and muttered under my breath as I returned to the window.

CHAPTER SIXTEEN

"What's going on out there?" Brian asked.

"Some big, chubby fellow just bought your bedroll," I replied, my voice sour.

Brian frowned at that, and I grunted as I watched another item sell.

"There goes our coffee pot."

"Now it's getting personal," Brian muttered.

"I can't watch anymore," I replied, and I turned from the window.

"Those fellows must be bold, to just ride into town and start selling things that don't belong to them," Brian declared.

"They probably figured if anybody was looking for them they would head north toward the bigger towns," I replied.

"Probably so," Brian agreed.

I started to reply, but a knock at the door interrupted me. The deputy jumped to his feet and looked out, and then he unbolted and opened the door.

Maggie and Lewis walked in. She spoke in a hushed tone to the deputy, and then she walked over to our cell while the deputy closed the door and followed after her.

Maggie's eyes were cold as she stared at us. Several seconds passed, and she cleared her throat.

"Where's the money?" She asked.

"Money?" I raised an eyebrow. "What money?"

"My husband had just sold a very nice string of horses," she explained. "The money wasn't on Jacob, so you must have it."

Brian started to reply, but I cut him off.

"I'll tell you where it is," I said.

Brian shot me a wild look, but I ignored him.

"Yes?" Maggie looked at me.

"Walk over to the front window," I told her. "And take Lewis with you."

"What is this?" The deputy protested.

"Just do it," I said.

Maggie studied me a moment. Then she frowned, took Lewis' hand, and walked to the window. The deputy went with them.

"Look across the street," I told them. "Do you see a wagon?"

They looked, and Maggie said, "Yes, we see it."

"Recognize them?"

"I do," the deputy spoke up. "They pass through town every few months. They always have something to trade or sell."

"Tinker men," I said.

"Pretty much," the deputy agreed.

"Lewis," I said, my voice gentle. "Take a close look at them."

Lewis pressed up against the window. Then he looked back at us, and a puzzled look crossed his face.

"Are those the fellers that bushwhacked Jacob?" I asked.

"I'm – I'm not sure," Lewis said, obviously startled. "They do *look* like them!"

I heaved a sigh of relief. I glanced at Brian and looked at the deputy.

"Hear that, Deputy? If you search that wagon, you'll probably find the money."

The deputy was obviously displeased. He frowned and looked at Lewis.

"Are you sure about this, Lewis?"

"I – I just don't know," Lewis replied, frustrated.

The deputy nodded slowly. He thought it over and looked at Maggie.

"Well, I'll go find out," he declared.

"Deputy," I spoke up. "Don't go out there alone. They'll kill you."

"What do you suggest I do?" The deputy glared at me.

"Let us out, and we'll help," I said. "Brian and I have experience with such things."

"You are still my main suspects," the deputy declared. "You ain't going anywhere."

Before I could reply, the deputy turned to Maggie.

"You and Lewis stay here," he told her. "Bolt the door behind me, and don't open it until I return."

Maggie nodded, and they walked toward the door.

"Don't do this," I called after them, but they ignored me.

CHAPTER SEVENTEEN

I hurried to the window. I spotted the deputy walking across the street, and his movements were abrupt and stiff.

His hand hovered over his gun handle, and I could tell the deputy was nervous. Limber looked up and spotted him, and he met him in the street.

They talked a moment. And then, in a blink of an eye, Limber palmed his Colt. His movements were smooth and easy, and a stab of flame exploded from his barrel before the deputy could even react.

The slug took the deputy in the chest. His body was flung backwards, and he landed hard on his back.

Screams erupted, and folks ran for cover. A few shots were fired, but none came close as Squatty and Limber untied the horses and jumped into our wagon. Limber encouraged the horses forward, and they took out in a dead run.

I looked back at the deputy, and he was clutching his chest and rolling around. He was hurt bad, but at least he wasn't dead.

"What happened?" Brian demanded, but I ignored him as I turned from the window.

Maggie had been watching from the front window. She turned toward us, and her eyes were wide with fright.

"You've got to let us out, Maggie!" I urged. "They're getting away!"

"I'm – I'm not sure I should," she stammered.

"We're the only ones in town that can catch 'em," I declared. "We're innocent! Surely you know that by now!"

Maggie hesitated a moment, but then nodded as she came to a decision. She glanced around the jail and spotted the key hanging on a peg. She grabbed it, hurried to our cell, inserted the key, and ground it back.

Our cell door swung open, and we rushed to the gun cabinet. Our Colts and rifles were there, and we grabbed them and strapped on our gun belts. Next, we checked our firearms to make sure they were loaded, and then we turned towards the door.

"Let's go," I said.

Brian hung back. He looked at Maggie, and they stared at each other.

"I'm sorry about your husband," he said.

"Jacob was a good man," she replied, and she fought back tears.

"Seemed like," Brian replied.

An uncomfortable silence filled the room, and I cleared my throat.

"We'd best be going," I urged.

Brian nodded. He took one last look at Maggie and followed me out the door.

CHAPTER EIGHTEEN

A crowd had gathered around the deputy, and nobody noticed us as we hurried down the street.

A pony express rider couldn't have gotten out of town any quicker than we did. We reached the livery stable, threw our saddles on our horses, mounted up, and left in a lope.

We slowed to a trot once town was behind us. We studied the surrounding landscape, and we spotted boiling dust in the distance.

"There they are," I gestured.

"What's the plan?" Brian asked.

"Don't have one."

"I've never chased down a wagon. Usually, folks are chasing *us*."

"Always a first time," I replied, and we kicked up our horses to a lope.

A few minutes passed. I could tell we were gaining on them, but then the dust settled.

I slid my horse to a stop. Already he was lathered up with sweat, and was breathing hard.

"Looks like they stopped," I said.

"Do you suppose they're waiting for us?"

"Could be."

Brian frowned at that and said, "I reckon there's only one way to find out."

I nodded, and we continued on with a wary eye.

We rode about half a mile, and I spotted the wagon. It was in an open spot, and I pinched my face as I studied the layout.

"Not a good place to make a stand," I said. "I would have left the wagon in those trees over there. Better cover."

Brian nodded as he squinted ahead.

"I only see two horses," he announced.

I looked back at the wagon and frowned in confusion.

"They had four horses when they left town," I said, then added, "They must have rode out and left the wagon."

"Makes sense," Brian replied. "They can travel faster without it."

I nodded, and we nudged our horses forward.

Something didn't feel right, and I studied the surrounding landscape as we approached the wagon.

We were about a hundred yards from the wagon when my eyes caught a flicker over in the trees. I looked again, and I spotted the back end of a horse.

"It's a trick!" I yelled, and we dove off our horses.

As soon as I yelled, rifle shots exploded from the wagon. Bullets whined all around us as we hit the ground and crawled toward cover.

There was a slight incline in front of us, and Brian and I reached the base and pressed ourselves as flat as possible. Meanwhile, our startled horses scampered away.

We only had our Colts, and we grasped them as we lay there. Meanwhile, bullets continued to pepper the ground all around us.

"You all right?" I gasped.

"I think so," Brian replied. "You?"

I studied our surrounding area before I replied. There was no cover, only open ground.

"We're in a bad spot," I said.

"You don't have to tell me!"

I looked back at the wagon. Squatty and Limber were behind it, shooting at us from behind the wheels.

I narrowed my eyes as I studied the horses. They just stood there obediently, and I recognized them both.

"The horses," I said.

"What about them?"

"They're still hitched to the wagon."

"So?"

"If they were spooked, they'd take off and take the wagon with them."

"But they're used to gunfire. They won't move."

"They'd move in a hurry if one of them was nicked in the rump," I replied.

"You'd shoot your own horse?"

"Actually, I was hoping you would."

"Just a scratch, eh?"

"That's what I was thinking."

"That's actually a good idea."

"Glad you like it," I replied, then added, "Ready anytime you are."

No more words were spoken. I held my Colt ready, and I ignored the bullets that were still peppering the ground around us.

Brian raised his Colt and took careful aim. He fired, and the nearest horse jumped in surprise. He took off in a run, and the other horse went with him.

Squatty and Limber yelled in surprise. They stopped shooting, jumped to their feet, and lunged at the wagon. However, they weren't fast enough, and they were exposed as the wagon left them.

I jumped to my feet. From my hip I aimed at Squatty and squeezed off two shots. His body lurched backwards under the bullets' impact, and he landed on his back.

Limber spun towards me, and his face was twisted in hate. He raised his Colt, but I fired into him before he could shoot.

He staggered backwards and dropped his Colt. A terrified look crossed his face, and he fell face first.

I kept my Colt trained on them, but neither one moved. I was finally satisfied, and I reloaded my Colt and holstered it.

"You all right?" I asked Brian.

Brian nodded, and his face was grim as he studied Limber and Squatty's still forms.

"Their plan almost worked," he said. "They wanted us to *think* they had left the wagon."

"Sure did," I nodded.

"Well, now what?"

I glanced at the sun.

"Be dark soon," I said. "We might as well make camp and head back in the morning."

"Sounds good."

I nodded and looked around. The horses and wagon had stopped over by the trees, so we walked toward them.

The horses were still startled. Brian spoke soothing words to them, and after they settled down he studied the horse he had nicked on the rump.

"How is he?" I asked.

"He's just fine," Brian replied. "Barely even a scratch."

"Good thing you can shoot straight."

Brian grinned and puffed out his chest.

"You can just call me Wild Bill Hickok from now on."

I sighed and grunted in response.

CHAPTER NINETEEN

We rolled back into town midmorning. Town was busy, and a crowd quickly gathered around us.

Nobody spoke as I climbed down. I tied the horses to the hitching rail, and Skinny pushed through the crowd and stood in front of me.

"Did you get them?" He asked.

"They're in the wagon," I announced.

"Dead?"

"They sure are."

Cheers erupted, and folks stepped forward. Some shook our hands; others patted us on the back.

"Sorry for the misunderstanding," Skinny said. "We sorta jumped to conclusions."

"You sure did," I replied with a tight smile, then asked, "How's the deputy?"

"Doc dug the bullet out. Said he's going to pull through."

"Good. I'm glad," I said.

I spotted Maggie and Lewis coming down the street. Maggie's face was tense and anxious, and her eyes were on Brian.

They stopped at the wagon. Brian stared at her, and a silence came over the crowd.

"You're back," Maggie said, her voice hoarse.

"That's right," Brian replied, then added, "We got them."

"Good."

A thought occurred to Brian, and he grinned and reached inside his pocket.

"We found Jacob's money," he said, and he pulled out a bag of coins and handed them over.

"Thank you, Brian. This is really going to help."

"It's the least we could do," Brian replied. He hesitated, then added, "I wish I could do more."

Maggie nodded, and it fell silent.

They both looked like they wanted to say something, but they couldn't find the words. Instead, they just stood there and looked at each other.

Finally, Maggie took her eyes off Brian and glanced at me.

"We spread the word, and folks are bringing back everything they bought yesterday."

"I appreciate that," I grinned.

"I cooked a big breakfast," Maggie offered. "Ya'll could eat while we're waiting."

I didn't think for long.

"Lead the way," I said.

Maggie nodded. She glanced at Brian, and then she grabbed Lewis' hand. She hurried up the street, and Brian and I followed after her.

CHAPTER TWENTY

It took half a day to gather our belongings. Even then, we were short a blanket and two forks.

It was finally time to go. I hustled about the wagon, making sure everything was ready, while Maggie and Brian said their goodbyes.

"You take care," Brian said, his voice husky.

"You too," Maggie replied.

"Mebbe I'll come see you sometime."

Maggie studied Brian a moment, and then nodded.

"I'd like that."

Brian grinned at her, and he climbed up onto the wagon seat beside me.

"How's the sheriff?" He asked.

"He's fine," Maggie replied.

"I'm glad to hear that."

Maggie nodded, and they stared at each other some more.

Several seconds passed. I just couldn't take the silence, so I encouraged the horses forward. They took off in a trot, and we put the town behind us.

Brian watched her as long as he could. Then, he sighed in contentment and turned around. I glanced at him, and he looked pleased.

"Did you hear what Maggie said?" He asked. "She said we could visit."

"I heard that," I said.

"What do you think about that?"

"Not much."

"What?" Brian was startled.

"You visit anytime you want," I replied. "Just leave me out of it."

"You won't come with me?"

"Nope."

"Why not?"

"This is the second time we almost got hung here," I explained. "And you know what they say about the third time."

"Aw, you're being superstitious."

"No, I'm being realistic."

Brian frowned at me, and then changed the subject.

"I hope Maggie will be all right," he said wistfully.

"She'll be fine."

"But running a ranch is a lot of work," Brian objected. "Especially by herself."

"She's not alone. She has Lewis," I reminded, then added, "Besides, a woman in her position won't be single long."

"What do you mean?"

"She has a lot to offer," I replied with a straight face. "You know, a nice little ranch and all."

"She won't marry just *anybody*."

"She married you," I pointed out.

Brian scowled. He had no reply for that, and I chuckled as we bounced along.

The End

About the Author

Born in West Texas, Tell Cotten is a seventh generation Texan. He comes from a family with a ranching heritage and is a member of the Sons of the Republic of Texas. Besides writing, he is also in the cattle business, and he resides in West Texas with his wife, Andi, and their two children.

Tell is the award-winning author of The Landon Saga. His novels have won Gold, Silver, and Bronze in the Readers' Favorite Awards, and Tell also won Best New Western in the Laramie Awards and Bronze in the Global ebook Awards for CONFESSIONS OF A GUNFIGHTER.

For announcements of new releases and all other information, please like The Landon Saga Page on Facebook https://www.facebook.com/TheLandonSaga Or, you can join The Landon Saga Fan Group https://www.facebook.com/groups/784798154926122/ You can also visit Tell Cotten's website http://tellcotten.wordpress.com/

You can find Tell's books on Amazon here: https://www.amazon.com/Tell-Cotten/e/B00BTNWC4Y/ref=dp_byline_cont_pop_ebooks_1

Acknowledgements

I would like to thank my wife and my family for all their help and support. Without them this wouldn't be possible. I'd also like to thank God for the gift of writing.

Storm Warrior

The Legend

By

WL Cox

About The Series

This story goes back in time and involves a lost story never before told in the volumes of Charles' life with the Sioux.

It is important for new readers of the series to start with Volume one, Traveling To America, and follow the stories in sequence. Book II begins where Book I left off.

Charles Crawford, aka, Storm Warrior, was raised in China. His father traveled from England to China to buy land to create an orchard of select grapes only grown in China to be shipped to his winery in Winchester, England.

Charles' father discovers a Chinese Lord of great wealth owns the land he wants to buy. He learns the land was set aside as a dowry for his daughter when she marries.

He agrees to marry the beautiful Chinese girl and acquires the land. Charles is born a year later, and at the age of five, his parents are murdered by Hong Xiuchuan, an evil warlord with an army of warriors determined to take over the country.

When the attack occurred, Charles was placed down a hole in the floor that led to a tunnel in the mountain. Charles' father ordered him to climb Song-Shan Mountain near Dongfeng City and seek protection at the Shaolin Monk's Monastery.

Charles never saw his parents again. Hong Xiuchuan's army murdered them, and the workers on the plantation before burning the buildings.

Charles was found by a Monk hiding in the garden. He was frightened, cold, and hungry. The Monks raised and educated Charles. At the age of twenty-one, Charles knew the life of a Monk was not for him. A ship was hiring help to haul freight to America, and Charles hired on and agreed to work for no pay in exchange for a one-way trip to America where he had heard land was free for the taking, and wildlife, fish, and fowl were plentiful.

Charles' life changed dramatically once the ship was out to sea. All of the Chinese laborers was taken prisoner and they were destined to be sold on the open slave market in Boston upon arrival.

Charles had other ideas. After docking a quarter of a mile offshore, the captain went ashore to sell his goods. The evil co-captain was left on guard duty after the other hands had gone to bed.

Charles slipped from the hold of the ship and killed the co-captain and escaped by swimming ashore during a thunderstorm.

After walking west for months, Charles encountered two criminals on the plains hiding from the law. One wanted his prized knife given to him by a Martial Arts Master at the Monastery when Charles earned his Master's level.

Charles killed one criminal when he pulled a gun and injured the other. Charles took one of the men's horses and turned the other horse loose.

Charles eventually crossed the Missouri River hours ahead of a bounty hunter that had tracked him from Boston.

Charles was captured by Sioux Indians and eventually was accepted into the tribe. For the first time in his life, he had a family. Charles rode on many war parties and set up a training camp in the Sioux valley for the young Braves that wanted to learn the art of hand to hand battle.

The Sioux give Charles the name, Storm Warrior, after watching him pray, and shortly after a horrible tornado hits and wipes out the war party of Pawnee that was following them.

Unknowing to Charles, his father had left his England winery in the hands of a law office in London. The law office hired a man to track down the surviving son, and heir to the winery. After six years of blissful living with the Sioux, two men come to the Sioux Nation, and after many long talks, it was determined that Charles was the missing heir that they were in search of.

Charles agreed to return to England to honor the wishes and memory of his father. Charles' life was never the same after that. He began to develop an empire in America, and ten years later he was a millionaire, by the winery, construction companies, thousands of acres of ranch and farmland, and racing.

CHAPTER ONE
The Attack

Storm Warrior arose early, and after retrieving his horse from the herd, he rode to a hilltop and prayed as the sun's rays crested the Eastern peaks.

Storm Warrior had learned to pray daily during the years he was raised by the Monks in China. He was told by one of the ancient ones in China that he was blessed with the ability to converse with God in a way few would ever enjoy.

The Sioux would often look at the distant hill and observe him praying and could see the glow of light that beamed from his body as he prayed and meditated.

No one interfered with him during prayer, they knew he was receiving words of wisdom that would help protect the tribe and guide them to the location of the mighty buffalo herds that wandered the plains.

Storm Warrior sat quietly with his eyes closed and listened to the words that were spoken to him.

"Beware," he heard the voice say, "Trouble is upon you and the Sioux. Many are preparing to attack that will kill many and steal your horses. Go quickly, and warn the others."

Storm Warrior thanked God for the warning and picked up his prayer blanket, leaped on his horse, Wind Fire, and raced down the hill to the head chief's teepee, Red Bear.

Red Bear was sitting on a log near the fire in front of his teepee when Storm Warrior skidded Wind Fire to a stop and dismounted.

Sitting with Red Bear was Little Bear, Storm Warrior's father-in-law, Gray Wolf, Storm Warrior's adopted blood-brother, and Gray Horse, war chief.

"We have trouble," Charles said as the Chiefs observed him rushing to their fire. "We are about to be attacked by the Pawnee and Shoshone. Many will die, and they will steal many ponies."

"Are you sure?" Chief Gray Horse asked as he jumped to his feet.

"Yes, God warned me during prayer. They are preparing for the attack now. They will soon be here."

Gray Horse ran to the signal fire and began sending signals for the Warriors to arm themselves and prepare for an attack.

The Chiefs ran to their teepees to arm themselves and to warn the women to keep the children in the teepees.

Charles leaped onto Wind Fire's back and raced to his teepee. His Sioux wife, Sun Bird, was breastfeeding their infant son when Charles arrived.

"Quick, Sun Bird. Take Ghost to your mother's teepee. We are under attack."

Storm Warrior escorted Sun Bird and his son, Ghost, to Little Bear's teepee. Sun Bird's mother, Rain Bird, was pleased to have them stay with her and Sun Bird's sister, Gray Dove.

Sun Bird was armed with a knife, and Rain Bird held a rifle. Should anyone try to enter the teepee, the Sioux women knew how to fight. Little Bear would stay with the women while the warriors protected the camp.

Storm Warrior walked out of the teepee and looked north towards the hills and read the smoke signals. The Wolves that Gray Wolf had posted had been alerted and had signaled the northern camp located at the end of the valley.

Two thousand warriors were mounted and armed. The enormous horse herd had been pushed down towards the river near the main camp for protection.

One of Storm Warrior's prize students, Swimming Otter, and four of his friends rode up and asked, "What is happening, Storm Warrior?"

"Alert the other students, in prayer I was shown that Pawnee and Shoshone have joined forces and we are about to be attacked. They want to steal horses and kill as many Sioux that they can. Gather the students and stay close to camp to protect the women and the old ones."

Swimming Otter shouted, and they raced off to do as Storm Warrior had ordered.

Storm Warrior adjusted his quiver of arrows on his back and leaped onto his horse and raced towards where many warriors had gathered.

Gray Horse, the war chief, was shouting orders instructing his warriors of what to do and assigning Chiefs to lead different groups.

Then, rifle fire was heard coming from the top of the hill at the southern entrance to the valley. Then hundreds of warriors broke over the top of the hill, and they were racing down towards the main camp.

Storm Warrior heard rifle fire coming from the Northern Camp and realized they were attacking from two different locations. He kicked Wind Fire into a gallop, and the Sioux met the Shoshone head on in battle.

Storm Warrior drew his bow and fired an arrow at a warrior and struck him in the chest. The warrior fell from his horse as he notched another arrow. A mighty Shoshone warrior hit a Sioux with his war club and knocked the Sioux from his horse. Storm Warrior fired his arrow at the warrior, and the arrow hit him below the rib cage, and as he bent over in pain, another Sioux rode by and hit him in the head with his tomahawk, and the Shoshone fell from his horse.

The Sioux and the Shoshone were mixed and involved in hand-to-hand battle. Storm Warrior dropped his bow and pulled his knife.

Storm Warrior dispatched two more warriors with his knife, and the Shoshone Chief ordered a retreat. Four hundred Shoshone raced for the southern entrance, and more than two hundred lay dead on the battlefield.

The Shoshone Chief was angry, he was sure that the attack would be a surprise. They had moved into position in the dark, and when the sun crested the eastern horizon, they were to coordinate their attack with the Pawnee. The attack went as planned, and they were shocked to find close to two thousand Sioux warriors mounted and armed for battle waiting for them. He had lost many Warriors and decided it was better to retreat and fight another day.

Storm Warrior realized he needed his bow, he turned Wind Fire and ran back to where he had dropped it and reached down and retrieved it from the ground. He glanced up towards the northern tribe and saw several hundred Pawnee heading for the horse herd.

Storm Warrior raced his horse back to the Warriors and shouted that the Pawnee were attacking as he pointed back towards camp.

Gray Horse decided to let the retreating Shoshone go and ordered his men to attack the Pawnee. Gray Horse knew he must protect the camp and horses at all costs.

The Pawnee saw the two thousand Sioux Warriors coming, so they decided to turn and run. Storm Warrior notched an arrow and fired at the fleeing attackers. One warrior fell from his horse when the arrow struck his back.

Storm Warrior saw his Braves, and the men left to protect the camp on the ground fighting with Warriors in hand-to-hand battle.

Storm Warrior spotted a large Warrior that had just clubbed a Sioux and was moving in for the kill. Storm Warrior leaped from Wind Fire and kicked the large Warrior in the back and knocked him hard on his face. The Pawnee rolled and stood to face the man that had kicked him.

He smiled when he saw Storm Warrior. Storm Warrior's fighting ability was famous with the Nations, and the

Pawnee Warrior knew that whoever killed him would receive great honor and admiration among the tribes.

He charged Storm Warrior in an attempt to knock him off his feet. He was surprised when Storm Warrior leaped aside, and with a powerful kick to his stomach, he bent over in pain as Storm Warrior spun and brought his heel down on the back of the man's neck. The powerful Pawnee Warrior's neck snapped, and he fell face first into the dirt and never moved.

Another Pawnee saw Storm Warrior kill his friend, and he raised his rifle to shoot just as a Sioux Warrior rode his horse past Storm Warrior and threw a lance into his chest.

The Pawnee fell back as his gun discharged. He was dead when he hit the ground.

Storm Warrior and the other Sioux dismounted to assist the Sioux braves that were in hand-to-hand battle with the Pawnee Warriors on the ground.

Soon, there were no Pawnee left standing. Warriors were scalping the dead Pawnee and removing weapons and ornaments from their bodies.

Storm Warrior looked around at the carnage and felt bad. There would be much wailing in the village tonight after the burials.

Swimming Otter, Storm Warrior's finest student in martial arts rode up on his Paint leading Wind Fire.

Swimming Otter said, "A Pawnee leaped on Wind Fire's back to escape, I killed him and brought your horse to you."

"Thank you, Swimming Otter. I am proud of the way you and the others fought today. Were any of the students injured?"

"Yes, three were injured, and two were killed by rifle fire."

Storm Warrior leaped onto his horse and looked around.

"Let's ride to the Northern Camp and see what damage the Pawnee have done."

They rode through the mass of bodies on the ground and galloped the mile distance between the two camps. Pawnee bodies were lying on the ground as they rode, ponies were grazing, most were Pawnee ponies, and however, there were also a few Sioux ponies near their fallen riders.

A dozen warriors joined Storm Warrior as he rode to the Northern Campsite. The Northern Camp had been hit harder than the southern camp. Over a thousand Pawnee Warriors had hit the Northern Camp, and only six hundred Shoshone had hit the Southern Camp.

The ground was littered with hundreds of bodies, and most were Pawnee. It would have been much different had Storm Warrior not warned the Sioux of the pending attack.

Chief Spotted Elk of the Northern Tribe rode his horse to Storm Warrior and said, "We were prepared when the Pawnee attacked, and we hit the Pawnee from two sides. There are 318 dead Pawnee, and we lost 86 Sioux, many more are wounded. Two hundred Pawnee got through and charged the southern camp."

"Yes, they are all dead."

"That is good, this means five hundred Pawnee died today."

Storm Warrior said, "The southern camp was hit by over six hundred Shoshone. Over two hundred Shoshone are dead. They must have had the attack planned to hit both camps at sunrise. Their goal was to steal the horse herd, they would have stampeded the horses north through the Northern Camp to make it hard for the Sioux to attack. They would have killed as many Sioux as they could as they passed through."

"Running Calf and Red Elk led a thousand warriors after the Pawnee. With their numbers cut in half, it will be a short battle if they catch them."

Chief Spotted Elk added, "The Pawnee had many guns. Why would the whites sell the Pawnee so many guns?"

"They didn't sell them, the Pawnee and Shoshone attacked the white man's fort near the Knife River Villages in the central Dakotas a month ago. The fort was being built, and the attack took the whites by surprise. It is said all of the whites were killed. All of their weapons and food supplies were taken."

"This will anger the whites; they will send their armies to attack the nations."

"Yes, it is said more than three hundred white soldiers died. The Pawnee and Shoshone have the white man's guns."

"Many guns are lying on the ground. We will collect them, and the ammunition. We will use the rifles to kill the Pawnee."

Storm Warrior said, "When Gray Horse, Red Elk, and Running Calf return, we will hold council and decide how to avenge the attack."

Strom Warrior turned his horse and rode back to the Southern end of the valley where the main camp was set up.

Dead enemy warriors were stripped of their clothing and were being dragged away where their bodies were going to be dropped into a deep canyon a mile from camp. There, the wolves, coyotes, bear, and buzzards would feed on their bodies. The injured and dead Sioux were placed on a travois and carried back to camp where they would be treated for their wounds, and the dead would be prepared for burial.

Hundreds of Shoshone and Pawnee ponies were grazing. The horses would be divided up and given to the warriors. Storm Warrior was glad that his stallion, Wind Fire, wasn't injured or lost in the battle.

Red Bear had awarded Wind Fire to Storm Warrior last year for bravery. The Pawnee had stolen Wind Fire from a small wagon train that they had raided and killed all the whites. Storm Warrior knew that this horse was a

Thoroughbred, and its owner must have been a wealthy white man.

Storm Warrior had learned of the different breeds of horses and cattle in China where he had been raised.

Charles' first concern was his wife, Sun Bird, and his son, Ghost. He rode to Little Bear's teepee and was happy to see Sun Bird sitting with her mother, Rain Bird, and her sister, Gray Dove.

Charles dismounted, and Sun Bird ran to him and hugged him. "I was worried," Sun Bird said, "So many were killed, and I had not heard from you."

"I am okay, Sun Bird. Is everyone okay?"

"Yes, the Warriors never attacked the camp."

Little Bear approached and said, "It is said that you fought well, my son. I am proud of you. Your God's warning saved many lives."

"Thank you, Little Bear. I must get back with the Warriors. I wanted to make sure you and the family was well."

"Yes, thank you, Storm Warrior."

Storm Warrior leaped onto Wind Fire's back as Sun Bird ran to him and handed him a large piece of buffalo meat she had cut off from the meat hanging over the fire.

"You must eat, Storm Warrior."

"Thank you Sun Bird," Charles said as he bit off a piece of meat and turned Wind Fire and galloped through camp.

CHAPTER TWO
The Aftermath

The war parties that had followed the Shoshone and the Pawnee returned to camp at dusk.

A large fire was built in front of the main lodge and warriors were dancing around the fire to the beat of the drums as they imitated the battle and killing of the enemy.

The chiefs from the Northern Camp arrived for the powwow, and Storm Warrior joined them in the large council lodge.

Storm Warrior took his place between his blood-brother, Gray Wolf, and War Chief, Gray Horse.

When Chief Red Bear was confident that all were present, he lit the pipe, took a draw, and passed it around the fire for the wise ones to smoke.

No one was permitted to speak until Red Bear asked them to speak, so everyone remained silent during this opening ceremony.

When the pipe reached Red Bear, he placed the pipe on the ornamental pipe holder and spoke.

"Today, the winds of evil spirits blew across our land. Our brave warriors faced the evil spirits and drove them away, and chased them into the clouds of defeat. Our nation owes much to the wisdom of Storm Warrior's warning. We lost many warriors today, but many more would have been lost if we didn't have the time to prepare."

"I ask Chief Red Elk of the Northern Sioux to tell of your battles."

Chief Red Elk took a step forward and said, "We saw the smoke signals, and alerted the tribe. Warriors armed themselves, and we moved our horses to a protected location near the camp. The warriors were mounted, and armed when the Pawnee attacked."

"The Pawnee had many guns and began firing. Our warriors were in two groups, and we hit them from two sides with arrows. Many Pawnee fell, and then we charged and were fighting by hand before they could reload their rifles.

"A party of two hundred warriors passed through camp and headed for the Southern Camp. We could not give chase and leave our camp unprotected.

"Our archers were posted and kept firing arrows, while many other warriors were in hand-to-hand battle.

"The archer's aim was true, and many Pawnee were hit with arrows. A Chief shouted retreat when he saw that he had lost many warriors, and was losing more Warriors every time the archers fired their arrows.

"Running Calf and I gathered our Warriors, and we gave chase. We gave up the chase when the Pawnee crossed the river. We did, however, kill another fifty-eight enemy during the chase. Content knowing that they had lost half or more of their attack force, we returned to camp. We lost seven warriors during the chase. We collected their bodies and brought them back to camp with thirty-four Pawnee ponies. We left the dead Pawnee on the prairie after we had taken weapons and ornaments from their bodies. The wolves and coyotes will eat well tonight."

Red Bear nodded and said, "Very well, Red Elk, you did well. Does anyone have questions for Red Elk?"

A hot-blooded warrior, Standing Bear, spoke up and asked, "The Pawnee will retrieve their bodies. Shouldn't we lay wait and kill them when they come?"

Red Bear looked up at Standing Bear and said, "No, warriors that come to carry the dead home come in peace.

"The spirit of someone who is not buried properly or whose grave has been desecrated would be doomed to walk the earth, unable to rest. We will let them retrieve their dead in peace."

Red Bear looked at Gray Horse and said, "Gray Horse, tell the council of your battle."

Gray Horse stepped forward and said, "We were mounted for battle and were heading for the southern entrance to the valley when six hundred Shoshone broke over the hill shouting war cries and began firing rifles. We charged them and began shooting arrows. Soon, we were in hand to hand battle.

"We overpowered the Shoshone, and they turned and ran after losing many Warriors. Gray Wolf and I gave chase, and Storm Warrior shouted that Pawnee were attacking from the north.

"We turned and attacked the two hundred Pawnee. Minutes later, all of the Pawnee were dead. We turned and gave chase to the Shoshone.

"We caught them in the valley of the dry lake. The Shoshone were walking the ponies, and we attacked. They fired their rifles and ran. We chased them for two miles, and they crossed the river. We killed a hundred and fourteen Shoshone during the chase. Some were wounded and fell from their ponies; we killed them as we passed. During the chase, we lost eight Warriors to gunfire, and five were wounded. We retrieved ninety-three good ponies. The other ponies were of poor stock, and we left them."

Red Bear said, "You were wise not to cross the river. Both the Shoshone and the Pawnee lost many warriors. I want to thank Storm Warrior for the warning. Without warning, we would not have been prepared for battle, and many more would have died today."

Chief Running Calf asked, "Should we plan for the attack? We need to avenge their attack."

Chief Red Bear looked around at the faces and said, "No. To seek revenge now would be a mistake. They will be expecting us to attack and will set a trap. We would lose many warriors.

"To the East, we will post many wolves that can watch the river. If they cross again, we will know. I will assign this duty to Gray Wolf. You will pick high points where Wolves can watch a great distance. If Warriors cross the river, smoke signals will be sent. Post three Wolves at each location, and give the rifles to two of the Wolves. If a large party crosses, the Wolves are to send the smoke signals and then retreat to the safety of the camp. The number of warriors crossing the river must be in the signal.

"Gray Wolf, I want this done tomorrow."

Gray Wolf said, "We will head out at first light, it will be done."

"Due to Storm Warrior's warning, I will allow Storm Warrior to choose three of the Pawnee ponies of his choosing. Next, I will allow Gray Horse, Gray Wolf, Red Elk, and Standing Elk each five ponies for their leadership. The other ponies are to be given to the warriors in today's battles. Rifles will be used by the Wolves. I have much to talk with the wise ones. That is all."

Everyone knew that was the signal to leave the council lodge so the wise ones could discuss Sioux business.

Everyone left the council lodge and began gathering in groups to discuss to battles, and the decision not to avenge the attack.

Storm Warrior was asked by another Warrior, Angry Hawk, "Don't you think we should avenge the attack?"

"No, Red Bear has much wisdom. They lost many warriors because we were prepared, and they rode into a trap. If we cross the river, we too would be riding into a trap, and we would lose many warriors."

"Today, they lost many more Warriors than we did. It is a lesson they will not soon forget. It will be many moons before they try to attack our camp again. They will know that we have Wolves posted, and they will know they cannot attack again without losing many Warriors. They will be aware that we will know they're coming."

Sun Bird walked up holding Ghost. Storm Warrior hugged her and took Ghost in his arms and walked with Sun Bird through the camp and stopped at campfires and visited with others. It was a nightly routine that Storm Warrior enjoyed.

After visiting many families, Storm Warrior said, "I feel a need to pray. I must thank God for the vision I received this morning that saved many lives."

"I will go home," Sun Bird said, "Don't pray long."

"I will walk you to our teepee."

CHAPTER THREE
Miracles

After leaving Sun Bird and Ghost at the teepee, Storm Warrior mounted Wind Fire and rode to the hill where he liked to pray.

Storm Warrior prayed and asked grace for the fallen Warriors, including the enemy Warriors. He thanked God for the warning and for the safety of Sun Bird and Ghost.

Storm Warrior meditated and began receiving messages. "You are to go to the river, cross the river and a warrior, Black Hawk, will meet you. Black Hawk will escort you to the Shoshone Camp, and you will speak to Chief Blue Bull. Explain that I sent you, and you will not be harmed. Offer peace, to prove that you are following my orders, I will allow you miracles to show my power."

"What miracles will I use?"

God answered, "The miracles of your choice. Use them as you need to. Just say, God declares it so, and it will be done."

Everything grew quiet, and Storm Warrior stood and rode his horse to the central campfire and asked one of the young braves to take Wind Fire to the herd.

He returned to his teepee and went to bed as he pulled Sun Bird close, and thought about what he was told he must do.

The following morning Storm Warrior was on the hilltop praying and asking for guidance. During meditation, he was not getting answers to his questions.

Finally, in desperation, he asked loudly, "Lord, are you with me?"

A booming voice responded, "I am always with you. You have been told what you must do. Go quickly and obey my command."

Storm Warrior arose and placed his prayer blanket over his horse's back and leaped on. He rode to the teepee and quickly ate with Sun Bird and told her that he was going to the Shoshone camp to talk to Chief Blue Bull.

"No," Sun Bird shouted, "They will kill you."

"I must do as my God commanded. He will be with me. I will be safe."

"When will you return?"

"I should be home tonight. It depends on what God wants me to do."

Storm Warrior stood after eating, kissed Ghost and Sun Bird, and walked out.

Sun Bird picked up his bow and ran after him. "Storm Warrior, you forgot your bow."

"I won't need it. I am going to talk peace, not kill."

Storm Warrior mounted Wind Fire and rode through camp. He was passing his adopted Sioux father's teepee when Chief Many Bears stood and held up his hand.

Storm Warrior stopped, and Many Bears asked, "Where is my son going so early in the morning?"

"I am going to the Shoshone Camp and speak to Chief Blue Bull. I will be back tonight."

Many Bears was shocked. "No, my son, they will kill you."

"No, my God will be with me. I am doing as I was commanded. I must obey. I will return tonight."

"If you do not return, three thousand Sioux will attack, and no Shoshone will be left alive."

Storm Warrior smiled, "I will return tonight, Father."

"Be safe, my son."

Storm Warrior turned his horse and galloped away.

Storm Warrior passed through the narrow pass and waved to the Sioux Wolves posted in the trees above the pass. He broke out of the pass and turned Wind Fire southeast and headed towards the river.

Wind Fire enjoyed the exercise, and his long strides moved over the plains quickly. From time to time he passed Shoshone bodies lying on the prairie and continued as he looked straight ahead as though they weren't there.

Storm Warrior reached the top of the deep valley and could see the river below. He followed a game trail down the side of the valley and spotted smoke signals on the far side.

Storm Warrior reached the river, and without hesitating, he urged Wind Fire into the river and walked him across.

Three Shoshone Wolves were posted on the far hillside, and one warrior mounted his horse and rode down to see what this Sioux wanted as he cocked his rifle.

The two Shoshone that waited ordered him to shoot the Sioux and take the beautiful pony.

Storm Warrior rode up onto dry ground and walked Wind Fire towards the advancing Shoshone Warrior with a cocked gun on his lap pointed at Storm Warrior's chest.

As they drew near, Storm Warrior stopped and raised his hand. "I come in peace, Black Hawk. I need to speak to Chief Blue Bull."

"How do you know my name?" Black Hawk asked as he tightened his finger on the trigger of the rifle.

"My God said that I would be greeted by a great warrior by the name of Black Hawk and that you would take me to Chief Blue Bull."

"Your God was wrong; Black Hawk will kill you and take your scalp and your pony."

"Your rifle will burn and melt in your hands, God commands it so."

"Ha," Black Hawk said as he laughed. "Your God has led you to your death. You are a fool, Storm Warrior. The name Black Hawk will be spoken by all warriors across the plains as the mighty warrior that killed Storm Warrior."

Suddenly the rifle turned red and burst into flames. It was too hot for Black Hawk to hold and he dropped it to the ground as he blew on his burnt hands and the rifle was soon reduced to ashes and melted iron.

"Do not ridicule my God, if you do not follow my orders, your tribe will be eliminated from the plains."

Storm Warrior looked up and said, "Thank you, Lord."

God spoke to Storm Warrior as his body glowed in the light. "Order him to lead you to Blue Bull."

Black Hawk saw Storm Warrior's body glow and his eyes flashed a brilliant light as he asked, "Are you a God, Storm Warrior?"

"No, I am not a God, but my God is with me. Take me to Chief Blue Bull, now."

Black Hawk's hands were blistered from the burning rifle and he had a hard time holding the leather reins on his pony.

Storm Warrior saw the large blisters and said, "Stop, hold out your hands."

Black Hawk looked doubtfully at Storm Warrior, he thought Storm Warrior would kill him.

"Why?"

"I will heal your hands."

Black Hawk held out his hands, and Storm Warrior placed his hands over Black Hawk's hands. Storm Warrior looked up at the sky and said, "Please heal these burnt hands as my God commands it so."

Storm Warrior removed his hands, and both of Black Hawks hands glowed a brilliant light. Black Hawk cried out in pain, and then he stopped when the light left his hands. Black Hawk looked at his hands and couldn't believe it, his hands had been healed.

Black Hawk rubbed his hands together, and there was no blisters and no pain.

Storm Warrior looked at Black Hawk and said, "If any warrior attempts to attack me, or shoot me, my God will strike him dead. My God commands it so. Take me to Chief Blue Bull now."

Black Hawk was amazed. He turned his pony and said, "Come with me."

The two Shoshone on the hillside were angered that Black Hawk didn't kill the Sioux. One of the Shoshone spat angrily and said, "When he passes by I will kill him myself."

"No," the other warrior said. "You saw Black Hawk's rifle burn, the warrior has great powers. We must wait and see what he wants."

"You can wait, but I will not. My brother was killed by a Sioux, I will avenge his death."

As Black Hawk and Storm Warrior neared their location, the two Shoshone stepped out onto a rock, and the angry Shoshone pulled the hammer back on his Spencer Carbine. The audible sound of the hammer clicking was loud.

Black Hawk held up his hand and said, "No, he comes in peace, we will speak to Chief Blue Bull."

"I will take his body to Chief Blue Bull," the Shoshone said as he shouldered his rifle.

"No!" Black Hawk shouted as a bolt of lightning struck the warrior and killed him instantly. The gun fell to the ground and burst into flames.

Storm Warrior looked up at the smoldering body of the Shoshone and said, "My God will kill anyone that tries to harm me. Hurry, we must speak to Chief Blue Bull immediately."

Black Hawk was scared of Storm Warrior's power, so he did as Storm Warrior demanded and began heading up the hill by following the heavily used trail.

Storm Warrior followed, and as they climbed to the top, they passed three young Braves coming down the hill on their ponies.

The young Braves were shocked to see a Sioux being taken to their camp. They stopped and followed to see what was happening.

Black Hawk broke over the top of the hill, and the Shoshone Camp was plainly visible. Hundreds of warriors had gathered when word reached them that Black Hawk was bringing a Sioux to their camp.

Storm Warrior looked at the faces of the warriors, and hatred was plainly visible. He followed Black Hawk, and they stopped in front of a teepee with four older Shoshone sitting around a fire.

Black Hawk said, "Chief Blue Bull, I have brought Storm Warrior to talk to you. He has come alone and is unarmed."

A large majestic looking Shoshone stood and walked to Storm Warrior. "Dismount, I will not speak up to a Sioux."

Storm Warrior dismounted and said, "Chief Blue Bull, I have come in peace to talk to you about making peace. We do not need to kill each other, there is plenty of land for all. We must learn to live in peace."

Chief Blue Bull said, "It is hard to talk of peace while my son lies dying."

"Take me to your son."

"Why, so you can kill him?"

"No, my God will heal him to prove that we wish peace, not death, with the Shoshone. It is as my God commands."

"Come, if you do not heal him, you will die."

Storm Warrior followed the Chief to a nearby teepee, and they entered. A warrior lay on some blankets and had a severe wound on his body. A squaw was sitting on the floor next to him and was crying as she wiped his face with cold water. She looked up at Blue Bull and said, "You are too late, he is dead."

"Ask her to step away," Storm Warrior said as he looked at Chief Blue Bull.

Blue Bull ordered his son's wife to move away.

She looked up at Blue Bull and said, "You don't understand, he is dead."

Charles looked skyward towards the opening in the teepee and in Chinese he prayed. "Lord, as you commanded me to do, please heal this injured warrior and make him whole again."

God spoke to Storm Warrior in Chinese as Storm Warrior's body glowed in the brilliant light. Chief Blue Bull had never seen anything like this, and his eyes opened wide in amazement.

God said, "Kneel and place one hand on his head, and one hand on his heart. Chief Blue Bull will think you are hurting his son, so tell him what you are doing and not to worry."

Chief Blue Bull had never heard the Chinese language, and Storm Warrior turned and looked at him, and Blue Bull's face showed fear.

Storm Warrior's eyes were brilliant and appeared to be on fire. "Do not worry, I will heal your son. Stand back and do not interfere."

"He is dead, you will die!" Blue Bull shouted.

"No, he will live," Storm Warrior said as he knelt and prayed, as he placed a hand on the Warrior's head, and then put a hand on his heart, and he asked God to heal this broken body.

The warrior's body began to glow and levitated a little as Storm Warrior spoke praises to God and his healing power. Storm Warrior could feel the shock passing through his body as he kept his hands on the warrior's body. The powerful energy passing through his body was transferred into the dead warrior's body, and he began moaning loudly and struggled.

The shocking power began to lessen, and the warrior's body was lowered back to the blanket, and Storm Warrior felt severely weakened.

Storm Warrior gasped for air, as the warrior stirred and tried to sit up. Storm Warrior almost fell as he tried to stand, and the warrior looked up and asked, "What is the

Sioux doing in my teepee?" As he coughed and choked for air.

Chief Blue Bull looked at Storm Warrior in disbelief.

The warrior's wife cried out with joy as she hugged the warrior and wept.

Storm Warrior looked at Chief Blue Bull and said, "I must rest," as he collapsed to the ground.

The injured warrior stood, and Chief Blue Bull asked, "Are you okay, my son?"

"Yes, I will kill this Sioux," he said as he pulled a knife.

"No," Blue Bull said as he stepped in front of his son, "This is Storm Warrior. He healed you, you were dead, now you live."

Chief Blue Bull looked down at Storm Warrior. "Put him in your bed, he transferred his energy to you so that you may live again. No one will harm him."

Black Hawk and Blue Bull's son, White Wolf, put Storm Warrior on White Wolf's bed and they stepped outside to show all that White Wolf had been healed.

Chief Blue Bull selected four mighty warriors and ordered them to guard the teepee and not allow anyone inside.

A loud roar of approval was heard when White Wolf stepped from his teepee.

Blue Bull walked to the central fire and raised his hand to silence the crowd of Warriors.

"My son, White Wolf was dead when we entered the teepee. Storm Warrior restored his life. Storm Warrior came to our camp in peace, and he will leave in peace. No harm will come to Storm Warrior."

"Where is Storm Warrior?" One of the Warriors asked.

"He is sleeping. He transferred his energy to White Wolf in blinding light and is exhausted. Look, the wound on White Wolf's body is gone."

One of the old men sitting nearby asked, "Is he a God?"

"Only a God could bring my son back from the dead, and heal his wound as though he was never injured."

Black Hawk said, "We saw Storm Warrior coming across the river. I volunteered to go see what the Sioux wanted. Otaktay ordered me to kill the Sioux warrior. When I drew near, I cocked the rifle. Storm Warrior said he wanted to talk to Chief Blue Bull. I said, no, I would kill him and take his horse. I started to lift my gun, and the gun turned hot and burned my hands. The gun was on fire, I dropped it and the iron melted, and the wood burned to ashes. He demanded me to take him to see Blue Bull."

Black Hawk looked around at the faces of the men that didn't believe him. My hands were badly burned, I had blisters and could not hold the reins. Storm Warrior told me to hold out my hands, and he would heal them. I held out my hands, and he touched them, and I was healed.

"We approached the post where Otaktay and Kohana were waiting. Storm Warrior warned me that if anyone tried to harm him that his God would strike them dead.

"Otaktay raised his gun to shoot Storm Warrior. I shouted at him, no, but he wouldn't listen. A bolt of lightning struck Otaktay and killed him, and the rifle fell to the ground and burned. Storm Warrior has great powers, his God is with him."

Chief Blue Bull said, "It is as if his God lives within him. When he awakens, we will listen to what he has to say. I have spoken, and it will be so."

The Shoshone crowd thickened as everyone talked to each other about the miracles they had heard. Some believed, and others did not.

Storm Warrior awoke, and God spoke to him. "You must rise and talk to Blue Bull. Time is short."

Storm Warrior stirred and stood. A squaw was sitting off to one side of the teepee and had a frightened look on her face. "Thank you," he said as he walked to the flap in the teepee and left.

The four great Warriors were standing and turned to look at him. They allowed him to pass by and he walked to where Blue Bull and the others were seated.

The crowd of Shoshone grew silent as they watched him walk to Chief Blue Bull's teepee.

Blue Bull said, "Storm Warrior, thank you for saving my son's life."

"I didn't save his life, God saved his life. He allowed me to perform the miracle so you would know that the words I am about to say are true."

"Please, sit Storm Warrior," Chief Blue Bull said as he lit a long stemmed pipe and handed it to Storm Warrior.

Storm Warrior knew it was customary to speak only after the pipe was passed. Storm Warrior took a draw on the pipe and handed it to the Shoshone sitting to his left. After all had smoked, Chief Blue Bull sat the pipe down and looked at Storm Warrior.

"You came to talk, what does Storm Warrior say?"

"My God is angered that the Shoshone and the Pawnee joined forces to attack our camp. I was ordered to come and speak to you about peace. No one wins in battle. Friends and family lose their lives, and bitter feelings are felt by all. After the dead are buried, plans are made to avenge the fallen. Then more are killed, and no one gains anything."

One of the older Chiefs sitting near Blue Bull said, "The Sioux have killed many Shoshone. Are you saying we should not avenge the deaths of our Warriors?"

"That's right, the Shoshone attacked the Sioux. The Sioux did not attack the Shoshone. We were defending our land and our people."

Another older Chief sitting by Storm Warrior asked, "How did you know we were attacking? It is said the Sioux were armed and waited."

"Yes, I knew you were attacking from the south, and the Pawnee were attacking from the north."

"How did you know?"

"My God spoke to me and warned me. God also told me to come and warn you to live in peace, or great sorrow would fill your camp."

"What would he do?" Blue Bull asked.

"I don't know, it could be famine, disease, great storms, fire, or perhaps an earthquake that would split the ground and swallow the tribe."

The old chief sitting next to Blue Bull asked, "Are you a God?"

"No, I am a man, the same as all of you."

"How do you explain your great powers?"

"I have a close relationship with God. He performs great feats through me, and many think I am the one doing it. Actually, it is God that is performing the miracles, not me. I have no special powers."

Blue Bull said, "You restored my son's life, I saw you do it."

"No, it was God. He asked me to place a hand on White Wolf's head and heart. God used my body to transfer power and energy into White Wolf's body. I am merely an intermediary, God is the real power."

Chief Blue Bull asked, "Why is it that you have this power, but we don't?"

"Anyone that prays daily has a pure heart, and believes in God could be blessed. I was raised in a faraway land called China. My parents were killed when I was five winters old. I was found by a Buddhist Monk. Monks are a religious group of people that live alone in a Monastery located in the mountains. They prayed daily and taught me to pray. Praying is a habit that I still do to this day. It was through prayer that I was warned of your attack. I pray daily for guidance and advice when I am facing a tough decision, and I don't know what to do. God guides me, even when I don't think it would work."

Blue Bull said, "When you prayed, you spoke a language I have not heard before. Is that the language of the Gods?"

"I was praying in the Chinese language."

Storm Warrior looked at the Chiefs sitting around the fire and said, "We must declare peace and live in peace. Too many have died for nothing. It must end, and we must live in peace."

One of the old chiefs looked at Storm Warrior and said, "Many Shoshone were killed by the Sioux, many will not forgive, or forget."

"Many Sioux died because of the Shoshone. We must learn to accept what is, let go of what was, and have faith in what could be. The survival of the Nations depends on the tribes living in peace, and helping each other."

Storm Warrior looked at the Chiefs and said, "As I rode over today, I noticed a lot of dead Shoshone lying on the prairie. You should come and bring them home for burial."

"Yes, and the Sioux will kill us."

"No, leave your weapons, if you come in peace, you may leave in peace. We do not kill those that come to collect the dead. I must return home. Do I have your word that there will be peace, and we will have no more attacks?"

"We will talk, if there is to be peace, we will send smoke signals. Three smoke signals will be peace, no smoke signals will mean no peace."

"I will tell our Chiefs," Storm Warrior said as he stood and shook Chief Blue Bull's hand.

"I will assign warriors to escort you safely to the river."

"Thank you, Chief Blue Bull."

Blue Bull shouted to a Brave to bring Storm Warrior's horse and selected six warriors to ride with him to the river.

Storm Warrior leaped onto Wind Fire's back and headed back down the trail with six warriors riding with him.

They reached the river, and Storm Warrior crossed the river and saw the hill on the far side was lined with Sioux Warriors. He climbed the side and was greeted by Gray Horse, the war chief, and his blood-brother, Gray Wolf.

Gray Wolf said, "Storm Warrior, that was foolish to ride to the Shoshone camp alone. I am surprised to see you alive."

"My God was with me and protected me. Let's go home. The Shoshone will come to collect their dead to take home for burial. I promised them that as long as they were just collecting their dead, we would not attack."

Gray Horse looked at Storm Warrior and said, "We must get back to the camp before dark," and kicked his horse into a gallop with the others following.

CHAPTER FOUR
A Time Of Peace

They arrived back in Sioux Valley just as darkness fell upon the valley.

There was a great celebration that started as they rode into camp. Storm Warrior, Gray Wolf, and Gray Horse dismounted in front of the council lodge and Braves took their horses to the river for water before releasing them with the herd.

The council of wise ones was sitting around the fire when they entered, and many warriors were standing to hear of Storm Warrior's journey.

Chief Red Bear passed the pipe, and after it had been returned, he set the pipe in its cradle.

Red Bear said, "Chief Many Bears alerted the tribe that Storm Warrior left alone to travel to the Shoshone Nation. Tell us, Storm Warrior, why did you go?"

Storm Warrior stepped forward and said, "Last night, when I was praying, God instructed me to go to the Shoshone camp and talk to them about peace. God promised he would protect me and would be with me, and he was.

"I told the Shoshone Chief, Blue Bull, that to wage war on each other was foolish, and asked why we couldn't live in peace. Blue Bull said he would talk to the other Chiefs, and if they agreed to peace, they would send three smoke signals tomorrow. No smoke signals would mean no peace."

"We all think that what you did was foolish. Why did the Shoshone not try to kill you?"

"One did, but God struck him dead with a bolt of lightning. Another pointed a rifle at me, and God burnt the rifle to ashes and burned the Warrior's hands. God healed his hands, and the Warrior led me to the camp."

Storm Warrior told them the story of the Chief's son that had died just moments before he had arrived, and how God breathed life back into him and healed his wounds.

After the Warriors had been dismissed, Storm Warrior and the others left the council lodge.

Sun Bird was waiting and was holding Ghost. She ran to him, and they hugged, and he kissed her.

"Storm Warrior, I was so worried. I am glad you are home."

"I am happy to be home too," Storm Warrior said. "God kept his word, he was with me all the way and protected me."

They walked through the camp and talked to different families. Storm Warrior walked Sun Bird home and said, "I must go to the hill and thank God for bringing me home safely."

"Don't be long," Sun Bird said as she kissed him.

Storm Warrior walked to the hill and prayed. He thanked God for being with him and protecting him and prayed for peace.

God answered, "Tomorrow, you will see three smoke clouds, well done." Then it grew still and quiet.

Storm Warrior stood and walked back to camp. He approached his blood brother, Gray Wolf. "Alert your Wolves. Tomorrow, they will see three smoke clouds from the Shoshone, they will want peace."

"I hope you're right, Storm Warrior. Now, all we have to worry about is the Pawnee and the Black Foot."

"Perhaps God will have me visit them as well."

"You are walking dangerous waters, Storm Warrior. Many wish to kill you, and you could anger the wise ones."

"I do as my God commands. He does what is right for the Sioux. My God protects, and watches over us."

"I hope you're right," Gray Wolf said. "Many were worried about you."

"I must return to my teepee, Sun Bird and Ghost are waiting. Good night, my brother."

Storm Warrior walked to the teepee as he thought of the day's events. He knew the Shoshone, and the Pawnee would talk, and he wondered what would be said. Would the Pawnee grow angry?

As he reached his teepee, he relaxed. If there were a problem, his God would inform him.

Storm Warrior lay next to Sun Bird, and she snuggled close.

"Storm Warrior, you have never told me much of your white parents, why?"

"There isn't much to tell," Storm Warrior answered. "I was a child of five winters when my white parents were killed. I was raised by Shaolin Buddhist Monks, and they educated me, and trained me how to fight hand to hand. They called it, Shaolin Kung-Fu. It is the oldest style of Chinese Martial Arts.

"My father was English, my mother was Chinese. I don't remember much about them, our time together was so short, I can remember my mother was kind and gentle, my father was proud and strong.

"My mother's name was Shuang. It is pronounced, Shwank, and in Chinese, it means, Jolly. My father had a hard time pronouncing Shuang, so he called her Sun Flower."

"Maybe we will name our daughter, Sun Flower."

Storm Warrior chuckled, "Don't tell me you are pregnant."

"No, but one day we will have a daughter."

"If we do, I will call her Little Sun Bird, after her mother."

"What was your father's name?"

"I was told that his name was Charles. The monks called me the Asian version of Charles, it was Charlemagne. I haven't heard that name in a long time."

Storm Warrior wrapped his arm around Sun Bird and pulled her close. "We need to sleep, I am tired."

The next morning Storm Warrior was up early and walked to the hill to pray.

An hour later, he returned to the teepee and ate with Sun Bird. Storm Warrior felt refreshed after a good night's sleep.

Sun Bird asked, "What were you told in your prayers?"

"I was shown that two white men from England are in China searching for me."

"Why?"

"I don't know. But I was told that one day they will come to the camp."

"Do they mean you harm?"

"No, I do not think so. I was told they have a message for me from my white father."

"How will they find you?"

"I do not know, but I think God will lead them here. But it will not be until next summer."

"What if they want to take you away?"

"Do you really think 3,000 Sioux Warriors would allow them to force me to leave? I will never leave you and Ghost. If I find that I must leave, you and Ghost will go with me. I would never abandon my family. I must get to the training camp," Storm Warrior said as he stood.

Storm Warrior left the teepee, and a Brave was waiting outside holding Wind Fire. "Thank you, Takoda," Storm Warrior said as he leaped on Wind Fire's back and rode to the training camp.

Storm Warrior arrived, the Braves were already there. He released Wind Fire to graze and greeted the boys with a smile.

"Show me the Horse Stance," Storm Warrior said.

The Braves immediately stood with their feet wider than the shoulders, with the feet parallel, and noticed the bend in the knees as they sat their bodies down. Storm Warrior knew that this basic move and hand technique served several purposes. First, the stance would strengthen the legs and would teach the students how to relax down into their stance so that their center of gravity is lowered and the chest is not pushed outward.

Storm Warrior addressed two of the newer students that did not do it properly and then after he was satisfied, he said, "Stand, show me the Forward Stance."

This position moved the body forward, with the front knee bent, and the back leg is held straight. From the side, it resembled a drawn bow. Storm Warrior walked to the side and addressed the two new students and had them correct their stance.

Storm Warrior explained, "This position is critical. It forms a very stable base for generating power and further forward movement.

"Stand, show me the Cat Stance."

Storm Warrior explained for the benefit of the newer students "This position is used for transitional movements and affords mobility. The weight is on your back leg. The front leg rests on the toe or the ball of the foot. It resembles the way a cat puts his paw out to take a step, with no weight on it. Your front leg is able to step into another stance quickly, or to kick your opponent.

"Stand, relax. Now, show me the Twist Stance."

Storm Warrior explained, "This is another transitional position. This position is used to advance or retreat. This is a great position to untwist and change directions, and also contains a hidden kick and joint locking application.

"Stand, and show me the Crane Stance."

Storm Warrior explained, "This stand imitates the way a crane stands on one leg, by raising the other leg. From this position, you can kick the opponent or evade attacks."

After Storm Warrior was satisfied with the five basic stances, he asked the Braves to break off into pairs and practice the five basic stances on each other.

Most of the students were advanced in their lessons, and he pulled Swimming Otter aside to work with him on hand and arm techniques. He worked with Swimming Otter on the back fist, the elbow strike, hammer fist, haymaker punch, hook punch, jab punch, knife hand strike, palm strike, slap, straight punch, and the uppercut punch.

After he was confident that Swimming Otter had mastered these hand strikes, he brought over another advanced student, Yellow Calf, and worked with him on the same moves.

At the end of the day, before he released them, he had them stand and once again went through the five stances.

"Remember," Storm Warrior said to the students before he dismissed them, "Tomorrow is the tournament. I know you will all win, but should one of you lose, I expect you to show pride and respect. Anger has no place in Shaolin Kung-Fu, dismissed."

As they began to walk away, Storm Warrior said, "Swimming Otter, a word please."

"Yes, Storm Warrior," he asked as he stood before him.

"You have advanced ahead of the other students. I am proud of you. Be careful in tomorrow's tournament. I do not want you to injure your opponent."

"I will be careful, Storm Warrior."

"I saw you in battle, and you quickly disabled Shoshone Warriors that attacked you. That is the time to use your might and power on the opponent. You did well."

"Thank you, Storm Warrior."

"Come, let us go home. Soon, the council will be meeting."

They mounted their horses and crossed the stream and rode to their teepees.

Sun Bird had food boiling in the pot, and as Storm Warrior took a seat, he looked at his son that was sound asleep.

After eating, Storm Warrior left the teepee and went to the council lodge.

Red Cloud announced that the Wolves reported seeing three smoke clouds from the Shoshone. "Our Wolves returned the smoke clouds as a sign of peace acceptance."

Chief White Buffalo scoffed and asked, "How long will it be before they break the peace?"

"I don't know," Storm Warrior answered, "But it is a good start."

"We will see," White Buffalo said with a sneer.

Chief Red Bear said, "Tomorrow is a new moon, are your students ready for the tournament?"

"Yes, all but the two newest students. They have only been in training for a week, they are not ready, but the others are."

"Yes, I agree, Little Hawk, and Red Deer will not compete. Gray Wolf, have you selected your Warriors to compete?"

"Yes, they are ready, and I have nine Braves to fight tomorrow. They will choose their opponent."

Storm Warrior smiled, "I know my brother has chosen the nine largest and most powerful Braves, it will be a great victory for my students."

Red Bear said, "The matches will be held at first light before the other contests. It will be a day of celebration."

Everyone left the council lodge except for the wise ones.

Once outside, Gray Wolf teased Storm Warrior about the matches tomorrow. "I hate to see your training camp lose, but my Braves are trained and ready."

"Is that so? Tonight as I was dismissing them, I asked them to go easy and not to hurt your untrained Braves."

Gray Wolf laughed. "My brother, you always make me laugh. I will be judging the matches tomorrow."

"Yeah, so will I, that's the only way your Braves could win."

"Will we use the three-point rule tomorrow?"

266

"Yes, a solid hit, or a fall to the ground counts as a point. Three points and the match is over."

Gray Wolf asked, "Who is your finest fighter?"

"You know Swimming Otter is, why do you ask?"

"Standing Bear wants to join the matches. Standing Bear is large and powerful. He killed three Shoshone in the battle. I don't want him to pick out one of your weaker students. I will instruct him to choose Swimming Otter."

"Swimming Otter also killed Shoshone. It will be a good match."

Gray Wolf saw Storm Warrior looking towards the southern hills and asked, "What is wrong?"

"In prayer, it was shown to me that two white men are in China searching for me. In one summer, or maybe two summers they will come to the camp and will find me."

"If they come to harm you, they will die."

"No, I was told that they have a message for me from my white father."

Gray Wolf scoffed, "That is too far to travel just to give you a message. They will give up and will not come."

"It depends, Gray Wolf. It will depend on how important the message is."

"Nothing could be that important. Come, let's visit with the others."

Storm Warrior returned to his teepee after telling his students to get to bed early. Sun Bird had just finished feeding Ghost and had put him to bed.

Storm Warrior was up early and rode Wind Fire to the prayer hill, and as the sun began to crest the horizon, he returned to the teepee and escorted Sun Bird and Ghost to the tournament field.

A large area had been roped off to act as the arena. Storm Warrior had his students' line up inside the arena along the side, and Gray Wolf had his Braves line up on the opposite side facing them.

It was customary for Gray Wolf's Braves to pick an opponent from Storm Warrior's students. This would be the sixth match, and so far, Storm Warrior's students had won all of the matches.

Many gathered to watch the matches, including the Chiefs and the wise ones.

The first Brave to pick an opponent was Lame Hawk. He walked across the arena and smiled as he looked at the students. Lame Hawk stopped and pointed at Yellow Calf. "I choose Yellow Calf," he said as he chuckled.

Yellow Calf was smaller than Lame Hawk. However, he was almost as good as Swimming Otter. Storm Warrior knew that Lame Hawk would soon regret his choice.

Storm Warrior and Gray Wolf acted as referees should the matches get out of control. Storm Warrior walked between the two challengers and announced for all to hear. "The Shaolin Martial Arts consists of seventy-two types of attacks using the hands and feet. My students are trained only in the five basic stances. As the students' progress in their training, I will teach them more moves."

Storm Warrior bowed to Lame Hawk, and then turned and bowed to Yellow Calf who in return nodded to Storm Warrior.

Storm Warrior backed away and clapped his hands, and the matches were on. Lame Hawk smiled and approached Yellow Calf as he flexed his muscles. Instead of backing away, Yellow Calf went into a Twist Stance and waited.

Lame Hawk gave Yellow Calf an odd look and reached for Yellow Calf's arms. Yellow Calf spun and kicked Lame Hawk's legs out from under him. Lame Hawk went down hard and quickly leaped to his feet.

As Lame Hawk approached a second time, Yellow Calf went into his Horse Stance. The position caused Lame Hawk to laugh, and he swung a fist at Yellow Calf's face.

The blow was blocked, and Yellow Calf kicked Lame Hawk in the stomach, and it caused him to bend over in pain. Yellow Calf spun and kicked Lame Hawk in the shoulders, and it knocked him off his feet.

Lame Hawk got up slowly, and when he had regained his breath, he advanced once again. This time, Yellow Calf went into the Cat Stance. Lame Hawk once again was surprised when he thrust a fist towards Yellow Calf's face, and his punch was blocked by a leg kick, followed by an open-palmed punch to his stomach, and then Yellow Calf spun and swept Lame Hawks legs out from under him.

Lame Hawk landed hard on his back and moaned as he tried to stand and catch his breath.

Gray Wolf waved his arms, "Match is over, and Yellow Calf is the winner."

Everyone applauded, and Yellow Calf shook Lame Hawk's hand, and both returned to their position.

The matches continued for two more hours, and Storm Warrior's students had won all nine of the matches.

In China, different colored belts were awarded when students advanced. Storm Warrior had asked Sun Bird to make different colored headbands instead of belts.

Storm Warrior walked to the edge of the arena, and Sun Bird handed him nine red headbands.

Storm Warrior walked to face his students. "You have done well and have made me proud of you. Today, you surrender your green headbands and will be awarded red headbands.

Storm Warrior shook each of their hands and gave them the red headband and took the green headband to use another day when a yellow headband progressed to the green headband.

"Go, and enjoy the day. But remember always to keep an eye on the horizon and always know who is close to you. Danger can spring upon you at any time. Always be prepared. Do not brag about your victory today, honor your parents, and help the old and the young. Showing honor to your family and others is the greatest gift. You are all well on your way to becoming magnificent Warriors. I am proud of you. That is all, have fun today and be at the training camp in the morning."

Storm Warrior walked back to talk to Sun Bird as Red Bear approached. "Storm Warrior, your students fought well. They stand oddly, but it works well for them. Congratulations."

"Thank you, Red Bear," Storm Warrior said as they shook hands before Red Bear walked away.

Gray Wolf said, "Your students did well, Storm Warrior. I think the way they stand looks funny."

"Yes, however, it takes much practice to learn the stances, and it is almost impossible to defeat a man that learns these stances. They provide protection, and offer a quick response that will take the opponent by surprise."

Storm Warrior walked with Sun Bird and held Ghost as they stopped and visited with people. It proved to be a beautiful day. Charles and Sun Bird watched the archery matches, and the trick riding tactics that many of the Warriors had mastered.

Swimming Otter came to Storm Warrior and asked, "May I ride Wind Fire in the horse race?"

"Yes, be careful, he is fast."

"Thank you, Storm Warrior," Swimming Otter said as he ran to the horse herd and mounted Wind Fire.

Storm Warrior knew that Swimming Otter was an excellent rider, and wanted to watch the race. The race was held between the Northern and Southern Camps. A pole was erected at both ends, they would run to the north, turn at the pole, and race back. The entire race was about two miles. It was a good race to test speed and endurance.

It was a good race, and Swimming Otter won the race by a large margin.

Gray Wolf walked up and chuckled as he said, "Storm Warrior, it is not fair to race Wind Fire against the Mustangs."

"Yes, I know. Swimming Otter asked if he could race him. How could I turn my star student down?"

Gray Wolf chuckled, "You are too soft on your students, Storm Warrior."

"Yeah, I'm a real pushover," Storm Warrior said as he put his arm around Sun Bird and walked away carrying Ghost.

The End

BOOKS WRITTEN BY WL COX

Storm Warrior	Hunt-U.S. Marshal
Storm Warrior II	Hunt-U.S. Marshal II
Storm Warrior III	Hunt-U.S. Marshal III
Storm Warrior IV	Hunt-U.S. Marshal IV
Storm Warrior V	Hunt-U.S. Marshal V
Storm Warrior VI	Hunt-U.S. Marshal VI
Storm Warrior VII	Hunt-U.S. Marshal VII
Storm Warrior VIII	Hunt-U.S. Marshal VIII
Storm Warrior IX	Hunt-U.S. Marshal IX
Storm Warrior X	Hunt-U.S. Marshal X
Storm Warrior XI	Hunt-U.S. Marshal XI
Storm Warrior XI I	Hunt-U.S. Marshal XII
Storm Warrior XIII	Hunt U.S. Marshal XIII
Storm Warrior XIV	Hunt-U.S. Marshal XIV
Storm Warrior XV	Hunt U.S. Marshal XV
Storm Warrior XVI	Hunt U.S. Marshal XVI
Storm Warrior XVII	Hunt U.S. Marshal XVII
Storm Warrior Vol 18	Hunt U.S. Marshal Vol 18
Storm Warrior Vol 19	Hunt U.S. Marshal Vol 19
Storm Warrior Vol 20	Hunt-U.S. Marshal Vol 20
Storm Warrior Vol 21	Hunt-U.S. Marsal Vol 21
Storm Warrior Vol 22	Hunt-U.S. Marshal Vol 22
Storm Warrior Vol 23	Hunt-U.S. Marshal Vol 23
Storm Warrior Vol 24	Hunt-U.S. Marshal Vol 24
Storm Warrior Vol 25	Hunt-U.S. Marshal Vol 25
Storm Warrior Vol 26	Hunt-U.S. Marshal Vol 26
Storm Warrior Vol 27	Hunt-U.S. Marshal Vol 27
Storm Warrior Vol 28	Hunt-U.S. Marshal Vol 28
Storm Warrior Vol 29	Hunt-U.S. Marshal Vol 29
Storm Warrior Vol 30	Hunt-U.S. Marshal Vol 30
Storm Warrior Vol 31	Hunt-U.S. Marshal Vol 31

ADDITIONAL BOOKS

The Gray Brigade Vol 1
Participated in, Wanted, A Collection Of Short Stories

Find these books on Amazon:
http://www.amazon.com/WL-Cox/e/B00EN3AFP0/ref=sr_tc_2_0?qid=1456028836&sr=1-2-ent

About the Author

WL Cox, born 1947 in Middletown, Ohio, and helped farm for the first 18 years of my life near Germantown, Ohio. I worked retail sales for over 40 years and spent 6 years in the Air Force as an engine mechanic. Always being an avid western fiction reader for most of my life led to the western fiction writer that I am today. I hope that the readers of my books get as much enjoyment from reading them as I get from writing them.

www.ingramcontent.com/pod-product-compliance
Lightning Source LLC
Chambersburg PA
CBHW071234260626
47161CB00003BA/862